# Whispers of Liberty

By Heidi Sprouse

BYGONE ERA BOOKS

Published by:
Bygone Era Books, Ltd
7665 E. Eastman Ave. #B101
Denver, CO 80231

Book cover design and layout by
Ellie Bockert Augsburger of Creative Digital Studios.
www.CreativeDigitalStudios.com
Cover design features:
Beautiful woman in medieval dress: © darkbird / Dollar Photo Club
many old crosses in cemetery: © geraldas1 / Dollar Photo Club

ISBN: 978-1-941072-30-1

# Acknowledgements

They say it takes a village to raise a child. The same holds true when a story is born. Thank you to Noel Levee, Johnstown's historian, the Johnstown Historical Society, Joan Fudger, and Joan Loveday for all of your gems of knowledge. A shout out to Patricia Port Locatelli for historical photos and Mysteries on Main Street for your support of local literature. You keep the history of this fine town alive.

To the residents of Johnstown for being the memory keepers of their proud, Colonial heritage, past and present, you have my gratitude.

# Dedication

To Lise Wilson. Because of you, this sweet town has become my home, a slice of history has become a part of who I am, and Whispers of Liberty came to be.

To our brave, Johnstown Colonials, and all of the Patriots near and far. You dared to dream, fight, and sacrifice to give us America, the land of the free. Because of you, we still hear the whispers of liberty today.

# Chapter 1

*I HEAR THE WHISPERS* of liberty every day and its ghosts pass me by. The rustling of heavy skirts. A tricorne hat, head and shoulders above the others ambling on the sidewalk. A smattering of red coats scrambling across a farmer's field with blue coats in hot pursuit before vanishing into the woods. The crackle of musket fire making me catch my breath. The boom of cannons waking me in the night from a sound sleep. It's not surprising really. I have lived in historic Johnstown all of my twenty-two years, steeped in Colonial history like a tea bag in a dark, strong brew.

I can climb my family tree all the way back to the 1760's and some of the original settlers in Sir William Johnson's colony. My father, Martin Ross, is a major, history buff, particularly US history, with a full blown obsession for the American Revolution. While other children grew up with fairy tales, I heard "The Midnight Ride of Paul Revere" and the Declaration of Independence so many times the words are written on my heart.

Most kids went to Disney. Our family getaways and vacations took us to every point of interest in the battle for our independence. Boston. Breed's Hill. Lexington and Concord. Ticonderoga. Long Island. White Plains. Fort Washington. The Delaware. Trenton. Oriskany. Bennington. Valley Forge. Saratoga. Yorktown. I could rattle off more. The Battle of Johnstown holds a special place in my heart as my hometown's claim to fame; it was one of the final battles in the Northern theater of war. I can spin off more details about that distant day than an encyclopedia. Believe it or not, our brave Patriots fought six days after Cornwallis' surrender. No cell phones to spread the word back then.

As a double whammy, my mother, Clara, is a social studies teacher at the junior high. Not nearly as passionate about Colonial history as my dear father, she still managed to cheerfully humor and indulge his whims all of my life, which could be worse. Every costume, every oral presentation, every book report at school involved an important figure in full dress from those patriotic times, thanks to my mother's brilliant imagination and skill with a sewing machine. My father's burning desire for historical accuracy ensured they were right. Each time I had to give a speech, my classmates began to place bets trying to figure out who I was before I opened my mouth and spilled the beans.

All of those outfits are carefully packed away in my hope chest, reminders of my school days. Betsy Ross, mother of our flag. Molly Pitcher, alias Mary Ludwig Hays, who tended the wounded, carried water, and helped load the cannons at the Battle of Monmouth. Sybil Ludington, the brave heroine who rode more than twice as far as Paul Revere at the young age of 16 to save the day after the British raided Danbury, Connecticut. Deborah Sampson, who posed as her brother and actually fought for the Americans. Courageous, strong women that are a part of me.

To say I'm entangled in Colonial days is an understatement. I'm addicted to Assassin's Creed III, mainly because Sir William Johnson, founder of my town, is a character and his estate, only a few miles away from my home, has been recreated with incredible authenticity. When most people are watching the Walking Dead and an abundance of reality shows, I'm on the edge of my seat following "The Sons of Liberty" on the History Channel. I'm thinking about starting a petition because I can't live without a continuation. Instead of credit cards, I carry a membership card in my purse: *Charlotte Ross, proud member of the Daughters of the American Revolution*. I earned a history degree and opened a bookstore, the Colonial Book Nook, so I could indulge in my greatest loves, olden times in America and my own writing. I spend more time in a bygone era than in the 21st century.

I guess I shouldn't have been shocked that one day the past and present would collide.

*OCTOBER 25, 2014*, the anniversary of the Battle of Johnstown and a ghost walk was taking place in town. With only six days until Halloween, it was an opportunity that couldn't be missed. The air was brisk, hinting of the onset of winter as the dead leaves skittered by my feet on the mile and a half walk from my snug, rental cottage. I figured the exercise would do me good. I buttoned up my coat and moved along at a steady pace as the sun finally dipped below the horizon over my sleepy town. A full moon blazed high in the sky and lit my path.

I'd walked the roads of my town so many times I could find my way with my eyes closed, first holding my father's hand as a child, then on my own, soaking up historical sites everywhere I turned. The James Burke Inn, originally established for Robert Picken, Johntown's surveyor, 1765. Fort Johnstown, a.ka. the Tryon County Jail, 1772. . The Fulton County Courthouse, formerly known as the Tryon County Courthouse and the oldest working courthouse in New York, also dating back to 1772. Night or day, it comforted me to share my town with these enduring landmarks. I thought of them as old friends.

As I rounded the corner of St. John's Episcopal, I had to squash the perverse urge to spit on Sir William Johnson's grave. A major figure in pre-Revolutionary history, I could only think of him as a Loyalist through and through, a true British baron. I didn't care that the man was instrumental in ensuring we remained British colonies, not French, due to his part in the French and Indian War. It did not matter that he was the Great White Father to the Natives at the time. A true imperialist, he just had to take everything and keep it all.

Thanks to *my* father, I had a rather partial view that favored the Americans, rational or no. I lengthened my stride and resolutely turned my gaze away, moving swiftly down West Green Street, past the Colonial Cemetery. I'd done rubbings of many of the stones where Revolutionary notables slept. My feet were tempted to turn inside the gate and visit those honorable grave markers, but the ghost walk was about to begin.

Maynard Hughes, town historian and old crony of my father's, was the host of the evening, quite dashing in a cape and cap that was in style over 250 years ago. He stood on the Drumm House steps. A fitting location, it was supposedly built in 1763 for the first school master, Edward Wall, and acted as a museum. I'd taken many a trip to the tiny, colonial house with my parents and teachers. I gave Maynard a wave and joined the small crowd that had gathered.

The elderly gentleman doffed his tricorne hat and bowed his snowy head, flashing me a grin, his eyes twinkling behind wire-rimmed glasses in the glow of the moon. The man was in his glory and reveled in drawing his audience into the past to find out who haunted our noble town. As the wind kicked up, making the branches of the trees creak eerily, the stage was set perfectly. Maynard launched into a long-winded tale that dragged on and on.

*Get to the punchline, Maynard!* God love him, but the man could talk. There was many an evening that I nodded off on our couch while my father and the historian talked about the olden days. Fighting the urge to snooze, I decided to browse the cemetery after all. I broke away from the others and had only taken a few steps when a masculine figure passed by me, sending a draft of cold air my way that made me shiver and set my tousled curls to fluttering around my face. Goosebumps rose up on my arms, the fine hairs on the back of my neck standing on end, and I couldn't take my eyes off of him.

He was tall, broad of back, his shoulders firmly set, the kind of man who stood out in a crowd and would turn heads everywhere. He wore Revolutionary garb, his dark hair tied back in a tail, brushing a collar that stood up straight. Breeches that went just below the knee, stockings, and leather shoes with buckles gleaming in the light completed the ensemble. The man called to mind Ichabod Crane from that new Sleepy Hollow series on TV. *Wow. Someone is really getting into the spirit tonight.*

The stranger made his way through the gates, between the stones, as Maynard's deep voice droned on in the distance. Inexplicably drawn to the back of the graveyard, I followed him. He paused in front of a tall stone, one I had seen the day before while wandering through the cemetery on my lunch break as I often did. I'd planned to come back to take a picture or do a

6

rubbing, maybe do a genealogy search because it pulled at me. The writing was remarkably clear, the stone a pure white when others had been stained by time, yet I'd never noticed it before and the fire of curiosity started burning in the pit of my stomach. Tonight, it was a bonfire.

The man knelt on the dead grass in front of the stone and bowed his head. The clouds shifted as I approached, bathing him in a shaft of light, and the he looked up at me. His face was troubled, his dark eyes filled with longing. His hand lifted, palm up, and reached out for me. I couldn't resist his beckon, couldn't turn away. The sounds of the night, the low rumble of Maynard's voice, the rustling of the straggling, dry leaves scraping against the trees, the thundering of my heart, all faded away.

The man turned and rested his hand on the grave and I stared at the words that had already been etched in my mind. *Here lies Benjamin Willson. Died October 25, 1781 at the Battle of Johntown. Liberty's son, he bravely fought. To break tyranny's chains is what he sought.*

Trembling, I slowly lowered myself to the ground beside him, hoping to give comfort, and pressed my hand to the pale sandstone. *"Remember...I said I would find you,"* a low voice whispered softly in my ear. I felt like someone was tugging me into a deep, bottomless pit and I was falling pell-mell through the air into blackness.

# Chapter 2

*I HAD VERTIGO ONCE,* thought that's what must be happening now. My head was spinning, lights flashing behind my eyelids, making my stomach pitch. I felt like I was tumbling end over end, buffeted by an icy wind that chilled me through and through until my free fall came to a jarring halt. There was stillness.

At first, I was only aware of the sound of my breathing, coming in sharp, short pants. The rush of blood in my ears. The hammering of my heart. Something rough was poking at my cheek and I was lying down. I slowly opened my eyes and had to shield them from a bright sun blazing overhead. I took a deep breath and opened my eyes again. I was still in the cemetery...but not the cemetery that I knew so well.

Shivering even though the day was warm, I slowly pulled myself to my feet and took in my surroundings. There were a few grave markers before me, but they were scarce, pristine, still young. Benjamin Willson's stone was not there. I turned and glanced around me, my heart working even harder. Everything around me was vaguely familiar...yet oh so different.

The Courthouse stood on the corner, but looked shiny and new. The Drumm House looked as if it could have been built yesterday, rather than a place of advanced age that had been carefully preserved. Most of the other buildings that made up present day Johnstown had vanished. With a start, I saw the James Burke Inn stood on the opposite side of the road, just down a stretch, rather than a few blocks from my house. Spinning full circle, I saw a church standing in the place of St. John's, a much less imposing, simple, stone structure with a rounded cupola. *Remember? The original church burnt down in the early 1800's.*

The roads were dirt. There wasn't a scrap of pavement or sidewalk to be found. People strolling by wore breeches and long coats or dresses that swished as they brushed the ground. Horses and wagons rumbled by. It felt like a re-enactment.

There was only one problem. In re-enactments, I could never fully suspend my disbelief because of the modern day trappings that couldn't be erased; now, they were gone, sucking the air from my lungs. The bare bones of Johnstown were laid out before me, those few present day remnants giving me proof if I needed any...but the question was how?

*You're dreaming. You have to be dreaming. Too many forays into dusty, old journals, museums, and graveyards.* I grabbed my arm and pinched as hard as I could. "Ouch!"

I quick glimpse down and I let out a high pitched squeal. My hikers, jeans, and heavy coat were gone, replaced by a plain dress in dark brown with a form fitting bodice that buttoned to the neck and a full skirt, a pair of serviceable, leather boots poking out at the fringe. A basket hung on my arm, filled with vegetables and some other odds and ends. I reached up with trembling fingers to touch my head and encountered some type of bonnet, my hair tucked inside. I started to hyperventilate.

A girl stepped up beside me and looped her arm in mine. "Charlotte, don't look now, but Jacob Cooper is watching you. Start walking." I laughed faintly as we began to move, not even bothering to glance over my shoulder at any would-be suitors. I had bigger problems at the moment like figuring out what the hell was going on.

*Abigail. Abigail Andrews.* The name came to me with a jolt. I didn't know how or where it came from, but somehow I knew that was who was at my side...my friend. We walked along the town square where a small collection of shops stretched out before us and came to stop in front of one painted a dark green. A sign hung over the door, *The Needle and Thread.*

My dark-haired companion, somewhat plump and only five feet to my five foot four, tilted her head to glance up at me. Her forest

11

green eyes flashed as she gave me a merry smile and squeezed my arm. "Will you look at that gown? It's like something that would have been worn to one of the affairs at Sir William's. Remember how we used to dream of being invited to a social or a ball?" She sighed and gave me a playful wink. "Jacob would love to see you in that rose colored beauty. It would be perfect for you."

I nodded slowly, my mouth gone dry, clothing being the farthest thing from my mind. The reflection in the thick, rippled glass had grabbed my attention and was stealing my breath away again. The figure in the glass was more slender than the body I called my own, more delicate, but it was not the body that made me tremble.

The face that stared back at me was so similar to my own that it could have belonged to my sister, if I had a sister. The cheekbones were a bit higher and more narrow, the nose a tad longer and more severe. A stray curl tumbled out of my bonnet, the same as the hair I'd struggled to tame all of my life, calling to mind sun-kissed wheat, a blend of light and dark. I stared wide-eyed into a golden gaze that looked like mine, honey gleaming in a jar, while the color spilled from my cheeks and I went quite white. Weak in the knees, I began to sway.

Abigail grabbed my arm and held on tight. "Are you all right, Charlotte? You look as if you've seen a ghost."

Perhaps I had. I swallowed hard and wet my lips with a quick dart of my tongue. "I think the heat must be getting to me. It's rather warm, isn't it?" I was lying. I was chilled to the bone, ice running through my veins.

Abigail patted my hand and gave me a gentle tug. "It is quite mild for early September, more like summer. We'd best be getting home. You can get a cold drink from the well and sit a spell before your father comes home from the smithy."

We set off at a steady pace, kicking up a cloud of dust as a gentle breeze pressed my skirt against my legs, swishing over the ground. The buildings became sparse the further we walked, giving way to field and woodlands. My heart pounded harder with every step and I breathed deeply, trying to stave off a full panic attack, desperate to make sense of whatever had happened to me. Fortunately, the young woman at my side continued a steady stream of conversation that didn't require input from me, allowing me to think. To try and get control of my pulse. To get a grip on a situation that was completely beyond my control.

I didn't even notice that we'd slowed until Abigail stopped by a long lane and gave me a hug. "Here's where we must part. I'll be quilting on Saturday if you'd like to join me. Go rest a bit, Charlotte. You don't seem yourself."

*You don't know the half of it.* I patted her on the shoulder and pulled out what I hoped was a reassuring smile. "I'll be fine, Abigail. I'm just a little unsettled. I didn't sleep well last night. I think I'll take a nap. If I can get away, I'll come on the weekend." *If I'm still here this weekend.*

13

She kissed my cheek and continued on her way. I could hear the sound of her singing, a sweet hymnal, something soothing, drifting back to me. It gave me enough courage for the next leg of this strange journey.

The path was wide enough for a wagon and well-traveled. As I followed the meandering twists and turns, surrounded by trees crowding in closely on either side, my heart began to beat erratically. I had the strong sense of déjà vu, that I had been here before. I rounded a corner to be met by a small, cozy house, perched on a foundation made of fieldstone. It was very similar to the Drumm House, except it was a deep blue, rather than the buttercup yellow of that beloved landmark, with a barn, outhouse, and corral out back. A cow and horse grazed peacefully in the tall grasses. A small porch and plain, brown door reached out to me in welcome. *Home*, my inner voice whispered and I breathed easier for the first time since my adventure began.

I stepped on to the porch and had to grab hold of the railing to steady myself when I caught sight of the sign mounted on the shingles. *The William Ross House 1764*. William Ross. I knew that name well, imprinted in the deep recesses of my brain. When I was old enough to follow print on a page, even though I couldn't read it yet, my father had tucked me on to his lap and laid out the Ross Family Tree. He'd taken my hand and placed my finger on my name, then his, trailing up through all of the branches as far back as he could manage in tracing our origins.

To the family that had originally settled in Colonial Johnstown when our town was young. William and Mary Ross. Mary had died in childbirth after giving birth to my namesake. Charlotte Elizabeth Ross. *You...are...Charlotte...Elizabeth...Ross...the First.*

I closed my eyes and laid my hand on the door, that odd sense of a homecoming, washing over me. One deep breath and I took hold of the door knob. A gentle push and it swung open with a creak. The door clicked shut behind me as I stepped inside into a shaft of sunlight, dust motes dancing around me and somehow this place that was not my place felt like my own. *I guess that will have to be enough.*

To say the house was small did not do it justice. There was mainly one room with a large, stone fireplace and two chairs set before the hearth. A dining table with backless benches sat in a central area while a small, plain wooden table stood against the wall in the kitchen area, joined by a tall cabinet and some shelves. One bed stood in one corner against the wall, another bed standing across from it, also against the wall, most likely placed to benefit from the heat of the fire.

I set my basket on the small table and saw that the fire had died down. I stirred the embers with a poker and added a log from the metal rack off to the side, as if I was on auto-pilot. A large, cast iron pot hung over the fire. *The eighteenth century's version of a crockpot.* When I lifted the lid, I was met by a delectable

15

scent from a stew of some sort that made my stomach growl. I picked up the ladle hanging on a hook by the fireplace and gave the contents a good stir. I was tempted to have a bowl, but didn't feel right about it, like Goldilocks intruding on the three bears.

I replaced the ladle and turned back to survey the room, pressing a hand to my stomach in hopes of calming the mad fluttering of butterflies that were swarming inside of me. A blue stoneware pitcher sat on the table by my basket, a matching mug beside it. My hand shook as I poured the contents into the cup and took a sip. It was water, cold and pure. I drank the whole thing down and cleared my throat, wishing for something stronger. Much stronger. Maybe I *would* lie down for a little while. Go to sleep. Wake up and find out this whole thing really was just a dream.

The clip-clopping of approaching hoof beats made my stomach clench and it was hard to breathe. I wiped sweaty palms on my skirt and turned to face the entrance as heavy footsteps sounded on the porch and the door opened. "Charlotte, my blessing! How was your day?"

The door swung shut and a tall man stepped into the ray of light, his smile kind, his pale gray eyes like sun-warmed slate. His hair was the same color as mine, heavily threaded with strands of white. Time had carved deeper lines in his face than my father's, but he looked so much like the man who raised me that I ran across the room and hugged him hard, my eyes stinging with tears. It took everything I had not to break down in his arms.

# Chapter 3

*"WHATEVER IS THE MATTER, MY DAUGHTER?"* William Ross stepped back and cupped my cheek with his callused hand. His forehead creased in concern. "You seem troubled, my blessing. Did something happen in town today?"

*Something most definitely happened in town, but I can't tell you.* Playing along with the charade that had taken over my life, I smiled with false cheer and rose up on tiptoe to kiss his cheek. "Oh, I'm just worn out from Abigail's tongue wagging all the way into town and back. Sit, Papa. You look tired."

It didn't seem strange to call him father, but why should I question anything at this point? It was obvious that my ancestor's blood ran strong in our family line, leaving his stamp on Martin Ross so many generations later. Those similarities gave me an anchor. William was the same height, nearly six feet tall, but more compact than my scholar of a father, the muscles of his back, arms, and shoulders straining against his plain linen shirt. I recalled. Being a blacksmith was backbreaking work.

Right now, his weariness was plain on his face and in the slight stoop of his shoulders, yet my father from a previous generation set his discomfort aside to kiss me on the top of the head and squeeze my arm in passing. "You're right. That girl certainly can talk."

He crossed the room to the hearth, reached his hands over his head, and stretched hard enough to make his bones pop. Sighing heavily, William slowly sat and leaned toward the crackling flames. Going on instinct,—my own or the first Charlotte's, I wasn't sure which—I poured hot water from a tea pot in the coals, sprinkled in some tea leaves, and sugar, topping it off from a small pot of cream, everything readily at hand. I set the mug in William's— *Papa's*—hands and stood behind him. Tentatively, I reached out and began to massage his neck and shoulders, hoping to receive comfort by giving comfort.

"Oh, Charlotte, you do not know how good that feels. Some days at the smithy seem to go on an eternity. Give it your best, daughter. Press as hard as you can on these poor, overworked muscles."

Slowly, under my attentive touch, the knots under the skin came undone and my forefather's body went loose. He sagged against his chair and his breath came out in a rush as all traces of tension left his face. His considerably larger hand reached back and rested on mine. "Thank you, my blessing. You are too good to me."

Inside me, a river of love flowed, memories from my life in the future and impressions from the past jumbling together. I felt as if I'd known this man forever and that reassured me. No matter what happened, William Ross would be my shelter.

*THE EVENING WAS QUIET,* a slow winding down and early preparations for taking to bed. I served the stew with a crusty bread that waited in the basket I'd carried home. Our meal was accompanied by butter, made by the churn tucked in a nook, I was certain, and beer. A much stronger ale than what I was accustomed to in modern times, it was a sure recipe for feeling tipsy. I cleared, tidied up for the night, and followed William's cues.

When he pulled out a screen to change his clothing, using the chest at the foot of his bed, I investigated the matching chest by my bed. A plain, cotton gown in white and a robe waited inside, along with several other outfits. With a great sigh of relief, I wrestled my way out of my dress and quickly changed. Eying a table that must have acted as a nightstand, I took up a brush, sat on the feather mattress, and let down my hair. I started to work my way through the curls and nearly fell over. I was so exhausted, I thought I could sleep for a week.

"Charlotte, you are so weary you're swaying where you sit. It's because you do too much. Go to sleep now, love. Morning will be here soon enough." William had undone the ribbon that tied back his hair, allowing his long curls—*just like mine*—to fall down to his shoulders. He also wore a long, white shirt of sorts. He took the brush from my hands, pulled back the down comforter, and tucked me in. "Pleasant dreams, my blessing."

"Good night, Papa." My voice became choked and I turned away from the fireplace as he crossed the room and extinguished the oil lamp. I fought the urge to cry as I heard his covers rustling on the other side of the room. Unable to hold back any longer, quite undone after what had turned out to be the most bizarre day of my life, I stuffed the blanket in my mouth and let the sobs come. When my face and pillow became damp from my tears, fatigue finally won out. I cast up a final prayer before drifting off to sleep. *Now I lay me down to sleep, I pray the Lord my soul to keep...and before I wake, take me back to my bed in 2014.*

My sleep wasn't easy. I tossed and turned, entangled in a tug of war between past and present, all beginning with my slip through a crack in time. A thumping at the door woke me with a jerk. Disoriented, I rolled over and gazed, blurry-eyed, around the room. The fire was almost out, red embers the only light in the cottage, with the exception of a few tendrils of moonlight reaching through one of the windows. There was the sound of movement from the other side of the room and William's dark silhouette went to the door. "Who knocks at such an hour?"

"It's Jacob Cooper, sir. The militia is needed straight away." My ancestor opened the door a few inches, revealing a dark figure on the step. His hat and cloak nearly made him merge with the night, a choice in clothing that was surely intentional.

William drew the young man inside. "We've been called up, sir. We're setting off from the Andrews' farm." The messenger spoke in a low voice and he was breathless, from urgency or being in a rush.

This must have been the one Abigail had gone on about in town. I couldn't make out any features at the moment, except that he was shorter than my forefather by several inches and his hair gleamed red in the moon's glow. The two men talked for a few minutes in hushed tones, William patted his back in farewell, and Jacob Cooper slipped into the night. I did not know this young Patriot, although on some deeper level there was a sense of familiarity, but I prayed that God would keep him safe all the same.

Without hesitation, Papa, because that's what he was to me now, lit the oil lamp, pulled his clothes from the chest, and dressed swiftly. He took up a leather band and wrapped it around his hair, pulling it into a tail. Finally, he slid a musket from under the bed. I couldn't muffle my gasp.

At the sound, he took great strides to reach my bed, sit at my side, take my hands in his. "I'm sorry, Charlotte, but word has spread that British regulars are looting nearby in Palatine. We must move quickly to squash them and help those who need us most."

I gripped his hands, desperation rising up. This man was my haven, my sanity in a world gone mad. "But, why must *you* go, Papa? Surely there are others."

His eyes were sad, but his voice was fierce as he bowed over me to kiss my forehead and my cheeks. "My blessing, you know how heavy our losses have been. What able-bodied men are left must answer the call. We must be strong, Charlotte. If you think England was hard on us before, she would crush us if we were to fail in our act of rebellion, grinding us beneath the heel of her boot."

Seeing the fire in his eyes, listening to his conviction, I could finally understand why my father and I loved the American Revolution so. There was too much Colonial patriotism in my forefather to be contained in one generation's blood and bones. My father's fervor, the most passionate person I know, was a flickering candle compared to the bonfire of spirit in William Ross. A spark of energy crackled down my arm as he held my hand and tried to make me understand.

"I will come back as soon as I am able. You stay here and use the Brown Bess," he gestured to the hooks over the fireplace, "if you need it. One never knows when the sorry lot of Redcoats may come here. Take care of Belle and Bonnie, be on your guard, and pray for us as I will pray for you."

The slight stubble on his cheek scraped against mine as he kissed me once more and pulled me in close for a hug. With a catch in his breath, he took up his gun and left, the door swinging shut behind him with a bang.

"I love you too!" I called after him. As the hoof beats of his horse carried him away, I let out a wail. There was no one to hear me, no one to see. I sobbed my heart out, unable to sleep, until the first fingers of daylight tapped on the windows.

I sat up and swiped a sleeve across my face. Crying hadn't changed a thing. I was still trapped in the past and I was all alone. Unable to sit there any longer, I scrambled out of bed and began to pace. There had to be something I could do.

*You can try and get back where you belong.* It wasn't much of a plan, but it was something. I dressed in the same clothes I'd worn the day before because it was easier. A hunk of bread with butter and more water were all my stomach could take for breakfast. Poking my head outside, I was relieved to see no tell-tale signs of red. I started to set off down the lane when I remembered the animals. *Belle and Bonnie. Who was who?*

In the barn, I was met by two, sweet, brown-eyed creatures. A white cow with tan spots and a tan horse, with what looked like white socks, waited in two stalls. A quick glance around the small building and I found a pitchfork, hay, and a bag of oats. I quickly gave them food, dutifully waited for them to eat, tapping my foot all the while, and finally let them into the pasture. As the cow moved by, I stroked her warm back. *Belle* floated to the surface of my mind. I smiled and turned to the gentle horse next, patting her cheek. "You must be Bonnie. Goodbye, girl." My eyes began to burn. It would appear that my emotions were on a roller coaster ride as well.

Mission accomplished, I ventured down the lane once more, walking as quickly as I could. Clouds gathered overhead, hiding the sun, and the air became nippy. I rubbed my arms as I moved along, praying it wouldn't rain before I reached my destination. I had one goal in sight: get back to the cemetery and go back to the life I had known.

By the time I reached the town square, the first, fat drops were coming down. What little traffic there was began to clear out as people sought shelter from the weather. The wind picked up in intensity, snatching my bonnet, tugging my curls loose, making them a wild tangle around my face. I actually had to lean forward and push my way onward to get to the small gate by the cemetery. With my eyes fixed on the arch that was much simpler than the present day fixture, I took a deep breath, stepped through, and hit my knees in the spot where Benjamin Willson's grave had stood. Lighting crackled in the sky, a terrible clap of thunder nearly stopped my heart...and nothing happened.

"Please God...or Benjamin...whoever did this! Please! I want to go home!" The clouds opened up, sending down a torrent and the skies nearly turned black. *Not the answer I was looking for.* I waited...until I was soaked through to the skin, my teeth chattering, shaking with a chill that set into my bones.

I staggered to my feet as the lightning continued to streak across the sky like the fourth of July, a date that didn't even mean anything yet, and fought my way back to the Ross Homestead. Right then, it was the only place I had. I ran most of the way, my breath coming in great gasps, and put the animals back in the barn.

With my final burst of energy, I dashed inside and flung myself on the bed, begging for air, fighting off the urge to fall to pieces. I wondered if I clicked my heels together three times and said, *There's no place like home*, I'd finally get there. With a great sigh, I squeezed my eyes shut and listened to the drumming of the rain on the roof. *Dorothy, you're not in Kansas anymore.* The trouble was I was in Johnstown...but it wasn't my Johnstown and I had no idea what to do.

*I RAN ON ADRENALIN* for the next two days, up before dawn, wearing a track in the floor with my pacing. My hands and body followed a routine. Cleaning the house. Washing laundry in a tub in the yard, filled with boiling water from the kettle and some type of harsh soap. Tending Belle and Bonnie. Standing with my arms around the mare's neck, my head pressed to her warm face as the tears streamed

27

down. My mind was cluttered with impressions from another life, faded and blurred, along with an intense desire to go home.

I pondered my trip to the graveyard, wondered why I was still trapped in yesteryear. I suspected it had something to do with the missing grave marker for Benjamin Willson. Would I have to wait for that poor soul to meet his fate before I could pick up where I left off in the 21st century?

My head ached with the relentless questions. I drew a chair to the window and drank in the sunset along with my cup of tea. Homesickness welled up inside me and it was a struggle to find any peace. At any moment, I would unravel at the seams. The tears threatened to break the dam. I let them come.

Full darkness fell, the moon hidden behind cloud cover, and I stared with sightless eyes into the inky blackness. I could only see my old life. I missed everything and everyone in it, bitterly. I bent at the waist, holding on tight to my stomach as the sobs poured out, making me begin to gulp for air. I didn't think I could stop.

A distant beating, faint and then louder, proved otherwise, pulling me out of my chair. I rubbed at my cheeks as footsteps pounded on the porch and the door swung open with a bang against the wall. William stood in the opening, a bedraggled, bloodied soldier by his side, arm slung over my forefather's shoulder, his head hanging low. "Charlotte! I need you. Help me bring this young man in before he drops where he stands!"

# Chapter 4

*I SPRANG FORWARD* and slung the stranger's other arm around my shoulder. Together, William and I managed to half drag, half carry the militia man across the room. I pulled back the covers and my forefather eased our unexpected guest onto his bed. He gently lifted up the soldier's legs, careful not to jar him. Even that movement made the injured man groan and toss an arm over his eyes. It was plain to see why. His breeches had been cut off to the top of the thigh on the left leg, a filthy, blood-stained bandage wrapped around it. With a start, I realized the bandage had been torn from the hem of William's shirt.

I turned to my forefather and hugged him swiftly, unable to contain my relief that he was home and intact. He kissed the top of my head and firmly pressed my shoulder. "His wound is a terrible thing. He'll need tending and whatever miracles your sweet touch can bring him. Do what you can for him."

I rushed to the kitchen area to gather supplies, pulse racing, stomach knotted. *What do I use?* I wasn't a nurse and there wasn't much available by the way of medicine in 18th century America. William spoke in a soothing tone while I grabbed clean rags, packets of herbs, homemade soap, and a basin of hot water. I set everything on the small table next to the bed and glanced up, resisting the urge to make the sign of the cross and throw in a few Hail Mary's. My mind latched on to words that had comforted me many times. *Our Father, who art in heaven, hallowed by Thy name. Thy kingdom come, Thy Will be done...*

My forefather gave me a smile of encouragement as he pulled up a chair next to the bed, sat, and set his hand on the soldier's good leg. "This is my daughter, Charlotte. You are in good hands with my blessing."

I took a deep breath. Where to begin? Perhaps, clean him up a bit first. I dipped a piece of cloth in the water, scalding myself in the process. A quick intake of breath, a dash of soap, and I swabbed the man's face. Covered in mud, soot, and blood, it was hard to find where the filth left off and the man began.

He shifted, hissing through his teeth with the movement, and lifted his arm. Taking my hand in his, his head tipped slightly even as his face went whiter under the dirt. "Benjamin Willson, your servant, miss."

My fingers tightened around his as my stomach went into a spasm, my heart fit to explode. I nodded shakily and pulled my hand away, turning swiftly to get a new rag and cover how rattled I was. Facing him once more, I continued to wipe off his face, my hand tingling from his touch. All the while, I catalogued his features and the blood thundered in my ears. The dark hair, pulled back in a tail at the nape of his neck. The coffee eyes. A quick sweep of his body confirmed the man was tall, his shoulders broad. A last pass of the cloth over his face and I was certain. Here lay my graveyard visitor, in the flesh.

I felt faint, a fuzziness creeping up around the corners of my vision as my head began to swim. Quickly, I turned back to the basin and plunged my hands in. The shock of the steaming water snapped me back to alertness; as an added bonus, I was sanitary. I took up a new cloth and proceeded to clean Benjamin's arms, saving the leg for last. I had a feeling that was going to take all of our strength combined.

Finishing up, I dipped my hands in the basin again, biting my lip at the thought of looking under that bandage; fresh blood had seeped out since we laid the man on the bed. William reached across his body and took my hand. "How about some tea first, Charlotte? We could both use some fortification."

I peered closely at my forefather for the first time since his return. Smattered in dirt and blood as well, he was pale with weariness, the lines etched even more deeply in his face. With a nod, I grabbed the basin and went to the kitchen area. As a precaution, I rinsed it with water from the kettle and filled it again before setting about making two cups of tea.

"I never expected such a gentle and lovely flower for a nurse," Benjamin said softly to the older man at his side. "How is it that she does not have a household of her own? She must be 20 at least."

William smiled warmly, his gray gaze pinned on me. "My blessing is nearly 22. I have encouraged her many times to take a husband, but she insists on taking care of me. We lost my Mary, her sweet mother, when she was born. It has been only the two of us ever since. What about you, my young friend? How old are you?

Benjamin moved slightly and gasped. My forefather's grip on his leg tightened and the man nodded slightly in thanks, swallowing hard. "24, although I feel twice that right now."

"I am sure you have seen a great deal of pain and loss in your short life." William's voice dropped down low as I returned and set a cup in his hands. He gave me a slip of a smile and returned his attention to our guest.

"More than anyone should see in a lifetime." Benjamin's eyes drifted closed for an instant, springing wide when I touched his hand. His lips curled up and he closed his fingers around the cup I held before him, but they trembled so that I had to hold on. I lifted his head with my other hand and helped him to take a sip.

He sighed, pleasure lighting his eyes, warming them like melted chocolate. "*Real* tea, with cream and sugar? However have you managed it?"

William laughed and walked away, returning with an earthenware jug. "I am the town blacksmith. Since the war started, people often don't have money. They barter in exchange for my services and I often get their hoards that have been carefully stashed away. I'm also lucky enough to have a cow." He uncorked the jug and the strong scent of alcohol wafted through the air. "I also have spirits. Not rum, I'm afraid. No one can get that anymore, but this whiskey is locally made and is damned good if I say so myself. Drink up some of this to ease the pain before Charlotte tends to your leg."

He poured a healthy amount in Benjamin's cup, then doctored his own. William's eyes drooped closed as he took a deep swallow, swaying slightly. The poor man was nearly dead on his feet, yet my ancestor demonstrated he was made of a strong mettle. The soldier in our bed would be placed first before my forefather attended to his own needs.

He'd opened his home, given up his bed, and offered all the comforts he could give. My heart swelled with love for this man that I hardly knew. Those qualities had been passed down to my father and I would be forever grateful to William Ross for planting such a strong seed for our family tree.

Benjamin drained his cup and licked his lip. "That is damned good. I haven't had anything better than horse piss in years." His cheeks became streaked with crimson as he bowed his head in embarrassment. "I beg your pardon, Miss Charlotte."

William laughed and reached out to cup my cheek with his palm. "It would not be the first time my daughter has heard such language. She spent many an hour with me at the smithy when she was growing up. Men do not remember the niceties when they gather. Neither did I when I would burn myself or hit my thumb with a mallet."

Benjamin laughed softly, but his face went tight. "Do you think I could have a bit more, please? My leg is on fire and throbs with every beat of my heart."

William didn't hesitate to fill it to the brim. "Drink every last drop, lad. You're going to need it."

I tipped the cup slowly and Benjamin took long, deep swallows until his breath came out in a rush. "That *is* damned good." His mouth tilted in a crooked grin that squeezed my heart. "All right, sweet Charlotte. I'm ready now. Do your best."

I nodded and set the cup down, steeling myself for the challenge ahead, resisting the urge to snatch the jug from my forefather's hands and gulp it down. William's strong, firm hand came up to grasp the nape of my neck and give a gentle squeeze, telling me, *You can do this, Charlotte.*

Staring at the bandage on my patient's leg, I saw that it was dried and stiff, most likely stuck to the wound. My forefather must have read my mind. He moved away, rifled through a basket by the fire, and returned with scissors.

"Thank you, Papa." He went to the foot of the bed and held Benjamin's leg steady while I began to snip at the material. The young man closed his eyes, but did not make a sound, not even when I peeled the filthy cloth away and pulled at the gaping wound in his thigh.

He moaned and his face twisted. I grabbed his hand. "I'm sorry. I didn't mean to hurt you."

Somehow, he managed a grin in response. "You didn't. A damned Lobsterback did."

I had to bite down on my tongue to keep from crying out as I returned my attention to his leg. The hole was large and ragged, black around the edges and an angry red was radiating outward. Blood and an awful green puss oozed from the wound. My stomach turned, not at the loathsome sight of it, but in fear. Infection had already started to set in and I had nothing but hot water, herbs, and a tenuous faith. Tears sprang to my eyes and I turned away. "It has to be cleaned," I murmured.

Benjamin's hand came up to take mine, sending a jolt through me, making the blood hum in my veins. *I know you*, my heart said with every beat. He managed a weak smile. "With your sweet touch, it will be all right."

I gave him back what I hoped was an answering smile and dipped a clean rag in the fresh basin of hot water. The best I could do was use new cloths each time to be as sanitary as possible. Taking a deep breath, I wiped the top of his leg first before working my way down. His skin was hot to the touch. His hands tightened into fists as he held on to the edge of the mattress, his knuckles white. I continued, trying to finish as quickly as possible.

When his whole leg was clean, I dipped another rag in the water to wipe my hands, took up a fresh one, and swabbed the wound as deeply as I could. Benjamin's teeth clacked together as his jaw clenched and his back arched. "I'm sorry. I'm so sorry."

I couldn't hold back the tears seeing his pain. I grabbed another rag and squeezed the hot water into the wound, getting a dreadful groan in answer. Finally, I sprinkled the herbs in the water, soaked another cloth in the mixture, and set it on his leg. His whole body went stiff and I feared that he forgot how to breathe.

"Drink some more, young Benjamin. You've earned it." William held the cup this time, filled with whiskey once more. His own eyes were wet as he lifted the soldier's head and helped him to drink it all down.

While I put everything away, my forefather pulled up the down comforter for our guest and set a hand on Benjamin's head, perhaps in prayer. He left our guest's side only long enough to wipe his face, arms, and hands. Finally, he changed into his night shirt and sat down at the bedside once more.

"So, Benjamin. Why don't you tell us a bit about yourself?" William glanced up at me as I joined them, drawing the other chair from the hearth. "We are barely acquainted, my blessing.

Benjamin and other militia members joined us in a skirmish. When he was shot, I only took long enough to dig the musket ball from his leg and made for home as quickly as possible."

As my ancestor rattled on, I saw Benjamin's body slowly go loose, his hands letting go of the mattress. It would appear that William's efforts at distraction were working. Benjamin's tongue loosened and once he began to speak, a river of words flowed out. He needed to talk, a purge of sorts, and we let him.

"I'm from Boston." My hands clasped each other tightly in my lap as I thrilled to his revelation. To think that someone from the birthplace of the Revolution, the very heart of Independence, was in the same room with me. Not a book. Not a faded scrap of paper. A real man of flesh and blood.

Benjamin did not seem that impressed. Rather he was crushed with weariness and sorrow. His face was turned to the fire, his eyes staring into the flames, yet I think he saw a distant scene. "My mother died soon after the Boston Tea Party. As Britain tightened its hold and tried to stamp out the rebellion, my father's livelihood was ruined. He was a cooper, but only Tories could do business. When Mother became ill with pneumonia, there was no money for a doctor or medicine. At least she died with the both of us by her side, holding her hands."

His voice broke and he paused, closing his eyes as one tear slid down his face. When he went on, Benjamin was hoarse with barely restrained emotion. "My father went to fight at

Breed's Hill. You do know it was at Breed's, not Bunker Hill?" He looked at us for only an instant, waited for our acknowledgement, and gazed at the fire once more.

"I went with him. What other choice did I have? He blamed the British for Mama...and so did I. I had the privilege of holding my father's hand as well when Death took him on that bloodied hill."

The only sound in the room was the crackle of the fire and the occasional pop when a spark rose up the chimney, that and the sound of Benjamin's ragged breathing. I could not resist. Like that night in the cemetery, I was compelled to soothe him. I took his hand in mine and he held on tightly.

"From there, I became a drifter and went where the war would take me. To New York Harbor, Oriskany, and Saratoga. I wintered with Washington's camp at Valley Forge. I carried on with a small band of fellow Patriots from Boston, men I called friends, but lost them one by one. I wandered and took up with the Tryon County Militia because I *cannot* give up this fight, not until we hold victory in our hands or I take my last breath. I vowed it on the graves of my mother and father. I *always* keep my promises."

For the first time, all the patriotic quotes that had been spoon-fed to me in my growing up years had true meaning. I heard liberty's whisper in my mind: Nathan Hale's, "*I only regret that I have one life to give to my country.*" John Paul Jones', "*I have not yet begun to fight.*" Patrick Henry's, "*Give me liberty or give me*

38

*death.*" Studying the young man lying in the bed, his fervor was much bigger than the room could contain, the embodiment of the spirit of the red, white, and blue.

I pressed his hand in encouragement. "You ask not what this country can do for you, but what you can do for these United States of America." Borrowing the words of the great John F. Kennedy, I found them fitting.

Benjamin's mouth turned up in a ghost of a grin, a bit of hope pushing back the shadows that had darkened his eyes while he told his story. "Yes, yes you've got it, perfectly."

Finally, the well ran dry, pain and exhaustion catching up to him. The young soldier swallowed hard and met my father's eye. "I am grateful William and I crossed paths by some twist of fate. Thank you for saving my life and bringing me here."

My forefather leaned forward and gripped his shoulder. "Thanks are not necessary. You would have done the same for me. Now, I think that it is time for all of us to get some rest. This day has already lasted an eternity." He bent over the bed and kissed the top of Benjamin's head, then mine, before spreading blankets on the floor and lying down next to his bed. William would not listen to my protests or accept my offer to take his place.

Sighing at his obstinate chivalry, I went to Benjamin's side and rested my hand on his. "Good night, Benjamin. Try and get some sleep. You need it badly."

He pressed my fingers to his lips. "Thank you for caring for me and for your gentle ways. It is more than I deserve."

I was so tired I didn't even change my clothes. As I teetered on the edge of wakefulness and sleep, my thoughts began to wander. To a dark, tall soldier kneeling before a marker in the graveyard. To a date that was etched deeply in my mind, a date that was not that far off. To the man lying across the room. I was in his bed, his body entangled with mine as he proved to be healthy and hale. My breath came in a sigh, the blood boiling in my veins, my heart a trip hammer. In any instant, I would vaporize.

A ragged cry tore the darkness, pulling me from my dreams.

# Chapter 5

*I SHOT UP IN MY BED.* Benjamin had tossed the covers aside and was thrashing from side to side. William had already risen from the floor and grabbed hold of the young man by the shoulders in an effort to pin him down. "Benjamin! Wake up! You're dreaming, lad." He glanced over his shoulder at me. "Light the lamp, Charlotte. He's burning up."

Prodded by the urgency in his voice, I sprang out of bed, throwing a few logs on the fire along the way; the cottage had cooled since we went to sleep. As soon as the room was illuminated, I crossed over and laid my palm on Benjamin's forehead, snatching it back at the intense heat rolling off of his skin.

His eyes opened a crack and he reached for his leg, pressing down hard before I could stop him. "Lord help me!" Benjamin cried out.

William took one hand, I took the other, our patient's muscles rippling with the strain of holding on to us so tightly to get a leash on the pain.

I glanced down at his leg. The cloth covering his wound had fallen off and blood was forming a puddle on the bed, combined with puss that was oozing heavily. A god-awful stench came with it. William winced at the sight. "Get him some cold water and a cold cloth for the fever, my blessing."

"Yes, Papa." I scurried across the room, filled a mug from the waiting pitcher, thankful I'd filled it the day before. I poured some water in a basin and brought that as well, along with a rag. William wet the cloth and placed it on Benjamin's forehead while I helped the poor man to drink. The young soldier was shaking like an autumn leaf tugged by the wind.

"You'd best clean the leg again as well." I hurried to do my forefather's bidding as quickly as possible, although it was the last thing I wanted to do. Upon closer inspection, I could see that the entire, injured thigh was swollen with a webbing of red lines extending from the wound. The infection was worsening.

I had to bite the inside of my cheek as I swabbed the angry hole left by the ravages of war and poured boiling water in the wound, Benjamin's screams enough to unnerve me. Another poultice of herbs, strapped on with a rag, and the three of us were panting hard from our efforts.

William shook his head as dawn's first light slipped in, painting the inside of the cottage a pale gray. "I have to go for medicine, anything I can find. I've heard there's a healer in German Flatts, a woman who has learned the Indian's ways and ours."

He dressed quickly and went to the door. I followed close on his heels, terrified to be left alone with the injured man. My forefather took hold of me by the shoulders. "It will probably take me about a day going there and through the night before I will be back, barring any trouble. You have the Brown Bess over the fireplace. Keep the shutters closed on the front of the house and the fire banked. I'll tend to the animals. Don't let anyone in and don't go out. The King's soldiers are anything but honorable at this late stage in the war. There's no telling what some disgruntled raiders might do."

I couldn't speak. I flung my arms around him and wished that was enough to hold him back. He kissed me roughly on the forehead, both cheeks, and on my lips. "Pray that God is with me and that I am swift enough. Pray for him as well. I love you, my blessing."

"I love you too, Papa," I called after him as he went out to the barn, my hand lifted in a wave as his black stallion carried him away. I closed the door and leaned against it a moment, fighting to collect myself.

"I'm sorry I've caused you all this trouble." Benjamin's voice was practically a croak. I wiped my sleeve across my cheeks and forced a smile.

"Nonsense. *You've* caused nothing of the sort. Blame those damned Lobsterbacks!" That got a low chuckle as I crossed the room and patted his arm.

I went to the fire next and put together a pot of coffee, staring into the dying flames as I rubbed my arms, impatient for the brew to perk. The supply of tea was low and I might need it for medicinal purposes. The cottage was silent, birdsong the only sound. I assumed my patient had fallen asleep until I started to prepare two mugs and felt his gaze on me.

"Extra sugar, extra cream, hardly any coffee?" It was my turn to giggle, when all I wanted to do was cry. Squashing the urge, I set the cups down and propped Benjamin up with a pillow. He took the cup and made a valiant effort to drink unaided, but his hand trembled so hard the hot coffee began to slosh over the side. I helped him to take a few sips and he smiled, his dark eyes lighting in appreciation as a fall of hair fell in his face. "That's perfect."

I brushed the hair away, sat down in the chair by his side, and took a swallow from my own cup. "It's the only way to drink coffee as far as I'm concerned."

We sat in a companionable silence, our efforts to have a conversation dying out after a few fits and spurts. I helped Benjamin to finish his coffee before draining my own cup. His eyes drooped shut. Fighting off a fever and infection was troublesome work. I rose from my chair and returned with my brush, undoing my hair and working my way through the tangle of curls. I closed my eyes and felt the tension slipping away, the repetitive motion therapeutic.

"You are too beautiful to be alone. Any man would be a fool not to cherish you." Benjamin's gaze was focused on me, his eyes glittering, face flushed.

He extended his hand and I took it, nearly yelping he was so hot. He brought my fingers to his mouth once more and skimmed his lips across them before falling back against the pillow and letting go. "It has been a long time since I've known the tender touch of a woman, Charlotte, or any kind of tenderness at all. A man can be deprived of food, water, home and hearth...but if he has someone to care for him, he has enough. I am most grateful to you for sharing all of those things, but especially for putting me in your gentle hands."

I stood and kissed him on the forehead as William had the night before. "I am only too happy to do so for one of our bold Patriots. I only wish I could do more. Rest now. You need to conserve your strength." My words were wasted. He'd already slipped off.

I tended him throughout the day, bringing him broth, plying him with tea in an effort to keep him hydrated, piling on more blankets. The fever did not break. If anything, it worsened. He was so hot to the touch, I thought my skin would be singed. Thinking to wipe him down with cold water, I went to the pitcher only to find that it was empty.

"I'm going out to the well. I'll be right back." I snatched the pitcher and took two steps

45

toward the door when Benjamin's hand clamped down on my arm. Surely, I would be branded with five, scarlet fingers on my wrist.

"Don't go. Your father said to stay put. I don't need the water." The hectic color of his cheeks, his glassy eyes, and his flaming skin said otherwise. He actually raised himself up on one elbow. In his weakened state, it would be easy to pull away, to push him down or knock him over.

Instead, I set my hand on his and hoped my expression would give him reassurance, that Benjamin could not see that I was quaking inside. "I'll be quick as a wink."

With that, I dashed outside to the well and began to pump. The water gushed into the pitcher, washing over my fingers, freezing them. I plunged my hands in and splashed some over my face and on my neck, the wind whipping my hair around me in a wild tangle.

A prickling down my spine had me glancing over my shoulder to see a snippet of red at the edge of the forest. A heartbeat later, two figures stepped out of the cover of the trees. My breath caught in my throat.

Their coats were ragged, their white breeches torn and stained. There was no sign of a commanding officer. I had the distinct impression that the two men were loners, worse by far than an entire regiment of regulars. The prospect of any type of discipline or respect was remote.

I turned and ran for the house, wishing the door was closer, wishing I was faster, wishing none of this was real...except for Benjamin. The instant my boot hit the porch, someone grabbed at the skirt of my dress. I pushed on the door with all of my weight, making it bang against the wall.

"Charlotte!" Benjamin barked. He was standing by the fireplace, the musket on his shoulder, the barrel raised at eye level. Instinctively, I threw myself to the floor. There was a loud *CRACK*. The scent of gunpowder and smoke filled the room. The Redcoat fell back, blood blooming on his chest. The Brown Bess slipped from Benjamin's hand and he grabbed hold of a chair to keep himself from falling.

I had no time to react as the second Lobsterback stepped inside, over the body on the floor, his face twisted with fury. I scrambled to my feet, but he took hold of my hair, wrapped it around his fist, and reeled me in. Frantic, I scanned the room. The scissors, used to remove Benjamin's bandages and cut others, were on the bedside table. With a lunge, I grabbed them, fell to my knees, and whipped around. With all my strength, I jabbed them into my assailant's shin. He howled and dropped like a stone.

A fiery hand burned through my dress as Benjamin grabbed my shoulder and pushed me out of the way. The two men scuffled, rolling back and forth on the floor. Both were grunting and gasping for air, but the raw scream was Benjamin's when the British soldier grabbed his wounded thigh. In response, my Patriot tugged the scissors out of the Redcoat's leg and plunged them into his assailant's chest, directly over his heart, as deep as he could muster.

47

The light spilled out of the Brit's eyes and Benjamin rolled off of him, panting hard, fighting to catch his breath. I knelt beside him and offered him a cup of water from the pitcher I'd set on the porch on my way in, guzzling down my own cup before slumping down beside him.

"We have to get rid of them," Benjamin told me, his voice soft but insistent. He was right. Who knew if there would be more, if anyone would come looking for them.

"How? I can't carry them and you certainly can't, not in your current state." We lay there, side by side, staring at the ceiling, chests rising up and down in time with each other.

A hand fumbled its way to mine and took hold, a lifeline. "If I've learned anything during all these war years, when there's a will, there's a way." I turned my head and stared into Benjamin's warm, steady gaze. He was unshakeable; I could rely on him.

In the end, we wrapped the bodies in an old blanket. One at a time, we dragged them out behind the barn, next to the manure pile. How my injured Patriot kept to his feet, I do not know. Benjamin had to stop frequently, his body wavering like a tree bent by a fierce storm, but forged on. If all of our soldiers had the same strength of will, it was small wonder that the Americans would eventually win the Revolution.

I rounded up a shovel and set about digging a shallow grave, desperation pushing me on. My shoulders screamed at the strain, the sweat pouring off of me, my breath coming in sobs. Benjamin set his hand on my arm, calming me, and held it out for the shovel. Reluctantly, I passed it over, unable to do more.

He fell down several times, going whiter by the minute, the pulse fluttering madly at the base of his throat. I thought the poor man would collapse at any instant, but Benjamin carried on until there was enough room to conceal the dead. With a fierce growl, he rolled both bodies in and dropped to the ground next to the pit. "I'm sorry. I'm done in."

I patted his back and took up the shovel. This was the easier part of the job. An hour later, the pit was filled, covered with a few shovels full of manure for added measure. I returned the shovel to the barn and offered Benjamin my hand. His lips twitched, the closest I would get to a grin, and he gained his feet. The first step and his leg nearly buckled. "Dear God," he muttered between clenched teeth.

I slung his arm over my shoulder and we stumbled our way to the house, Benjamin falling onto the bed as soon as he reached it. I poured water from the kettle to brew him tea and clean us both up. As I wiped the sweat and dirt away from his face and hands, I couldn't help but stare at his leg. The bandage was covered in a mixture of livid, green pus and blood.

"I...I'm going to need to change your bandage, tend to your wound again." Damn my voice for cracking. I'm sure he knew how bad it was. It was his leg for God's sake. Benjamin didn't need to deal with me falling apart too.

He nodded and took my hand. "All right. Do what you must. I've made it this far. I can get through this."

His courage was enough for me to take heart. Steering clear of the bloodied scissors and dark stains on the floor that needed to be attended to, I found a knife in the kitchen and gathered other supplies. Benjamin had to be my first priority. I sliced through his bandage first and a moan rose up from his gut as I pulled the soiled cloth away. I couldn't hold back a gasp. The skin around the wound had turned black and crackled when I pressed down on it. Gangrene.

I spun around and bit my lip, praying for strength and a shot of confidence. As I plunged my hands into the basin of hot water, Benjamin whispered. "Charlotte...the whiskey...please."

I didn't hesitate, not even bothering to grab a cup. I picked up the jug and held it to his lips, allowing him to drink as much as he could take. Benjamin's head dropped back and he lifted his chin toward me, steel in his gaze. "Go on now."

I dipped a rag in the water and cleaned the wound once more, wiping away more pus as it gushed out of the hole. A cup of steaming water was next, poured directly into the wound and Benjamin wrapped his hands in the covers, pulling so hard they began to tear. Finally, I made a poultice that was more herbs than water and bandaged his leg. My nerves were stretched thin, ready to snap, and I was dizzy with fatigue.

I eyed the jug of whiskey and considered drinking myself to oblivion.

"Come here, sweet Charlotte." Benjamin spoke so low, I could barely hear him. His hand floated up in the air, so slowly it barely moved. He pulled me in close, pressing his lips to mine, scalding me with his touch, setting my heart to racing. "I beg your pardon, but if I'm going to die, I must know the blessing of your kiss. If I live, it will be because of you. Thank you for all you have done."

My tears came, falling on his face, making him blink. "Thank you for saving *my* life."

His eyes slid shut and a fevered sleep pulled him under while I tried to set the cottage to rights. Down on my hands and knees, I scrubbed at the floor, but the blood would not come up. As the hours crept by, Benjamin thrashed in the bed, groaning piteously, shaking. I went to his side and touched his forehead only to cry out. The fever was worse, much worse.

I poured a basin of cold water, pulled back the covers, and wiped him with a cold cloth everywhere that I could possibly reach, even lifting up his shirt and swabbing down his chest. His teeth chattered, his eyes only slits as he grabbed my hand. "I'm cold...so cold...so very cold."

I had to warm him. I covered him with blankets, grabbed everything off of my bed and added them as well. I built up the fire to a roaring blaze, yet he still shivered, moaning with the pain in his leg that burned even more with his shaking. At wit's end, I chose the last

51

alternative I had left to me. I climbed into bed on his right side, wrapped myself around him, and held on tight, propriety be damned. I may have seen the date Benjamin Willson died on a grave marker far off in the future, but perhaps the date was not permanently set in stone. If I didn't do something right away to fight off this fever and fearsome infection, my Patriot could slip through my fingers within the next few hours.

Darkness had fallen, the fire offering the only light when hooves pounded down our lane. I didn't even have the energy to move or worry that it might be an intruder. At this point, whatever happened, happened. The door opened and William was framed by the moonlight. His clear, gray gaze scanned the room, took in the blood-stained floor, the wreckage left from my attempts at doctoring Benjamin, saw his unmarried daughter in bed with a young man, unheard of in those early, Colonial days.

He wearily smiled and cleared his throat. "I'm glad to see you've had everything under control in my absence."

# Chapter 6

*I SLIPPED OUT OF BED* and went to his side as he closed the door, taking his arm. "Benjamin is raging with infection and fever, Papa. He was so cold. I tried everything to get him warm, but climbing in beside him was my last resort." Even from across the room, we could see the bedding shaking with his trembling.

William lit a lamp and turned so that he could look at me, his hand cupping my face. "My blessing, there has always been nothing but trust between us. You do not ever need to give me justification for your actions and decisions. I am sure, when there is time, you will tell me why the Brown Bess is on the floor and where those giant blood stains came from, but young Benjamin is our priority right now."

His face was grim, his gray eyes clouded with worry as he approached the ill militia man.

My forefather rested his palm on the top of my patient's head. Benjamin's eyes opened, bright with fever, two angry streaks of red marring his cheeks. "Sir...you've returned...I can explain...about Charlotte...and..."

William set a finger to his lips. "Not to worry, young Benjamin. The only thing we need to think about right now is taking care of you." He took a bag off of his shoulder and handed it to me.

"You'll find a small packet of herbs in there, Charlotte. That one is for a willow bark and yarrow tea for his pain and fever. The larger packet is Indian sage and honey for a poultice to treat the infection. As soon as they are ready, we are going to need to cleanse the wound and cut any dead skin away." My ancestor pulled back the covers and the smell of Benjamin's wound was horrible, the swelling worse, red streaks running down to his toes. "Hurry, Charlotte! We've no time to waste or it will be an amputation next and even that might not save him!"

I spun around and ran to the kitchen area, my hands shaking so badly I dropped everything several times. Gripping the small table, I closed my eyes and counted to ten while the pot of herbal tea brewed, the other herbs steeping in a hot basin of water. I gathered up more rags and another basin of hot water. Finally, my hands slippery with sweat, I grabbed a carving knife, its blade long and dangerously sharp. After two trips, I had everything lined up on the bedside table.

54

Benjamin lay quivering, his eyes fixed on the ceiling while I dipped my hands into the water and William cut away the bandages. We both turned away for only an instant and I had to cover my mouth, fighting off the urge to be sick. The wound was hideous, the skin appearing to be bubbled where it was not blackened around it, pus oozing out and dripping down his leg. I swabbed the wound as quickly and lightly as I could. Benjamin's body went as rigid as stone.

I picked up the knife next when William set his hand on my arm. "No, wait." He crossed the room to grab the whiskey and returned. "The healer told me to pour that on the knife and into his wound, but first I think we need to pour it into young Benjamin."

My forefather was gentle as he held the young man's neck and raised him, helping him to drink. "Take as much as you can, Benjamin. Drink yourself senseless."

When the whiskey was dribbling down the militia man's chin, William handed me the jug so I could treat the knife. "One more thing before you continue, Charlotte." He rummaged in his pocket and pulled out a musket ball. Taking Benjamin's hand, he pressed the small, round ball of metal into his palm and closed his fingers around it. "This is the ball I dug out of your leg, proof you defeated death once. Use it now and draw on that strength to cheat death once more."

With that, my forefather met my gaze and gave a nod before using his considerable strength to pin Benjamin's legs down. Instinctively, our patient took hold of the bed, drew in a deep breath, and closed his eyes tightly. It was now or never.

Whispering a hasty prayer, I doused the knife in whiskey and poured more into the nasty wound. Benjamin's back arched and he swore up a storm, blistering curses that I'd never heard before. Rattled as I was, I didn't hesitate, swiftly digging the knife into his leg and cutting away the damaged skin. The screaming was horrible, tearing the night apart until Benjamin had no voice left and blood poured on to the bed. I grabbed more rags and cleaned it best I could, pressing on the flaming, swollen skin to force as much of the infected pus out as possible. Finally, I rinsed it with scalding water and covered the wound with an herb-covered poultice. Only then did any of us breathe.

Benjamin's chest rose and fell with short pants, his face twisted in agony, hands gripping the sides of the bed as if for dear life. William covered him and offered more whiskey, which the young man eagerly accepted, drinking until his throat must have burned and there would be a fire in his stomach. He coughed and sputtered, turned his head, and vomited over the side of the bed, before taking more. "I'm...sorry," came his hoarse croak.

I went to his side and rested my hand on his cheek, staring down into his fevered eyes. "You have nothing to be sorry for. The only thing you need to do now is get well." On impulse, I bent down and swiftly kissed his lips before moving away to clear up the mess.

William helped me, cleaning up the vomit himself, putting things away. He poured hot water into two cups, prepared tea from our dwindling, bartered stash, heavy on the cream and sugar, laced with whiskey. He took me by the arm, ushered me to a chair, and pressed a steaming mug into my trembling hands. "Drink this, my blessing. You need it tonight." A kiss was planted on the crown of my head and he settled into the other chair to drain his own cup. So began our vigil.

All through the night, on the hour, we bathed Benjamin with cold water and pressed damp rags to his forehead. At the same time, I continued to change the poultice on his leg. William kept the fire burning high, heaping on the logs until the room felt like a furnace.

Drenched from our efforts, tired to the bone, I leaned my elbows on Benjamin's bed and pressed my hands to my forehead, forming a steeple with my fingers. As we fought for Benjamin Willson's leg and life, I wondered what it all meant, why I had seen that grave marker, and if I could change his destiny. Over and over in my mind, I could only think these words: *Please God...Save him...Save Benjamin...Please God.*

A hand touched my shoulder and I jerked, my head snapping back. I'd dozed off, my cheek pressed to Benjamin's good leg. "My blessing, go to bed. Rest a while."

"But Papa, you are exhausted too and you rode all day and into the night." I rested my head on his sturdy chest and his arms came up around me. It felt so good to lean on him, to feel like *my* father, Martin Ross, held me again.

"That is what a father is for, my blessing, to shoulder the load and ease the burden for his young ones. I will do all I can, give everything I have for you and Benjamin, our future. Sleep a while and you can relieve me. I will get my rest when I can, but you are about to drop on your feet."

I didn't argue any more, simply kissed his cheek, gave him my love, and tumbled instantly off to sleep when I fell on my bed.

*THE SUN WAS PRICKING* at my eyelids the next morning, meaning my day was starting much later than normal at the Ross household. William was usually up before dawn and I with him. I glanced across the room. My forefather's head was on the foot of the bed and he was sound asleep, snoring softly. I couldn't help but smile at him. *My* father could bring down the roof with his racket. I used to sleep with ear plugs while I still lived at home. My mother still did.

I slipped out of bed and rested my hand on Benjamin's forehead. He was blessedly cool, his hair damp with sweat, tendrils sticking to his face and neck. At my touch, his eyes opened, no longer clouded with fever, rich and warm as dark chocolate. A grin stretched across his face. "I guess I will live another day to receive another kiss."

There was such hope and longing in his voice, I couldn't resist. I bent over him and brushed his lips with mine. My soul began to sing.

"It does my heart good to see young Benjamin is feeling better." I backed away in embarrassment, but there was no need. There was a smile in William's voice as he patted the young Patriot's arm and slowly gained his feet. He wavered and put a hand to his head, moaning softly.

Eyes wide with alarm, Benjamin tried to rouse himself, but could barely lift his arm. I pressed him down and told him firmly, "You stay put and rest. As for you," I ducked under my ancestor's arm. "Unless you want to drive yourself into the ground and give me two ill men to tend to, it's off to my bed with you, Papa."

He grazed my cheek with a kiss. "You are incomparably wise, my blessing." William was out the moment he hit the pillow.

I busied myself straightening up the cottage, putting more herbal tea on for Benjamin and coffee for myself. I went outside, filled the pitcher at the well, took care of Bonnie and Belle, letting them out to graze. I stood at the fence for a few minutes to draw in the fresh air, soak up some sun, and give thanks for a new day even as I peered watchfully at the surrounding tree line. Thankfully, there were no flashes of red in the woods today.

Back inside, I doctored my patient's leg while he was in a deep sleep. He twitched and shifted, muttering softly, but did not wake. I felt his forehead and breathed easy. Still cool with no more sign of fever. I intended to keep it at bay.

59

I poured myself a cup of coffee and sank into the chair at his bedside, sipping slowly, allowing myself to simply enjoy the sweet, creamy indulgence. I gazed at Benjamin, the way the dark, tousled waves of his hair framed his face, how peaceful he looked in sleep. Younger somehow...and hard-to-breathe handsome. "What are you looking at?"

I jerked at his hoarse whisper and nearly dropped my cup. "You. Quite a good view."

He laughed softly and extended his hand to me. "Mine is much better."

I entwined his fingers in mine and in a reversal of roles, kissed them one by one, the pit of my stomach going tight. Surprised at myself and flustered, I stood up quickly and pulled away. "I have more tea for you. You'd best drink as much as you can, while you can."

I daren't waste any more time on words. His eyes were already drooping, his hand falling back on the bed as if the weight was more than he could bear. I quickly poured a mug and brought it to his side, managing to get half of the brew down before Benjamin was gone. I sighed. He'd have to drink the rest cold.

I watched him for a few more minutes and checked on William; he slept soundly. Unable to sit still, I went to the kitchen area and began to make preparations for dinner, starting with a bread recipe I found in the tiny cabinet. I made a hardy soup next, thinking Benjamin's stomach could manage the broth. Those tasks done and at odds with myself, I moved the window and stared out at the field, the animals lying peacefully in the tall grass, and the woods beyond. Still no sign of intruders today.

I stood and rubbed my arms absently, all the while pondering my situation. I was more confused than ever, filled with questions and no answers. If Benjamin was going to die in late October, why had he brought me here the night of the ghost walk? Was I meant to save him or to be a witness to his life and death so I could share his story? Worse yet, had William and I fought to bring him through the trial of his injury only to lose him at the Battle of Johnstown?

"You're thinking very hard. I expect to see smoke coming off the top of your head." Benjamin's voice broke the silence, light with humor, carrying over the crackling of the fireplace, the bubbling of the pot on the hearth, and William's snores. "What *are* you thinking about?"

I turned to face him. He was so endearing, face whiter than the pillow, dark eyes pinning me down and setting my heart to beating. I crossed the room. "I'm thinking about what I'd like to do with you once you're well." I picked up the cup of tea and held his head while he finished every drop.

Benjamin let out a low chuckle. "Right now I am about as strong as a kitten. A good wind would knock me over. When I am whole again...I have a long to-do list and every item includes you." He drew me in and pointed to his cheek. "I would not scandalize you in your father's house, but another one of your kisses

61

right here will go a long way to helping me accomplish all of my plans."

I dipped in and kissed him on one cheek, then the other. "There. You're two kisses closer."

His finger caught one of my curls and wrapped it round and round. He stared intently at the heavy strands of hair. "Beautiful. Like sun-drenched wheat I saw in the farmer's field in Saratoga." His gaze met mine and his thumb skimmed my cheek next. "Those eyes. They are sweeter than the honey my mother scooped into my tea when I was sick as a boy. You...are every good reason to fight for America, a place to call home, worth dying for."

The hair rose on the back of my neck and I shuddered inwardly at his words, that cemetery stone looming large in my mind. I laid my hand on his. "I'd rather you say I was worth living for."

"You are, Charlotte. Forever isn't long enough to get to know a woman like you." His voice trailed off as his head tipped to the side. The flickering flames danced in his gaze before sleep took him once more. I took the opportunity to check his leg and sagged in relief. The gaping wound was still an awful sight, but the signs of infection were gone. I put together another poultice, set it on his leg, and drew up the covers.

"I wish you could come under the covers again. This time I wouldn't be out of my mind with pain. I could truly enjoy the experience. I don't suppose I could convince you that my healing would be faster? I didn't imagine the whole thing, did I?" His hands came up, trembling with weakness, to take hold of my arms.

"You were supposed to be sleeping!" I smiled and wagged a finger at him, only to set it to my lips as William shifted and gave a great stretch. He had slept enough.

I went to my forefather's side and kissed his cheek in greeting, receiving one in return on my forehead. "How are you feeling, Papa?" The longer I lived in these shoes, the more the name fit. After all, when in Rome...

"Well-rested and famished! I hope that meal is nearly ready? The divine scent of your excellent cooking dragged me from my sleep." I nodded and dished out three bowls, sliced the bread, slathered on butter, and poured William coffee. He took the cup with thanks and sat beside Benjamin. The two spoke quietly while I carried over the other dishes and more tea for my patient. Once everything was set down, my forefather and I managed to get Benjamin propped up against the pillows, a bowl of broth in his lap. His hand trembled, but he managed to eat more than he spilled.

The three of us enjoyed a companionable meal and talked well into the night. I caught Benjamin rolling the musket ball in his fingers as he stared at the fire, strange shadows dancing over his face, sorrow in his eyes, fatigue crowding in. My father, seeing his melancholy, spoke up. "Tell us of one of your remarkable adventures, young Benjamin. I'm sure you have had many with your lively past."

"I met George Washington." That had me sputtering in my cup of milk before bed while William drew himself up, eyes bright with fascination. Benjamin continued to stare into the fire. "He was...everything they have said about him. Larger than life, about my height, broad shouldered, and with such a presence about him. Admirable, bold, and strong. I'd made my way to New York Harbor and he was distributing leaflets of the Declaration of Independence to his troops. By the time he finished, we all would have marched straight into the fires of hell for the man. I saw him again at Valley Forge...and I tell you. That man is the main reason those men made it through that terrible winter."

He fell silent, likely watching the reel of images from his past. "Other than that, I've done nothing remarkable." Benjamin's voice fell flat and the words died out. He seemed deflated somehow.

I took his hand, drawing his coffee eyes my way. "You have lost much, paid the price for liberty, and nearly died fighting for us. I'd say that is quite remarkable."

Benjamin gave me a smile sweet enough to make me melt and pulled my hand to his lips. "Not as remarkable as you, Charlotte," he let go and extended his hand to William, "and you, sir."

William stood and bent over the young man, giving him his customary kiss on the head, a benediction and sign of deep love. "You underestimate yourself. I think we all should turn in. Morning will be here soon enough and I have to get to the smithy tomorrow."

A pat on Benjamin's shoulder and he gave me a kiss as well. "Good night, my blessing. Sleep well."

Benjamin murmured goodnight as my forefather extinguished the oil lamp and banked the fire. He stretched out with a groan and his snoring began almost immediately. I rolled over and stared across the room. In the faint light of the moon, I could see that Benjamin was wide-eyed as well, watching me. I gave him a little smile and his mouth turned up at the corner in answer. Closing my eyes, I held on to that welcome sight. It took everything I had not to tiptoe across the room, slip under the covers, and kiss him senseless. I'd never felt so strongly about any other man, but after all that had happened since October 25, 2014, I wasn't about to question this intense force of attraction. I opened my eyes once more. He was still watching me and I had the feeling that if Benjamin could get out of that bed, by my side was the once place he'd choose to be.

HE KEPT TO HIS BED FOR SEVEN DAYS, weak as a baby, asleep more often than not. I cared for him, got lost in conversations when he awoke, and eagerly awaited William's return after long hours at the smithy. I found a rhythm to my days, immersing myself in life at the Ross Home of 1781. As more time passed, the 21$^{st}$ century faded into the background. This seemed real, William and Benjamin the threads that wove me into the fabric of the past.

I looked forward to getting out of bed each morning, knowing Benjamin was waiting for me. I held his hand, laughed with him, and watched him sleep. I fell harder for him with every day that passed. I also took heart. The longer I kept Benjamin in Papa's bed, in this house, the less likely that headstone in the Colonial Cemetery would come to be.

On the eighth day, Benjamin insisted on getting up.

"Be careful, young Benjamin. We did not put all of our efforts into saving your skin only to have you fall and break your neck." William stood at the door in a shaft of sunlight, his smile wide as he prepared to leave for the smithy.

The young militia man, now nearly as much a part of the family as I was, pulled himself up into a sitting position. His whole body trembled as he hung his legs over the side of the bed, swaying where he sat.

I shook my head and went to William to kiss him goodbye. "Have a good day, Papa."

He kissed my forehead, cheeks, and mouth in his farewell ritual. "It will be, my blessing, because you are at the open and close of it. Oh, I almost forgot something."

Papa stepped outside and returned with a beautifully, carved walking stick, topped by an intricately carved deer. He crossed the room and handed it to Benjamin. "If you're going to attempt to stand, this could be helpful."

Benjamin's eyes lit. "Another barter, sir?"

William laughed heartily, a sound so like *my* father's, it made me go still and reminded me

I was from another time. "Yes, I accepted it from one of my customer's for when I am old and feeble. This is only a loan for you until it is no longer necessary." I knew better. So did Benjamin.

Our young guest extended his hand and shook my father's. "You are too good to me, sir."

Papa's hand came down on the nape of his neck. "I could never take your father's place, but I can stand in for a fallen Patriot, give you a shoulder to lean on, a roof over your head, food from my table, and a gentle touch." *And my daughter's hand.* His words hung unspoken in the air as my forefather gazed meaningfully between the two of us. He cleared his throat. "I will see you at dusk. Make sure he does not overdo it, my blessing."

We were both quiet as the sound of hoof beats retreated. Benjamin took a deep breath, determination lighting his dark eyes. "All right. Let's give it a go." His hair tumbled into his face as he took hold of the cane. I moved in close, in case he should lose his balance. The air came out between his teeth as he pulled himself to his feet and his face lost all color.

"Are you all right?" I asked, setting my hand on his arm. I could feel the tension running through him, a live wire.

He nodded with a jerk of his head, clenched his jaw, and took a step. One more. Another. I could see that every inch of progress was bought with pain, his face covered in sweat, his body shaking...and yet Benjamin Willson

67

made it to the door. He turned and started to wobble. "Charlotte!" He gasped.

I ducked under him and caught him, just before he hit the floor and an ungodly moan rose up from somewhere in the region of his toes. "That's enough. Back to bed with you."

We made excruciatingly slow progress. I tucked him in, made him willow bark and yarrow tea with whiskey for the pain written all over his face, and took his hand. The both of us were breathing hard, quivering, but Benjamin's smile went from ear to ear, all the way to his eyes. He was on the mend.

The next day, he made it back to the bed on his own, the day after that to the privy. Another day and Benjamin insisted on going with me to the barn, to help with the chores. I eyed him dubiously. "Really? I almost had to drag you back from the privy by your hair yesterday."

He laughed, a sound I had come to truly love, one that Benjamin did not make often enough. His hair was getting longer and needed a trim, the dark strands always falling in his face. He had pulled it back with a piece of leather and the lines around his mouth and dark eyes were not as deep as they used to be. "I'll make it. I promise. I always..."

"Keep your promises. All right then, let's go." I grabbed the pitcher and we went outside. "Stand here a moment while I fill this. Might as well kill two birds with one stone." I hurried to the well, all the while glancing back at Benjamin, comforted by his presence, the memory of the British raiders still all too fresh in my mind. I had broken down and sobbed when I was finally able to tell William what happened while he was gone. He held me, hugged Benjamin fiercely, and brought home a rug from town the next day, "Another barter," to cover the stains.

Water mission accomplished, I joined Benjamin again as he stood still, saving his strength for the rest of the walk. I could see him measuring the distance to the barn. Further than he'd gone as yet, I knew he'd pay a terrible price. No matter, Benjamin did not shy away from a challenge. I stayed close by his side and patiently waited while he inched along all the way to the barn and started to sway. I set the pitcher down and lunged for him, only to be brought down in a tangle of limbs.

Both of us were breathless with laughter. I wagged my finger at him. "If you think I'm carrying you back, think again. The man is supposed to carry the woman."

I moved off of him and he snatched my hand. "You have carried me...with your caring ways, carried me to good health, and you've carried your father all these years by giving him a home and your love. You are a strong woman, the strongest I have yet to meet." His hand moved up to cup my cheek. "You are most precious, Charlotte. I am grateful to have such a gift in my life for however long we may have."

With that, he kissed me. My heart began to flutter and his thumb grazed the pulse beating by my collarbone. I closed my eyes and heat rose up in my face. A minute...maybe more and we pulled apart. "I...I think you are precious too. Now, Bonnie and Belle are waiting for me. What am I going to do about you?"

Benjamin smiled and glanced at his cane. "Between this and you, I should be able to get up again." He managed, biting is lip, but he did it. While I took care of the animals, my Patriot sat on a hay bale, steeling himself for the return journey. I went slowly with my chores to give him more time and when I was done, he took my hand. "Let's go. We can do this, together."

Several falls later, a few more stolen kisses, and his words proved true. Once he made it to the bed, I eyed him closely, my head tilted in speculation. "I think you need a bed bath and your hair needs a washing. You haven't had either since you first arrived. Strip yourself down, cover your...modesty...and I'll have you taken care of in no time."

I poured steaming water in a basin, always kept warm in a kettle on the hearth, gathered rags, and found my supply of soap. I could feel Benjamin's gaze following my every movement.

He had been so ill. We'd come so close to losing him, so close to making a liar out of that grave marker. I'd feared I would never learn what my connection to Benjamin Willson was. This was the first time that either one of us could focus on anything beyond survival. There was a heightened sense of awareness between us. I could see it in the militia man's dark gaze, the way he went still. There was the flurry of his pulse at the base of his throat that I was sure was in time with mine.

I'd never felt this way about any other man in my life, this fierce force of attraction. My heart skittered at his touch. My breath caught when I met his eye. My whole body hummed at his mere presence. Stepping next to his bed, my hands trembled as I set down my supplies on the table. I swallowed hard and gave a little nod. "Are you decent?"

His mouth quirked up at the corner and mischief sparked in his gaze, warming it like my coffee before the cream. "Your innocent eyes are safe." Sensing my inner turmoil, Benjamin threw back the covers. He'd covered himself from the waist to his thighs with his stripped shirt.

I set to my task. Benjamin's eyes closed and he let a deep sigh loose as I stroked the warm, soapy cloth over his face, neck, arms, and shoulders. His chest was next and the pulse at his collarbone danced madly. I almost paused and let my hands rest on his firm body, nearly set my lips to that mad beating. He was a fine specimen of a man, slowly regaining his strength and losing the sharp edges that had been brought on by deprivation, injury and illness.

I cleared my throat and carried on, washing his legs next, taking great care with his wound. It was healing but pained him terribly; I'd seen what it cost him in his face and his eyes. He drew in a sharp breath when I applied pressure, but did not complain. Finally, I rested my hand in his. "I'll do your hair now. I have a homemade soap with sunflower and rose petals in it. If you don't mind smelling like me, it will do."

"I will be only too glad to smell like you. Every time I breathe in, I can imagine I'm holding you in my arms." He smiled and *I* couldn't breathe as he pinned me with those beautiful, brown eyes. I pulled my hand away, covered him, and went to the head of the bed.

"Lift your head up, please." I spoke softly, nearly a whisper, but Benjamin obliged. I began by untying the leather strip holding his hair in a tail. I threaded my fingers through the thick, dark strands and wanted to lean in, feel his lips on mine. Fighting the temptation, I rinsed his hair with warm water and rubbed soap on my hands. I worked it through to his scalp, the fragrant scent rising up around us. A rinse and I dried it with a cloth.

His eyes were closed, his body loose. "That was heavenly. Thank you."

I squeezed his shoulder. "How about I cut your hair? You can barely see."

A nod of agreement and I continued with my efforts, asking him to sit up first. I hesitated before picking up the scissors. The same scissors used to cut his bandages...the same scissors used to stab and kill a Lobsterback. My hand trembled when I finally held them in my hand. He closed his fingers over mine, making me go still. Understanding passed between us and I took a deep breath, able to go on.

I started with the hair over his eyes before running my fingers through the strands at the end. I began snipping away, taking a few inches and felt him begin to shudder. "Charlotte...I cannot take much more. It feels so good, but I am afraid I will not be able to control myself and behave as a gentleman."

One last snip and my hands gripped his shoulders as I clamped my eyes shut, need and want tugging deep inside of me. "I...I feel the same way." Benjamin reached up and set his hand on mine. A moment longer and he brought it to my lips.

"Thank you, sweet Charlotte. For everything, since the day I set foot on your doorstep." The thanks should have been mine from the moment Benjamin Willson set foot in my heart.

*"THAT'S IT. YOU'RE GETTING SOME FRESH AIR TODAY.* You're much too pale. A healthy dose of sunlight will do you good." It was the tail end of his week out of bed and my patient was rather peaked; I didn't like the look of him.

Benjamin stood at the door, his feet planted, leaning more heavily on his cane than I liked to see. He'd walked the entire length of our lane the previous day, and was practically crying by the time we made it back to the house. I rested a hand on his arm. "I know. We'll have a picnic."

The young militia man stared at me as if I had grown two heads. "A picnic? Isn't that a bit frivolous? I need to walk, get my strength back, make myself useful." He'd pushed himself more each day, unwilling to be an imposition, working hard at his recovery. Benjamin wanted to show

73

his gratitude by making a contribution to my forefather, but his injury continued to take a toll on him, sapping his strength and dampening the light in his eyes. Some R and R was in order for his own good.

"A little frivolity wouldn't kill you. Don't worry. We'll be sure to squeeze in some walking in our day, but first, *I* need some rest. I'm plumb worn out." I knew that ploy would work.

Ever the gentleman, Benjamin was immediately contrite. "I'm sorry, Charlotte. I do not mean to be a burden on you. I know how hard you work around the homestead and I've only added to your load. As soon as I am well enough, I will be able to ease the weight you carry." He caught my hand in his and brought it to his lips to brush it with a kiss.

A shiver ran through me at his touch and I closed my eyes, fighting the urge to fall into him. I set a finger to his lips, stopping any further protests. "I meant nothing of the sort. I only wanted you to agree to come. I don't want to waste a minute with you." I knew only too well how long we had...if the stone in the Colonial Cemetery did not lie.

Realization, that I had played on his sympathy, dawned on his face, warming his dark gaze as his mouth quirked up at the corner. "Why you little sneak!" A deep rumble of laughter from way down deep had him shaking. Benjamin gave a little bow. "Let's have at it then." He looked like a little boy, half torn between a pout and annoyance. I darted in and kissed his cheek and he couldn't help but grin. "Will there be more where that came from?"

I shrugged and scurried to put together a simple meal of bread, cheese, apples, and ale. I feared he'd changed his mind if I didn't hurry. He insisted on carrying the basket and we stepped out to meet the day. It was unseasonably warm for late September. A good soak in the sun and crisp air would do us both good, perhaps clear my head. Every time I was close to him, waking or sleeping, my mind became clouded with dreams about my young Patriot.

I scanned our surroundings, eying the forest and fields, looking for the perfect spot for our lunch. Off in the distance, I could see a meadow by a stand of pines, practically glowing in the midafternoon light. "There. It's perfect." I gestured with my hand.

His face fell at the sight; a considerable distance spanned between us. With grim determination, Benjamin inhaled deeply and gave a curt nod. "Let's get started."

"Stay here. I'll be right back." He sighed and leaned on his cane, humoring me once again because Benjamin Willson could not do otherwise. It was against his code of honor.

I went to the barn and gave Belle a pat before moving on to Bonnie. Talking to her in a hushed voice, I led her from her stall. I put her bit in her mouth, hoisted her saddle over her back with a great heave, and cinched it. A gentle stroke of her neck and we made our way outdoors.

Benjamin's puzzled expression turned to one of dismay as he contemplated the obstacle of mounting the mare, studying the space between the ground and her back. "I don't think horseback riding is a wise idea, Charlotte."

Undoubtedly, he was right. I had only been on a horse at the fair when I was a little girl and that was practically a pony on a rope. My rational mind told me to be sensible and keep my feet on the ground, while a voice from somewhere deep within its recesses told me I'd done this at least a hundred times. I pulled up short of him and crossed my arms. "You're *not* walking all the way to that meadow so you'll either stay here in the dust or get up on this horse."

Considering the glare he gave me in return, I had a formidable opponent. That said, Benjamin moved forward and gripped the saddle horn. One great heave and his bad leg was up and over. He went white at the strain, the lines around his mouth and nose etching their way more deeply into his face. He breathed out hard through his nose then pinned his gaze on me. His hand reached out for mine. "Well, are you planning on standing there all day or are you going to come with me?"

I tipped my head up to meet his dark eyes and a delicious burning began deep down in the pit of my stomach, sending a fire flickering through my veins. His face was brighter than the sun, dizzying as he smiled at me. I had no choice but to take his hand and allow him to pull me up in one smooth move.

Benjamin settled me against his chest, his body a warm, solid wall to lean on. His hand wrapped around my waist, holding me snugly in place, and I took up the reins. We began a slow mosey, the rhythm of Bonnie's swaying steps hypnotic as the sun beat down on our heads. Leaning back, my body grew heavy, completely at home in his arms. I felt safe...no longer torn between the past and the future...content to be in the here and now with him.

I hadn't slept well the past few nights. Nightmares of a plain, white stone, that awful date indelible in my mind, had torn me from a sound sleep. Unable to drift off, I would lie awake, staring at Benjamin's face, dimly illuminated by the dying embers of the hearth, trying to imprint it in my mind. With each passing day, I was all too aware that we were getting closer to the Battle of Johnstown, a date I was certain I could not change. The turn of events that had set that particular ball rolling could not be stopped. I was equally certain that the dark figure that led me to that stone was the ghost of Benjamin Willson and the thought of being parted from him filled me with dread.

"We're here," he whispered in my ear, his cheek scraping against mine, and I shut the door on the dark path my thoughts had taken. The day was ours and I had to snatch every minute.

Benjamin seemed as intent as I to enjoy this private moment. He rested his hand on my cheek. I turned to face him and his fingers worked through my hair, setting my curls free in the wind. "You are so lovely." He murmured softly and then his lips took mine.

I gave myself to the kiss. We'd kept a polite distance whenever William was home, but the inexorable pull between us grew stronger the more time we spent in each other's company. Now, alone with no threat of interruption, it was as if we couldn't get enough of each other. My head started to spin and he rested his forehead on mine, the both of us breathing hard. "Shall we get down?" I asked faintly.

"We'd best before you incinerate me with your touch." His smile was strained. Such strong feelings between a man and a woman could be painful.

I slid off with ease, my body knowing exactly what to do, and waited while Benjamin gripped the saddle horn and eased himself down beside me. His leg gave out, nearly pitching him to the ground and I ducked under his arm. "Are you all right?"

He swallowed hard, gave a nod. "Fine, just fine." Hooking the basket on his arm and accepting his cane, a few faltering steps were all Benjamin could take.

I sat to spare him and offered my hand. Benjamin eased himself down beside me on the carpet of tall grasses littered with leaves and the breath hissed between his teeth. I couldn't resist. I reached out and trailed my fingers over his hair. "I'm sorry it hurts you so."

I nearly choked on my words and my eyes filled. I glanced down at my lap and his hands were on my cheeks, forcing me to look at him. "It

78

hurts less because of you." One more light kiss, his breath brushing against my skin, and his thumb skimmed over my cheek, wiping away my tears.

If I sat idle any longer, I might do something I regretted—loosen my tongue about all of my fears...let my body lose all of its restraint. I squeezed his hand and turned to our picnic basket, laying out our meal. We took our time and ate everything, draining the jug of cider down to the last drop. It dribbled down Benjamin's chin and I dabbed at it, the both of us laughing...and all the while my heart was making a mad dance for him.

The strain was just as hard for my Patriot. I could see it in the rigid lines of his body and a tightness in his jaw that had nothing to do with his leg. He stretched out on the grass and gazed up at the sky, his chest heaving, his face flushed. Resisting the urge to lay my head on his heart, I followed his example.

Together, we stared at the canvas of blue above, watching the cloud formations float by. My hand wandered with a will of its own and found his. Benjamin's fingers closed around mine, holding on tight. We were quiet and my body hummed with his nearness. Searching for a distraction, I studied the shapes in the sky. "Look at that cloud over there, like a fat rabbit and that one...it's an angel."

"I see your face in every cloud." His low voice rolled over me. Benjamin was no longer looking above. His eyes were trained on mine as he turned and rested his palm on my cheek. "It is your face that I see when I wake, when I close my eyes, even when I am sleeping. When I was so ill, you were my candle burning bright, lighting my way back. I could never tire of seeing your face, Charlotte."

I couldn't speak, couldn't move, couldn't breathe. He shifted, easing his way closer, and grazed my collarbone with his lips...trailed upward to the hollow between my chin and my neck...then to my jawbone, finally pressing his mouth against mine. I closed my eyes, lost myself in him and cast a fervent prayer. *If I am meant to lose him, take me back now. Let this happy memory be my last.*

The wind picked up, sighing in the trees, tugging at my hair and our clothes. I reached out and grabbed hold of his shirt, fearful my prayer might come true. Benjamin's hand burned through the heavy material of my dress as he set it on my hip and I nearly cried out with my longing for him. In such a short time, this man had become my everything. I didn't understand the force of my feelings, but they were a hurricane, threatening to go beyond my control.

Benjamin moaned softly and sat up, a hand raking through his hair and pulling at the long strands. "I'm sorry...Charlotte...I cross my bounds. My feelings are so strong for you that being a gentleman is getting harder by the day." He took hold of his cane and pulled himself to his feet with considerable effort. With even more strength of will, he turned to me and offered his hand. "We'd best be going back. Your father will be home soon and I would not have him find me taking advantage of his only daughter out in a field."

I accepted his assistance and gained my feet. "Who's to say I didn't take advantage of you?" With that, I snatched a kiss and gathered up the remnants of our picnic. Benjamin could only shake his head, wearing a rueful grin. I untied Bonnie and led her to his side. He handed me his cane and took hold of the saddle horn. With a grunt, he was up and over. His face was drawn by the strain, but he said nothing of his discomfort. I mounted and we made our way to the barn at an easy pace, his hands at my waist, assuring me I wasn't going anywhere. My prayer would go unanswered for now.

In the barn, I dismounted. Benjamin did as well and suffered for it, immediately sitting on a nearby bale of hay. I turned away to allow him to deal privately with his pain. I went about putting the saddle away and wiping Bonnie down before putting her in her stall.

The barn was warm what with the late afternoon sunlight streaming in, the hay sweet. As I picked up a brush and began to run the bristles over the mare's body in a repetitive motion, I was soothed to the point of forgetting my struggles with time or even who I was. My mind was calm, my spirit at peace...until I felt Benjamin's hands on my shoulders.

"I do not know what the future holds, Charlotte, but I sincerely hope and pray that you are a part of it." He took the brush from fingers that went limp, set it down, and slowly turned me to face him. I was falling with no end in sight.

81

His hand came up to take hold of the nape of my neck, my face tipping to his as the flowers reach for the daylight, and I he gifted me with a kiss. As my hands found my way to his broad, firm back, I knew that I held my heart's content. *Forget my last prayer, Dear Lord. If You love me in the least, never make me say goodbye to this man.*

The kiss spun out until I was dizzy. A fine trembling ran through Benjamin's frame and he pulled me close, burying my head in his chest. We were walking a tightrope on our budding relationship, our hearts getting closer by the minute. At any moment, we could lose our balance...but I knew without a doubt, my Patriot would catch me.

I did not know how much time had passed, but the angle of the sunlight had changed, the day drawing to a close. Benjamin wrapped an arm around my waist and we walked to the house, taking the steps slowly, the pain rippling across his face. Once inside, he sat down by the hearth and rested one hand on his thigh, his fingers kneading at the wound, his hand tightening into a fist.

I set my basket down and went to the pitcher in the kitchen. "Would you care for a cold drink of water?"

Beads of perspiration had made his hair damp around his face and glistened on his forehead. I did not think they had anything to do with the heat, but rather the strain. The stubborn man insisted on pushing his body beyond its limit. He gave me the sweet smile I'd come to love. "Only if you will sit and have one with me."

I was pouring the second mug when the door opened and William filled the room with his cheerful presence. We'd been so focused on each other, neither of us heard the approach of his horse. "Greetings my blessing and Benjamin! I've good news. We've an invitation to dinner. I'm sure Benjamin is about to go out of his mind being trapped here so I'm springing him for an evening. Spruce yourselves up and we're off to the home of Richard Dodge."

The pitcher slipped from fingers gone numb as I grabbed hold of the table before my legs gave out. I didn't even feel the chill of the water splashing on my dress and feet.

# Chapter 7

"*CHARLOTTE, ARE YOU WELL?*" Benjamin sprang from his chair and was by my side. Forgetful of his injury, his jaw clenched as he took my arm, his forehead creasing in concern. He'd left his cane and had to grab hold of the table for support, but his other hand never let go of me. That endearing fall of hair had tumbled into his eyes and I wanted to stroke it, step into the steadying presence of his arms, assure myself he was real. Solid. Here.

William crossed the room in great strides to take my other arm. "Do you need to sit, my blessing? You've gone white as snow." He studied me closely while Benjamin bent down and picked up the pitcher, the air hissing through his teeth.

"I'll get more water." He turned toward the door, but my forefather shook his head.

"No, I'll do that. I think you've been overdoing it. Sit, young Benjamin, and you as well, my daughter. First, tell me what is the matter."

I smiled shakily and kissed his cheek in greeting. "Nothing...nothing, Papa. I thought I saw a mouse. I'm fine. I'll get the water." I don't think they believed me judging by the doubt in their eyes, but neither man questioned me.

I took the pitcher and darted out the door, leaving the dumbfounded men behind. At the pump, I wrapped my hands around the handle until my knuckles went white and closed my eyes. Another grave stone in the Colonial Cemetery blazed in my mind, one that had been erected only a year before...if we went back to my own time.

Brigadier-General Richard Dodge. He'd served in the Revolutionary War and again in the War of 1812. The man had also held the title of Johnstown's first postmaster. The Johnstown Historical Society had made great fanfare of General Dodge Day as they re-dedicated his new cemetery stone and rolled out a host of events in his honor.

I'd dressed in costume, marched in the parade, attended the ceremony, enjoyed a trip down Memory Lane with my fellow town's people. Pictures filled my photo album at home in the 21st century and now I was about to meet the man who would one day sleep in that tiny plot of ground. I doused my hands in icy water and splashed my face. Would I ever get used to these brushes with history, up close and personal?

I returned to the house. William had already changed his clothes and Benjamin was wearing a brown jacket and clean breeches, his dark hair neatly combed and tied back, face washed. I nodded to them both with what I hoped was a casual air and set the pitcher in the kitchen. I had to give myself credit. My hand hardly shook at all as I drank a mug of water in great swallows. Taking a deep breath for fortification, I went to my chest and rummaged through my clothing, drawing out a blue floral print with a matching bonnet.

As I pulled the screen to block the view, both men turned their backs. I could hear the low rumble of their conversation while I dressed. Reaching up to check my hair, I was dismayed to find I'd forgotten to pull it back up after our picnic. What must William think? I hastily brushed at my curls, hard enough to catch a few snags and make my eyes water.

My forefather gazed at me, a small smile tugging at his mouth as he watched me tuck my hair into a neat bun. I had the strong suspicion that he was aware Benjamin and I had been doing more than simply talking. On several occasions since the militia man had been on the mend, my ancestor had made hints about a future together. Was he trying to play his hand at matchmaker?

William's eyes shone brightly as he took my hand and kissed the top of my head. "You look beautiful, as always, my blessing. I'm going to hitch up the wagon to spare young Benjamin. Otherwise, I am certain the mule would insist on walking the entire way. Besides, these old bones are tired." He tossed Benjamin a wink and left us alone.

Our houseguest stepped forward and stood before me. He took my hand and made what could only be considered a courtly bow, grazing my knuckles with his kiss. "Your father does not do you justice. You are brighter than the sun and all the stars above, Charlotte, more beautiful than anything I have ever seen. I am thankful for whatever twist of fate or destiny brought me to your door."

My mouth went dry as I drank him in and felt the burn of his hand on mine. Gazing at this tall, straight figure of a man, the set of his shoulders, the jut of his chin, I had never seen anyone that could compare...past, present, or future. When he touched me, I felt a sense of homecoming for my heart, as if I had been waiting for this man all my life...or for many lives and the thought nearly made me throw myself into his arms. What if my soul had been looking for him generation after generation, only to made whole when we were together again?

"Charlotte? Are you sure you're not unwell? Perhaps you need to lie down." I'd begun to sway and Benjamin wrapped an arm around my waist to steady me. "I'm going to tell your father you need to rest."

I shook my head and pasted on a bright smile. "Nonsense! I'm fine, Benjamin. I'm just excited about our dinner invitation. I look forward to introducing you to Brigadier-General Dodge." *And meeting him myself. Maybe Thomas Jefferson, Benjamin Franklin, and George Washington will round out the group.* I had to bite my tongue to hold back the hysterical laughter that threatened to bubble over, making me giddy.

Benjamin stared at me intently, eyes clouded with doubt, but he did not argue. He took my hand firmly in his and we went outside. William waited with the wagon just a few steps from the door, Raven and Bonnie paired up to pull us on our way. I was filled with gratitude for my forefather's considerate intuition. My Patriot was truly battling with his leg, limping hard after his exertions from the day before. The shorter the distance, the better.

Benjamin placed his hands on my waist and lifted me up, no matter how I protested that I could manage. Jaw set, he boosted himself up next. His breath came out in a rush and we were off. A half hour later, following the meandering road outside of town, past Sir William Johnson's estate, we pulled up next to a home that was impressive by the standards of the time. Twice the size of ours, it was painted a dark green that complimented the stand of pines that pressed in close.

William tied the horses to a hitching post and walked around back of the wagon. He helped me down first, an easy task for a man that battled with metal on a daily basis. Brooking no argument, he came to Benjamin's aid next, allowing the young man to lean on his shoulder, sparing him from putting any weight on his bad leg.

"Thank you, sir. Your kindness knows no bounds." The militia man bowed his head, a crimson tide rising up to his ears. He was embarrassed by the need for assistance.

My forefather clapped him on the back. "You saved my daughter's life the day the British came to my home. I'd say that I'm forever in *your* debt. Kindness is free and easy to give away."

William reached for my hand and pulled me along with him. The love that I felt for this man squeezed my heart. So many qualities of my ancestor had been instilled in *my* father and not for the first time, I felt a pang of longing for the man who had raised me. I only hoped that the same seeds were blooming inside of me, growing by the day. We paced ourselves for Benjamin's sake and the door was opened wide the instant we hit the porch.

"William, Charlotte! Welcome! It has been too long my friends!" A tall man with an easy smile and neatly trimmed dark hair greeted us. He slapped his old friend on the back and kissed my cheek, leaving me with that odd sensation of familiarity for someone I had never seen before in my life...or had I?

Our host's hand reached out to take mine in the easy camaraderie of friends. My mouth went dry and my heart batted against the cage of my ribs. Every run in with the past was a shock and I couldn't help but wonder if I would be yanked back to the future. Benjamin stepped in close and took my arm, watching me closely. I made him my anchor and pulled out a smile, flashing it his way and turning my attention to the brigadier-general. I was still here, though only time would tell for how long.

Richard's blue eyes twinkled with lively interest as he offered his hand to Benjamin next. "You must be young Benjamin. I'm Richard. I was dealing with an ambush further down the way the day you were injured and did not have the opportunity to make your acquaintance, but William told me all about you. How's the leg?"

Benjamin tapped the floor with his cane. "Knock wood, I'll be better soon, thanks to the generosity and care of the Ross family."

Richard put an arm around the young man's shoulders. "They are something beyond belief. You are in the best of hands, especially sweet Charlotte's." He gave me a wink and a knowing look passed between him and William. "Do come in and meet the rest of my guests. I'm glad you could join us...and our militia. We need every able-bodied man to band together in this fight. Losing simply is not an option."

"I will be able-bodied soon, sir, I promise." *And Benjamin Willson keeps his promises.* I shivered as the image of his gravestone rose up to taunt me once again. I knew without a doubt that my Patriot would fight again...and if I could not do anything to stop it, he would lose his final battle. Giving myself a hard, mental shake, I accepted William's hand and we joined the others in what must have been considered the parlor. The room was large with an ample hearth and many chairs scattered about, allowing seating for his many guests.

We were greeted by other members of the Tryon County Militia, a veritable who's who of those who populated the Colonial Cemetery in 2014. Captain John Little; he would be wounded at the Battle of Johnstown, but go on to live a long life. I almost giggled at his name. Like Little John from Robin Hood, he was a large man, burly and boisterous with a great head of fair hair and pale blue eyes. Talmadge Edwards would be responsible for starting the glove industry in America with his tanning process. "How about a nice pair of gloves for a pair of shoes, William?" The sandy-haired man asked with a wink, eyes such a brilliant green, I couldn't help staring at him.

Jacob Cooper approached next. It was my first opportunity to actually study the man up close; I hadn't even looked at him on the day of my arrival and he'd been cloaked in darkness that first night when the young man acted as a messenger for the militia. Considerably shorter than Benjamin, he was a picture in contrasts, light to my Patriot's dark, his copper hair blazing in the confines of the enclosed space, eyelashes dusted with gold unable to dim eyes of a blue as bright as a cloudless, summer sky. He was brawny and crackled with a vitality that could not be contained.

His gaze lit up at the sight of me and I wondered if there was any kind of history between us or simply wishful thinking on his part. He kissed my hand and bowed with a flourish. "Miss Charlotte, you are looking well."

William clapped a hand on his fellow militia man's shoulder. "Jacob, I'd like to introduce you to Benjamin Willson, the brave Patriot from Boston that I told you about. Benjamin, this is Jacob Cooper."

"It is a pleasure." Benjamin's tone was cold to say the least. I glanced at him and saw that he'd gone rigid and I doubted that his leg was the source of his uneasiness. He gave a polite nod but his eyes were shadowed. His hand pressed at the small of my back, urging me forward. An intense look passed between the two men as we proceeded. *Challenge given, challenge accepted.*

Flustered after that exchange , I couldn't help but be amused by Benjamin's jealousy. The man was practically green and needn't have worried one iota. He had me from the start... beginning with a pale marker on a dark October night over two hundred years into the future while the ghosts walked among us. The familiar terror at the memory rose up and threatened to smother me.

I fought to steady myself when William put an arm around my shoulders. "Charlotte, Benjamin, these are friends of Richard's, William and Sarah Irving and their children,...." The names of their little ones were rattled off, William Junior, Peter, Ebenezer, Catherine, a toddler, John Treat, baby Sarah, all of them a blur in my mind except for one. Ann Sarah.

I was dizzy as I shook her hand and held on a moment longer than I should have. A slip of a girl, not more than 11, smiled and peered at me curiously until I finally let go and struggled to get control of my breathing. Benjamin was eying me as well as we sat down to dinner, but I only gave him a nod and pretended to focus on the meal.

All the while, my mind was hinged on my latest acquaintance, Ann Sarah. In only six years, she would marry our host. Years later, she would be buried with him in our Colonial Cemetery. Right now, she helped mind the litter of Irving children, laughed, and chatted cheerfully with no idea that Richard would be her husband. Marriage was the last thing on her mind. She was just being a girl, closer to childhood than adulthood at that moment. Several times, I caught Richard watching her with speculation. Perhaps the foundation for their relationship was being built tonight.

After a pleasant meal, we all took a seat around the parlor. The women were talking housekeeping, cooking, and childrearing. The men were talking war and politics. With Benjamin by my side, I couldn't help but be drawn into conversation that revolved around the militia. A part of me wanted to cover my ears even as I listened in fascination. These events were no longer distant facts and a re-telling in a history book, but rather recent enough to have shaken these people to their core, leaving them raw.

"They have already taken enough. We cannot let them have anymore, not after the Cherry Valley Massacre in '78 and just last year that bastard, *Sir* John Johnson, coming through here with the Burning of the Valleys. Blocking our supply routes to Fort Oriskany and Fort Rensselaer. Leaving nearly 200 dead. It has to stop and it has to stop now!" Jacob Cooper banged his fist on his knee, his blue eyes burning with the fire of youth and patriotism combined.

Beside me, the tension radiated off Benjamin. I knew the stories of war hit him hard, having destroyed his life as he knew it and robbing him of all he loved. I glanced at his face. His dark eyes were pinned on the young, copper-haired militia man across the room. Following his gaze, my breath caught as Jacob fixed his attention on me. His mouth curled in a playful grin and then, the unheard of. He winked at me.

Benjamin stiffened, his hand tightening around his cane until his knuckles bulged and turned white. At any moment, he'd be across the room and the two men would be at it, like two bucks clashing their antlers over a prize doe.

Taking hold of my companion's shoulder, both to calm him and in reassurance, I pulled myself to my feet. "How about a story?" I asked rather breathlessly, hoping to stave off a fearsome confrontation. Fighting over a woman might be romantic in theory. The harsh reality could only be messy.

The chatter died out as all faces were directed my way, lit in anticipation. After all, there was no television, radio, or theatre. Books were scarce, most reading material confined to patriotic leaflets. The art of oral storytelling was highly appreciated and most welcome. The children in attendance settled on the floor by the fireplace, including Ann Sarah Irving. Taking in her wide-eyed expression, her lips parted as she sat up straight, a bit of mischief inspired me to launch into two tales that would become favorites in the near future, Rip Van Winkle and the Legend of Sleepy Hollow.

I gave it all I had, a lively performance. After all, it was the dress-up of a lifetime, except this time I didn't wear a costume and it was for real. No one moved. No one barely breathed, their rapt attention hanging on my every word as I moved around the room, stepping in close from time to time, using voice effects and facial expressions for dramatic effect.

By the end of the Headless Horseman's tale, the children were rushing off to their mothers, some of them burying their faces in their laps, and the room broke into applause. I gave a little curtsy and glanced up to see Benjamin staring at me in open admiration. My cheeks burned and my heart raced, still high with the thrill of having a captive audience. I enjoyed their animated approval, but I only had eyes for *my* Patriot.

As I returned to his side, Benjamin stood, bowed over my hand, and kissed my fingers. "That was amazing, Miss Charlotte. I'd no idea you were such a talented storyteller, but then nothing you do should surprise me. You are incomparable."

I dipped my head at his praise, my heart fluttering with his affections . Others gathered around, asking me questions, squeezing my hand, patting me on the back or wrapping an arm around my shoulders. Jacob complimented me as well, but remained courteous and retreated immediately, not wishing to step on Benjamin's toes I would assume. One glance at my Patriot's formidable expression was enough to make anyone back off.

As we prepared to leave at the end of the evening, Ann Sarah grabbed hold of my hands and flung her arms around me. "That was wonderful, Miss Charlotte, simply wonderful. I'm going to go home and write those stories down. I won't ever forget them!"

Watching her leave with her family, I knew for a fact that she would not forget. In two years, her baby brother, Washington, would be born. I pictured the two of them, curled up in bed while Ann Sarah whispered my stories into his ear night after night. Perhaps I had interfered a bit in history myself, inspiring the creation of America's first bestselling novelist at home and in Europe. In twenty years or so, Washington Irving would pay a visit to Johnstown, a true sensation, his stories read round the world. The Legend of Sleepy Hollow and Rip Van Winkle would be the hallmarks of his success, classics that would continue to be shared for generations to come. A treasured volume of his works sat on the bookshelf in my little cottage in the 21st century; my father had read the stories to me so many times, I knew them by heart.

I was still thinking about planting the seeds for a legend when Jacob Cooper stopped before me and took my hand. "Good night, Miss Charlotte. It was a pleasure to see you this evening." With that, he gave a bow and then the charmer dropped a kiss on my cheek. *Whatever has possessed him?* Jacob whistled as he walked away, while I pressed my hand to my face, thrown of balance by his show of affection.

There was a sharp intake of breath by my side and Benjamin headed off to our wagon, moving rather quickly considering his injury. His back was ramrod straight, his shoulders tight. When I rushed to catch up, his eyes glittered dangerously, his jaw clamped shut.

William, an observant soul, squeezed Benjamin's shoulder and mine. "Young ones, I need to give John Little and his family a ride home. Do you mind if I drop the two of you at the end of our lane and go on to their place?"

We voiced our approval and Benjamin helped me up after the Littles boarded. I couldn't help but stare at John, his blonde head tilted toward his wife's, a baby in her arms and a boy nestled on his lap. The sight of them squeezed at my heart. John Little would fight at the Battle of Johnstown and survive being shot. His grave marker would not be far from Benjamin's in the Colonial Cemetery. A rubbing was framed and hung on my wall, far into the future. Tears rose to my eyes and I turned away. Benjamin's expression softened at the sight of my face and he took my hand. I leaned against his shoulder and closed my eyes, the tug of past and present wearing on me.

"I wish that I could have known my mother, felt a touch like Amy Little's." The words rang true. I missed *my* mother. A true confidante, she would listen to all of my fears and help me through this struggle. That I could talk to no one about the secret I carried was a great burden. Surrounded by all of these people, in many ways I felt like an island.

Benjamin proved otherwise when he kissed the top of my head, but even that comfort was fleeting. He would not be with me for long. "I understand, Miss Charlotte. I long for my mother often, especially at times like these when I see a woman holding her child close. I can only imagine what a hole has been left in your life, never having known that precious woman. You remind me to be grateful for the time I had." Loss. It was the cost of war...and there was still more to come.

The wagon rumbled to a stop a half hour later and William called out, "Here we are my blessing, Benjamin. I'll be home in an hour or so."

Benjamin lowered himself down, wincing with the pressure on his bad leg, and lifted me off the back of the wagon. With a wave and farewells from the Littles, we turned and began the trek to the cottage. We'd only made it several feet, when Benjamin grabbed hold of my hand roughly, pulled me to the side, and pushed me up against a mighty oak.

"What is this between you and Jacob Cooper?" He spoke through clenched teeth, practically a growl and he was trembling with barely controlled anger. He favored his injured leg, placing all of the pressure on his right, his hands braced on either side of my head. I could not possibly avoid him.

I set my palms on his shoulders and stared him in the eye. "Nothing, Benjamin, nothing more than friendship. I do not want anyone to be more to me than a friend except you."

He was breathing hard, his eyes squeezing shut for an instant, and then his fingers threaded through my hair. His mouth came down on mine and everything else was forgotten. There was no grave marker, no past or future, only this moment and this man. The kiss spun out until his body finally went loose and I fell against him. I felt so light I could float away if his hands did not tether me to the ground.

Benjamin pulled back and cupped my face with his hands. "I *am* your friend, Charlotte, but I want to be so much more." He took a deep breath and proceeded to pick me up in his arms, handing over his cane.

"What *are* you doing?" I batted at his shoulder helplessly. I might as well have tried to bend steel with my bare hands.

He moved forward, limping hard, grunting with the effort. "I'm carrying you of course. You said this is how it's done, that the man should carry the woman,...and I don't see

Jacob Cooper standing around or lurking in the bushes to sweep you off your feet."

"Benjamin, look at me." He stopped at my tone, breathing as if the man had just completed a marathon, but did my bidding. I stroked his hair, watched the line between his eyes disappear as his lip curled upward at my touch. "I don't want Jacob Cooper to carry me away. I never have. You already did—since the first moment I laid eyes on you." *In the Colonial Cemetery.*

He stared at me for only an instant before stealing another kiss. Shifting me in his arms, Benjamin moved forward. His steps faltered several times. I thought his leg might give, but my Patriot pushed on. I was in awe of him, his courage...his strength...and I hoped, his love.

We made it all the way to the house before he hit the door. We tumbled to the floor in a tangle of limbs, laughing breathlessly in the dim glow of the firelight. Benjamin nudged the door shut and then he was leaning over me, arms braced on the floor, making me lose my way in his dark gaze. "Are we more than friends, Charlotte?"

My hands came up to hook on the nape of his neck. "Definitely." I could not look away from him if my life depended on it. Benjamin Willson had that kind of power over me. I'd follow him anywhere. I'd already journeyed through time. If he asked me to go to the ends of the Earth, Benjamin need only tell me when. I would gladly go and did not care if I left everything I knew behind, as long as I had him. I'd done it once. I could do so again.

His head came down, his lips consumed my mouth, and the flames were rising higher in my blood, licking my veins. When the rumble of William's wagon approached, I was cinders in Benjamin's hands...and he was a cloud of smoke.

# Chapter 8

*BENJAMIN'S SCREAM SHREDDED THE NIGHT,* ripping us from our sleep. A terrible raw sound, we hadn't heard anything like it since the Patriot was burning with fever, consumed by infection, on death's doorstep. My heart thumped erratically. Had he taken a turn for the worse?

"No! Don't take it! Please! Not my leg!" The cottage was dark, the coals in the ashes casting a dim, red glow. A shaft of moonlight touched Benjamin's face and it was painful to see, twisted in agony.

William, still sleeping on a pallet of sorts on the floor by his bed, was first to reach the militia man. He grabbed hold of the young man's shoulders and gave him a firm shake. "Lad! Wake up! You're dreaming! All is well. Your leg—and you—are whole, safe."

Benjamin stared at my forefather with confusion, lost at first, and then his face cracked. He flung an arm over his eyes. His free hand held the musket ball taken from his leg and he rolled it over and over in his agitation.

William rested a hand on my arm. "I'm going to stoke up the fire, make something hot for all of us to drink. Why don't you sit with young Benjamin for a spell? Perhaps the words and touch of woman will soothe him." He rested his palms on my cheeks in a move that brought to mind my father. "Especially a blessing as lovely as you."

I pushed the loose hair from my face and pulled up a chair next to the bed. My pulse was still tripping from the abrupt jerk into wakefulness. In an effort to calm myself as well as my Patriot, I began to stroke his hair.

Benjamin let loose a deep sigh and his face relaxed. He lowered the arm that covered his eyes and studied me with a level gaze. "I am sorry for disrupting your sleep, for my weakness."

I snatched up his hand and pried the ball from his fingers. It was so warm from his touch, the worn, smooth metal nearly burned me. "You defied *this* inside of you and the bloody Redcoats when they barged through my door." My voice shook with the force of my emotions. "Yet *you* are still here. You are made of a stronger mettle than most, Benjamin Willson. Don't you forget that." I hoped my expression was fierce enough to hit home.

His gaze softened, rich and dark as chocolate. His mouth tilted up at the corner and he brought my fingers to his lips. "I'm not nearly as strong as you, sweet Charlotte." I didn't feel strong. In that instant, I was so fragile I could shatter to pieces at his touch. One kiss and I would be reduced to dust.

*"I'M GOING TO TOWN. I'LL BE BACK AS SOON AS I CAN."* Several days had passed since dinner at the Dodge's and the current of attraction continued to grow between us. What had begun as a slow trickle the night of Benjamin's arrival had swelled to a creek, then a river, and now rivaled Niagara Falls. If I stayed penned inside with him for one more minute, I would throw all caution to the wind, toss any sense of propriety out the window, and ravage *him*. My Patriot was feeling the strain as well; I could see him practically vibrating in his efforts to restrain himself and keep a polite distance. One look in his eyes and I began to smolder. Going to town was as good of a distraction as any. William had the horses and wagon for a delivery. A long, hard walk would do me good.

"I'm going with you." Benjamin rose quickly from the bed, cane in hand. He grimaced and pressed a palm to his injured thigh, smoothing his expression at my scrutiny while he limped heavily to my side. He made a slight bow, gesturing for me to precede him.

"Benjamin, I've gone to the market countless times. I'll be back shortly. While I would like nothing more than your company, it is

105

too far for you and you are not ready." Not only did his leg continue to ache terribly, but he was drawn and fatigued after another restless night. The nightmares had been plaguing him with alarming regularity, becoming more intense with each passing night. A premonition?

I reached for the door and his hand gripped my arm. "After what happened with those damned Lobsterbacks, you're out of your mind if you think I will let you go alone. Things have changed. Tensions are high. The frustration is rising in England's disgruntled army." I saw something dark shimmering in his eyes like a shark beneath the ocean's surface. "Trust me. You have not seen what I have. I may slow you down, but I will not rest unless I am by your side."

His hand brushed against his injured leg and I recalled William telling me in a private moment, *"Our attackers weren't even a part of a regiment, just a sorry lot of Redcoats that came out of nowhere with no other goal in sight than to do damage, and oh the damage they did to young Benjamin. I owe him my life, Charlotte. He stepped in front of me and took the musket ball that had my name on it. I am here with you because of him."*

No, I had not seen what he had. It was that bald assertion that swayed me. "All right, but if the walk is too much for you, we turn back." I gathered my cloak, basket, and slipped on my bonnet.

Benjamin walked beside me and caught a loose strand of my hair, tucking it behind my ear.

"I love the color of your hair, to watch it shine in the sunlight. You needn't hide it."

The heat rushed from my chest to my hairline as I pushed my cap back, letting it fall to my shoulders. Anticipation burned in the pit of my stomach, a candle flickering in my veins. As he walked by my side, the sun pressing down on my shoulders, I could not be more content. My inner voice snapped in my mind, *Have you forgotten the Battle of Jonstown, Charlotte?"*

I squashed my misgivings. Maybe I would change things simply by being here. Even if I couldn't, I vowed to fill my cup and drink every drop of whatever time I had with my ancestor, William, and my Patriot.

Our progress was as slow as molasses, slowing progressively the further we went. Benjamin's face went whiter if that was at all possible, the lines of pain etching their way more deeply into his face. I attempted to make it easier, feigning a twisted ankle to take a rest. The stubborn man would hear nothing of it. "If we don't keep going, we won't get there until tomorrow at this rate." He forced a laugh that was cut off with a curse under his breath when his leg nearly buckled. I waited by his side while Benjamin gripped his cane with both hands and breathed hard through his nose. A curt nod and we pushed on.

I had to admit that I was grateful for his company. I had not undertaken this journey alone since that day early on when I tried to travel back to my own time. I kept glancing over my shoulder, peering into the dense cover of the

107

forest on either side, feeling as if there were eyes on my back. What with the attack at the cottage, talk of war at the Dodge's place, and my own knowledge of what was to come, I was paranoid to say the least.

Benjamin must have sensed my unease. He hooked his arm around mine and gave me a smile to bolster my confidence. "Fear not, Charlotte. I *will* keep you safe, even if I have to use my body and blood to do it."

My heart nearly stopped at his words. I had no doubt of his utter seriousness. Men did not take vows lightly in such a tumultuous time. Before I could dwell on that thought any longer, he cupped my face with his solid, warm palms and dropped a kiss on my lips. "Stop worrying so. I'm sure we will make it there and back again without mishap. If we don't keep going, I'm going to fall down where I stand."

Eventually, we crossed the small wooden bridge that spanned the creek rushing by and I waved my hand with a flourish. "Welcome to John's Town. There you will see the Tryon County Courthouse and Edward Wall's place." I'd almost tripped on my tongue and called it the Drumm House, a title that would be earned much later on. "He was school master of the first free school here in New York."

Benjamin chuckled. "You sound like my teacher delivering a history lecture." We took pause as I pointed out other highlights of the town. In truth, I stopped because his face was tight and I did not think he could go on much longer. The homeward journey would be especially trying.

"I will test your memory on attentiveness later," I smiled and tapped him on the head. "Off that way, you will find the Tryon County Jail, currently acting as our garrison, Fort Johnstown. We've a hatter, a sword-maker, a breeches maker, a seamstress, a surveyor, a shoemaker, a tanner, a wheel wright, and a gunsmith. All courtesy of our deceased benefactor, the baron, Sir William Johnson." I finally ran out of breath, rattling off points of interest like a tour guide. Perhaps I would have to take up a new calling when I made it home, *if* I made it home.

Benjamin's jaw pulled taut; pain was not the source of his aggravation. "Not a conceited sort at all, was he, putting his stamp on everything?"

Pulling him away from grim reminders of the privileged members of English society, I ushered Benjamin into my father's smithy next. The place was dark and hotter than Hades as William alternated between the forge and the anvil, pounding away at a piece of metal work with a hammer, his arm arcing through the air in mighty swings. The sweat was pouring off of him, his hair damp around his face and neck. He had to be weary, yet his face lit up with a smile upon seeing us and he stopped for a brief visit.

Stepping outside to join us, my forefather swiped a sleeve across his forehead and dropped a kiss on the crown of my head, patting Benjamin on the back next. "Ah, young ones! What a pleasant surprise! Out to enjoy this

109

beautiful day are you? And well you should for the snow will fly before you know it and we will all be cooped up inside for much too long."

I saw a water bucket and cup by the door. Quickly, I filled a cup and pressed it in his hands. "You need to take it easy, Papa. You work too hard."

"Oh, I think not, my blessing. Anything I do to support you, our home, and our cause is not work enough. One need only to see Benjamin to understand that. What *are* you doing walking all this way on that leg of yours?" William eyed the young man closely, forehead creased in concern.

"I didn't want Charlotte walking alone, sir. I wouldn't have felt right to let her go, not after our much too personal encounter." He met my ancestor's eye and did not back down.

William pressed a hand on his shoulder. "You did right, lad. I greatly appreciate it, but promise me you won't do yourself damage on the way home."

Benjamin gave his word. We turned to leave when a wiry, dark-haired man in a coonskin cap strode up to us, a musket on his shoulder, several furs on his back. My forefather stepped forward and shook his hand. "Nicholas! How goes the trapping?"

Realization hit me with a jolt and I nearly cried out. *Nicholas Stoner!* The hunter, trapper, soldier, a well-known figure in modern day Johnstown, here in the flesh. In my time, there was an inn and a golf course named after him. Also of note was an impressive statue of his bold figure, looking out over the land, ready to take on the world; that monument nearly captured his essence, but not quite. I had the ridiculous urge to ask for the man's autograph...as if I could take such a thing with me. I forced myself to focus as the man who would become New York's first outdoor guide, and a man of great repute, began to speak.

"Quite well, William, quite! I'm off to the tanner's with my latest prizes. You will be joining me for a hunt soon, yes?" He was already in motion, someone who could not be tied down in any one place for long.

"Absolutely! I need some fresh game on my table. Take care, Nicholas!" William lifted his hand in a wave and turned his attention back to us. "Well, I must be back to work. I will see you at home later." He kissed my cheek and patted Benjamin's shoulder before returning to his furnace of a workshop. As we left, the hammer rang out on the anvil and I watched his back strain against his shirt.

"Your father works hard for a living." Benjamin said in awe. Watching such strength in action was impressive. A moment later, my ancestor was forcing a red-hot piece of metal to do his will, bending it until some sort of tool took shape, and the muscles in his biceps bulged to the point I thought his shirt would tear apart at the seams.

I shook my head as we walked on. "It's a wonder Papa is not completely exhausted by the time he comes home every day. Did you hear about Peter Townsend, the blacksmith who was hired by the Continental Congress a few years

111

back? He made links in a chain that were one foot wide and three feet long. The monstrous things were used to form a barrier that spanned the Hudson River at West Point. The Patriots put it on logs and the Redcoats haven't made their way through yet. Papa was bursting with pride when he heard that a blacksmith made such a marvel. I'm sure he could have done just as well...perhaps better."

Benjamin's expression softened as he took my hand, his eyes warm. "Of course he could. Your father is quite a man, Charlotte." His head tilted, his fingers grazed my cheek, and his voice dropped down low. "After all, he forged the likes of you."

Brighter than the sun. His eyes, his smile, his words, and his touch made me want to melt into his arms. Not being an option here in the middle of town, I laid my palm against his chest. The steady beat of his heart called to mine and the blood hummed sweetly in my veins, rising up in my face, making my lips part as I fought to catch my breath. "You are too kind, Benjamin."

He leaned forward, his breath warm on my neck as he whispered. "Kindness has nothing to do with it, Charlotte. I am an honest man and what I say to you is the absolute truth." A few people passed by, breaking the moment, but couldn't stop the sizzle that made my stomach tighten as Benjamin took my hand. I pressed a palm to my stomach and we resumed our walk.

We continued through the town square until we came to the open market. As the shadow of the church fell over us, I pointedly avoided the cemetery. The mere thought of the place made me shiver, fearful that something might happen if I went there with Benjamin. Either I would be yanked back to my own time or he might be swept away. I had no desire to tempt fate. At first, I'd wanted to leave. Now I hoped to stay as long as possible to see how things would play out with my Patriot.

We reached a stand in the market where a white capped woman, with silver curls and spectacles perched on her nose, smiled benevolently on all who passed by. Her dress and apron were ample for a woman who obviously sampled her wares. Her specialty: baked goods, cider, and the bounty of her garden. Ripe squash, pumpkins, and zucchinis, as well as bushels of apples made for a colorful assortment of goods. Homemade baskets were hanging on makeshift walls as well, providing customers with something for carrying their purchases home, the Colonial equivalent of the shopping bag.

At our approach, she rose from a stool and took my hand, her blue eyes sparkling with good cheer. "Why, Charlotte! It is so nice to see your pretty face today. A breath of fresh air, that is what you are. Who is this fine, young man you've brought along with you?" She actually blushed and batted her eyelashes, a flirt in the guise of an elderly woman.

I felt an odd frisson run through me at her touch, that sensation of knowing her, yet not knowing how. I could only compare it to déjà vu, a feeling that had overcome me many times since my tumble through time. "Grannie Brown," the name rolled off of my tongue, taking me by surprise. I stumbled on. "This is Benjamin Willson, a Patriot from Boston. He joined up with the Tryon County Militia in their latest skirmish and was injured. Papa brought him home to recuperate."

The old woman's bony hand squeezed mine tightly and took his next. Benjamin, always the gentleman, bent over and kissed her fingers, making her turn an even more brilliant shade of red. She giggled like a school girl. "Your servant, mam."

I almost started giggling myself and struggled to keep a straight face. "Grannie has the best cider and apple pastries that you have ever tasted. Do you think that Benjamin could have a sample, Grannie? He is quite done in from our journey. I'm afraid he's strained himself."

"Oh my! The poor lad is looking rather peaked. I'll fix young Benjamin up with my latest batch of cider, chilled in the creek just this morning, and some apple cobbler. You too, Charlotte. Lad, sit down before you fall down." The elderly woman set her stool behind the Patriot and gave him a gentle push. With that, she bustled off.

Humble soul that he was, Benjamin was rather flustered, his face crimson. I'd learned by experience; he did not want people to make a fuss about him. He gave me a crooked grin, a strand of dark hair falling into eyes that were as sweet as melted chocolate, effectively melting my heart. He accepted a small jug of cider with thanks and began to drink eagerly, his throat rippling with every swallow. Quite an intoxicating sight. I gulped my own, fighting the urge to unbutton the neck of my dress and fan myself.

Once I'd finished my cider, I turned away; otherwise I'd liquefy. To occupy myself, I browsed Grannie Brown's selection of goods. I chose a few squash and apples. High above, I eyed a large basket that would be more practical for carrying everything home. Behind me, I could hear Grannie showering Benjamin with attention, offering him tidbits of this and that, fretting over how thin he was. I glanced over my shoulder and saw misery while his eyes said, "*Save me. Please!*"

I turned back, chuckling softly, and rose up on tiptoe to reach the basket. "I'll get that for you." A deep voice rumbled at my shoulder and a freckled arm, covered in rust-colored hair, reached past me.

There was a flurry of motion behind me and Benjamin joined us, wincing as he leaned on his bad leg. "I can get that for her."

Jacob Cooper already had the basket in hand and passed it off to me. His grin was easy, laughter lighting his patch of sky blue eyes, framed by a mop of hair like carrots that had been tousled by the wind. "I know I'm not as tall as you, sir, but I can manage to help a lady in need."

Benjamin's face was strained, his lips forming a grim line, and his eyes were sparking with anger. "She doesn't need *your* help. I am quite fit, thank you."

"Of course," Jacob said with a nod and slapped his tricorne hat on his head. "Good day, Miss Charlotte. Mr. Willson."

I paid for my purchases and we began the return trip home. Benjamin was steaming, so angry that he forced himself to keep up a fast pace, his limp becoming harder with every step. The lines in his face looked like they could have been carved by a hammer and chisel and his eyes were so dark, they were nearly black. I didn't dare speak.

He pulled up short all of the sudden, breathing hard, his hands gripping his cane so tightly that I thought his knuckles would erupt through his skin. "Just what does young Cooper do?" He practically growled.

"His father is our town gunsmith. Jacob is his apprentice." I eyed Benjamin with trepidation. He looked ready to explode at any instant.

He sagged at my news, his eyes shadowed. "I know I may not be as good of a prospect to you as Jacob Cooper and I haven't been a part of your life for long," He spoke so low I could barely hear him. I moved in closer and rested my hand on his arm. His fingers found mine and took hold. "But I vow to you that I will work hard and care for you. When this blasted war is over, I will give you my body...my blood...my sweat...my tears...the air that I breathe...and my heart."

I moved to face him and set my hands on his shoulders, leaning in to kiss him tenderly. "I've never given kisses to Jacob Cooper, or anyone else, Benjamin. I've given you several. You know where my heart lies."

He took my hand and kissed it. "Why I am so blessed I do not know, but I will make sure I am worthy of you if it takes several lifetimes." He kissed me hungrily and his hands threaded through my hair, letting it tumble down my back. I laid my hand on his heart and every beat said, "You are mine." This, this was without a doubt why I was here. To experience the love of a lifetime…and perhaps, several more.

We lingered, breathing in the same air, oblivious of the chill because of the heat of our touch. The day was fading, the angle of the sun dropping further in the sky. Reluctantly, I murmured, "Benjamin, we'd best be on our way if we want to beat Papa…and the darkness."

He took my hand and we continued on. About half way home, Benjamin couldn't take another step. There was no use telling him he'd done too much too soon or should have stayed home. Catching sight of a large, flat rock by a burbling creek, I gestured to it. "Why don't we sit a bit? I've got some of Grannie's prize apples and," I wiggled my eyebrows and pulled a jug out of my basket, "one more dose of cider if you don't mind sharing."

Benjamin's teeth clamped down on his bottom lip as he eased himself down, a slow breath escaping him like the air from a punctured tire. He gestured to the cider. "Ladies first." I obliged and passed the jug off to him, watching the slow roll of his throat with every swallow, forcing me to look away. My temperature was rising off the charts and my heart wasn't far behind.

When I had calmed down enough to face him, I caught his fingers in mine. "Thank you for your company today. I know you shouldn't have come, that your leg must pain you terribly, but you made me feel safe. Going out alone, or being left alone, frightens me now."

"You have nothing to fear. I am here for you." He pressed closer, his breath grazing my cheek, and his lips met mine. "If I had only one leg and was on death's door, I would come with you. I am yours, Charlotte."

I leaned my head against his chest and held on tight; I didn't ever want to let go of him. "And I am yours, Benjamin. I am falling for you more deeply every day."

"Let's fall together." He smiled at me, a smile with his heart in it, and held me close. I shivered at his touch. It had nothing to do with the cold.

# Chapter 9

"*I'VE A YEN FOR SOME FRESH TROUT*, or maybe a nice bass. I don't suppose you've done any fishing, young Benjamin?" William eyed the Patriot's face with a grin, humor sparking in his eyes, making them as warm as sun-baked slate or the dawn just before it met the day.

"I used to go often with my father, sir. There was a river that ran just outside the city where we enjoyed many an afternoon together. I'd be honored to join you." Benjamin answered eagerly enough, although his gaze rested on me. The heat rose up in my face as it so often did at his attention, all the way to my ears. I studied the mending in my lap to occupy my hands, but couldn't tame my traitor of a body or my mind. I wanted to go too.

William stretched his arms over his head and forced a rather exaggerated yawn. "Actually,

I think I will lie down for a while. I'm rather overcome with fatigue today. Talmadge Edwards had me making all sorts of projects for him, from door hinges to gates, gate hinges, and an assortment of tools. I think he's preparing to go full swing into his glove making business. My arms and back are still aching. Why don't you two young ones go? My blessing is quite a catcher of fish if I do say so."

My forefather winked at me as I glanced up, unable to hide my excitement. It was a sleepy Sunday, a typical day of rest at the Ross homestead. We'd already shared breakfast and verses from the bible. I wasn't sure that fishing was truly acceptable on the Lord's Day, but William had made the suggestion. He had done everything in his power to give us private moments from time to time.

Whether my ancestor was that liberal-minded, it was based on the mutual trust between a father and a daughter, or he simply wanted to help us along in our relationship, I wasn't sure. One thing I did know with absolute certainty. As early October rolled in, Benjamin was becoming an integral part of our unit, like a son. I think William hoped to make him a son when this unsettled time was over.

My ancestor was a master with the forge in his smithy. He was also skilled at forging relationships; I already felt an unbreakable bond with the man, built on respect, love, and admiration for the one who planted the seeds of my heritage. A strong friendship had been formed between Benjamin and William as well.

What began in the throes of battle had developed into something much deeper, prompting my forefather to include the young militia man in his decision making and necessary tasks at the homestead. There had been hints dropped in conversation, talk of who would run the Ross home in the future, suggesting Benjamin would make a fine candidate.

It squeezed my heart each time I thought on it. I wanted nothing more than to make Benjamin my own to start our own family, but I had no idea if I was staying. Worse yet, the Battle of Johnstown loomed over me, only a little more than three weeks away, and a cold, white stone on a lonely plot far off into the future said Benjamin Willson would not make it off that field.

"My blessing, where did you go?" William had walked to my side and pressed a palm beneath my chin, lifting my eyes to meet his calm, steady gaze. "Are you well, Charlotte? You look troubled."

My eyes burned and the grief formed a knot that rose up in my throat and threatened to choke me. To lose Benjamin, just as we were getting so close...I could not bear it, but dare not speak of my fears. By denying them, they might not come true. I stepped forward and kissed my forefather's cheek. "I'm fine, Papa, just so happy for this bit of freedom. You are too good to me."

He smiled and patted my shoulder. "It is you who have always been such a blessing to me, Charlotte. I never would have survived those early years without your dear mother if not for your light shining brightly every day, pulling me from the darkness of my sadness. I will do all that I can to help you find someone who will complete you the way Mary did for me, to give you happiness." William reached out and took Benjamin's hand. "That goes for you as well, my young friend. I think that the two of you already give each other much happiness."

We were both flustered, darting glances at each other, as my ancestor walked away and returned with two, simple poles. Each had a line and a hook at the end with no reels. I couldn't help but grin. *Just like Tom Sawyer and Huckleberry Finn.* "There you are. Don't come back until you have enough fish for you supper. Go out and enjoy this beautiful day that the Lord has made. If this war has taught us anything, life is too short to be missed. Catch every drop on your tongue and savor it."

I hugged him hard enough to squeeze the breath out of him. Benjamin shook William's hand and we set out. The day was cool, but not uncomfortable, and we took our time, holding hands, going slow, avoiding stress on his leg. He'd stopped using the cane unless tired or strained by overexertion. I didn't mind meandering. It game me more time to revel in his nearness and bask in the warmth of his smile.

Eventually, we made our way to the creek that ran through town, choosing an isolated spot that was well off of the beaten path, making it feel like we were the only people on earth. Benjamin sat on the bank and pulled me down beside him. Seconds later, he pulled off his shoes and stockings, plunging his feet into the rushing water.

"Lord! It's like ice!" His shout rang out and he kicked up a great spray, dousing us both.

"Thank you very much, Mr. Willson! I wasn't planning on taking a bath," I sputtered. One look at his devilish expression and I removed my shoes and stockings as well, taking it a step further and walking into the creek, my skirt pulled up to my knees. The water was so cold my feet hurt and I began a little jig, whirling around and sending water right at his face with a forceful thrust.

"Oh, we're playing like that, are we?" He plunged in next to me and a water war ensued, the both of us drenched, shrieking, and overcome with uncontrollable laughter.

I was bent over, holding on to my side, when Benjamin froze, staring at me. The desire was written in his eyes and he closed the gap between us, taking my face in his hands. My skirt was forgotten, falling into the waters as I had to grab hold of him or I would fall. His strong, nimble fingers made quick work of setting my hair free of its pins and threaded their way in, cradling my head. I moaned softly as his lips took mine and my mind began to spin. To feel this way...I had never known there could be such a force of attraction between a woman and a man.

We swayed back and forth, rocking on our heels, and finally broke away. Both of us struggled to catch our breath. Benjamin wrapped me in his arms, my head tucked against his chest and I could hear the thundering of his heart. "Charlotte...you are killing me, more surely than any musket ball or Lobsterback ever could." A few more minutes to regain his equilibrium and he swallowed hard. "We'd best fish or I will be catching you instead."

He already had. The Patriot had hooked my heart and soul. I nodded shakily nonetheless and we returned to shore, baiting our hooks with some worms that Benjamin found under a pile of rotting leaves. We sat back and waited. Hours passed and several fine catches made it to the grass beside us.

I kept glancing at Benjamin out of the corner of my eye, watched the mad flutter of his pulse at the base of his neck, the crimson rising up in his cheeks, and knew mine must be the same. I fought the urge to step back into the creek and thoroughly douse myself, going completely underwater, and never coming back up if I could not hold him in my arms.

Finally, unable to take another instant apart, I flung my rod down on the bank and threw myself at him. Benjamin caught me and drew me into his lap. His mouth found a home on mine once again and I felt like we were built for each other, two halves of one soul. Our hands began to roam, over each other's bodies, the waist, the chest, the arms, and back. Not nearly enough. I wanted more. I wanted everything he had to give and would gladly surrender myself.

It was Benjamin's turn to groan, a low grumble that sounded from deep in his chest and had my belly tightening in anticipation. I opened my eyes intent on seeing his face and my blood ran cold.

"Benjamin...behind you!" I had time for no more warning than that as a native lunged from the cover of the trees, a blade in his hand. He jumped on my Patriot, who pushed me away, knocking me to the ground to keep me at a distance. They rolled on the ground and tumbled into the creek, thrashing, caught in a deadly dance of life and death.

I screamed and picked up rocks, taking aim and launching them at our assailant. He only grunted and fought with even greater ferocity, his knee coming down hard on Benjamin's bad leg. My Patriot's face blanched and he sucked in hard, but continued to fight with all his might.

A few more minutes that seemed to stretch on for an eternity and Benjamin wrenched the knife out of the Native's hand, brought it down hard in a mighty thrust, and put it through his heart. Our attacker fell into the water, blood spilling from his chest, and the light faded from his eyes.

Benjamin, breathing as if he'd just climbed a mountain, staggered toward shore, limping hard, his face tortured. His eyes sought mine and the shadows almost swallowed me. I ran to him and helped him up on the bank where he collapsed, taking me with him. I began to cry uncontrollably as I held on to him and he sat up, pulling me into his arms, cradling me as if I was a child. We rocked back and forth and he murmured words of comfort into my hair.

"That's twice now you've saved my life," I told him through chattering teeth. I was shaking uncontrollably, as cold as the winter's snow, and I couldn't stop.

He laid a hand on my cheek and stroked it with his thumb, his chocolate eyes reaching out to me. "And I would do it again, countless times. I would lay my life down for you, Charlotte, and not think twice." He held me, his arms strong bands that could carry any load, and eventually my heart slowed, the breath came more easily, and warmth began to seep back into my bones.

By unspoken agreement, we did not look back at the creek and the burden that slept there. I stood and offered Benjamin my hand. He stood gingerly, jaw clenched at the pain in his leg, but did not falter. We took up the fish and the rods, intent on getting back to the Ross homestead. Fishing had lost its appeal for the remainder of that day.

William was standing on the step when we turned down the lane. One look at the way Benjamin favored his leg and he rushed to meet us, hooking the young man's arm over his shoulder. "What happened, young ones? Did you hurt yourself, Benjamin, or just push too hard again?"

Benjamin related our mishap in brief terms, making every effort to leave out the great danger we were in or how terrifying the whole experience had been. My forefather's eyes widened in alarm and he grabbed hold of me, drawing me into a rough embrace, hooking an arm around my Patriot next. His gaze was bright with unshed tears, his expression fierce. "Thank you, Benjamin, for keeping my blessing safe. You have saved us both and I am forever in your debt."

Once settled inside, he went to his chest in the house and pulled out a pistol and a knife which he presented to Benjamin. "You will take these wherever you go from not on, Benjamin. I will not have you unarmed. I am too good-hearted, longing to believe that this town is still a safe haven. The war has taken that away from us. Even the Indians are no longer to be trusted. Without Sir William to guide them, many seek savage revenge, siding with the Loyalists. When I can, I will get you your own musket as well. Thank you again for being such a blessing to the both of us."

William sat on his bed between us and put an arm around our shoulders. If the man could, he'd be a dam, holding back the flood of life's storms.

*"BENJAMIN! WATCH OUT! BEHIND YOU!" The native lunged from the shore and landed on top of my Patriot, taking him completely unaware, his knife raised in a strong arm with muscles that bulged. A brief struggle ensued and the assailant plunged the blade into Benjamin's chest, over his heart.*

*"Benjamin! No! Not now! It's too soon!" I pushed the native out of the way and took the militia man in my arms. The crimson stain grew*

on the front of his shirt, the light fading from his eyes. "No! I love you, Benjamin! I love you! Stay with me!"

I wailed as one last breath gave out in a sigh and his body went limp. Our attacker grabbed my arm. I whipped around to face him, ripping my dress open, bearing my chest. "Here! Right here! Take me next!" I jabbed at my own erratically beating heart.

With a disgruntled scowl, he slapped me hard across the face. I relished the pain that blossomed on my cheek, a distraction from the agony in my heart. I tasted blood from where I had bitten my lip and the sobs rose up.

The native did not give me time to grieve. He grabbed my hair and wrapped it around his fist like a rope. A fierce yank and he began to drag me away. I held on to Benjamin, but he was too heavy. He slipped from my stained hands, drenched in his blood, and fell into the river with a splash. "Benjamin!" My screams bounced off of the silent, unyielding pines. No one came to my aid. No one heard my cries and my soul was torn to shreds.

"No!" I woke with a gasp, my heart fit to leap from my chest and I was trembling. I slipped out of bed, the floor cold on my bare feet, and streaked across the room, fighting my way outside. My lungs filled with great gulps of air and I dropped down on the step, knees drawn to my chest.

The door opened behind me with a creak and a blanket was wrapped around my shoulders. I was still wracked with uncontrollable shudders. I had never felt so cold in my life, as if my body was turning to ice from the inside out. Benjamin sat beside me and drew me into the shelter of his arms. "You dreamed about the Indian, didn't you?"

I buried my head in his chest. "I'm just sick of it all, Benjamin! The bloodshed, the war hanging over us. I just want a little peace."

He kissed the top of my head and let out a deep sigh. "I cannot end the war, although I wish that I could, and I cannot erase what you have seen, but I can give you peace, Charlotte. Here in my arms, at my side, with the warmth and solidness of my body. It is yours to take it if you will." I nodded and burrowed myself in against him. It was a reprieve, however brief. It would have to be enough.

# Chapter 10

*THE WAR WAS AN EVER-PRESENT CLOUD,* casting gloom over us, every day. We all went about our daily routines, Benjamin easily weaving himself into life at the Ross Home, making a valiant effort to pretend everything was normal...but nothing could be further from the truth. The colonies hung in a terrible state of limbo, their future uncertain, awaiting Britain's response. Would King George show his might and drop the hammer? Would the Patriots do the unthinkable, the impossible as a young, inexperienced upstart of a nation and prove to be victorious? Even though I knew the answer, that was little solace. America's future might be a sure thing...Benjamin Willson's wasn't.

I had experienced my own brushes with war, and it was much different from reading a book or watching a movie. Watching William ride away with the militia. Fretting over his return. Seeing the badly wounded Benjamin fall into our lives. Dealing with the Redcoats as they invaded our home. Nursing my Patriot to health and feeling death at our door. Listening to the talk of war at Richard Dodge's dinner, the anger, the fear, the passion. Facing the native's attack. My nerves were so frayed, I practically quivered trying to hold myself together.

The Revolution followed me to the market as people murmured and mourned over freshly turned mounds in the cemetery. I saw the marks of battle in the faces of militia men who had been wounded, permanently scarred and forever altered. It hovered at my shoulder every time I envisioned the blood stain under the rug in the Ross cottage. I felt as if William, Benjamin, and I were living in a bubble, tucked away from the outside world...but the Battle of Johnstown would make it burst in a little over two weeks. The pressure mounted inside of me until I thought I would explode.

"Charlotte, what is wrong? You haven't stood still since your feet hit the floor this morning." Benjamin shadowed me as I moved from one end of the cottage to the other, picking up random items only to set them down, cleaning a house that had already been cleaned meticulously. If my hands and body were kept busy, I might keep my mind from coming unhinged.

He stepped in front of me and set his hands on my shoulders. "Charlotte, stop."

I stared at the floor, the tears rising up and making my eyes burn. Benjamin lifted my chin, took one look at my face, and his gaze darkened, troubled. His fingers became entwined in my hair and his lips grazed mine, sending a fine shiver through my entire body. My heart began to thump so hard, surely he could hear it. "Tell me."

My tongue came so close to becoming untied, to spilling all of my secrets. About a cold night in a graveyard, a tumble through time, and the fast-approaching battle. Hardening my resolve, I kept my confidences to myself. I buried my head in his chest and told him in a muffled voice, "I am just weary of this war. I need to get out of this house and my head or I will scream. Will you take a walk with me?"

Benjamin didn't hesitate. He grabbed my cloak on the hook by the door and shrugged into the brown jacket that William had lent him. The crook of his arm presented the perfect spot for my hand and we set off.

The whispers of liberty rustled in the leaves at our feet, in the swaying branches overhead, and I wanted to grab hold of them. I wanted to truly experience freedom with Benjamin, to run away with him and never turn back, but thoughts of William stopped me. I could not break that man's heart and truth be told, I knew my Patriot would not flee. Honorable man that Benjamin was, he would not shy away from any conflict.

The sun was creeping up in the sky, heading toward the noon hour, but kept its distance. There was a nip in the air, sharp enough to prompt me to walk at a brisk pace. Benjamin was much stronger. Although his limp lingered, he kept up without complaint.

Still, I saw him begin to struggle and forced myself to walk in a more leisurely fashion. We went further than ever before, past so many places that belonged to Benjamin and I. The creek where we fished. The town square. The cemetery that sent a bolt of fear shooting straight to my heart. I hoped never to set foot there again, that I would somehow break the anticipated chain of events that involved the man at my side. Onward, our feet carried us to another place I had visited many times in the 21st century, but never before with my Patriot.

My lungs filled with great gulps of the refreshing, autumn air and I became pleasantly warm from our exertions. Benjamin took my hand in his and gave me his endearing smile, his dark hair falling into coffee eyes. Sliding a glance his way from time to time, I could not help but appreciate what a marvel of a man he was. With his tall, straight body, his broad shoulders set, and his head held high, I did not think I had seen anything more beautiful. We did not talk for the entire journey. Benjamin was a patient man and was giving me time to work through my turmoil. His approving gaze suggested that he was enjoying the view too.

Finally, we travelled down a broad, lengthy lane that led to Sir William Johnson's estate. The building looked very similar to the preserved hall in 2014. Cream-colored paint and shutters in a deep shade of red painted an attractive picture of the two-storied building that was the largest in the town, with two smaller stone buildings set beside it that could have been used for storage and defense as well, judging by the narrow slits in the walls. Compared to the humble Ross cottage, this was a veritable mansion.

Benjamin's eyes widened when he first surveyed the estate, then narrowed in contempt and his jaw tightened. We found a large, flat rock and sat down to rest, but I sensed his anger churning beneath the surface. As for me, melancholy rose up as I took in the disrepair and the hall's abandoned state. The historical marker of the future was well tended and had been a grand gathering place before the Patriots confiscated the property. Now, Johnson's pride and joy was in shambles.

"Sir William must be rolling in his grave to see his home look like this. This estate was the center of activity around here. Indian council meetings took place here, as well as important gatherings with prominent political figures. This was the picture of high society. My friend, Abigail, and I imagined going to a ball here, of dancing with a handsome prince of a man. We could never be invited, of course, but girls can dream."

Benjamin shot to his feet, cheeks stained with streaks of crimson, his eyes blazing. The wind picked up, whipping his hair loose from its binding and tossing it around his face. "This place only reminds me of all the ways the privileged have wronged us, taking from us, feeding off of our blood, sweat, and tears, simply because they could!"

His hand formed a fist and he shot it at the house. "I lost everything because of the likes of *Sir* William!" He spit the last words out, picked up a rock, and flung it at the walls. It bounced off and skittered across the ground.

My own anger began to bubble up and I went to him, banging my fists on his chest. "You are not the only one who has lost something! Have you seen the charred remains of the farms around here, the fields that were burned to rob us of their crops, the men missing their limbs and begging in town? The silver hairs on my Papa's head from the worry, every call from the militia only adding more?"

I turned away, struggling to catch my breath, frustration tightening around my lungs like a fist. "In 1779, the raid on Tillaboro happened not far from here. Our Captain Nicholas Rechtor lost a child. The raiders killed the little one and flung him over the bank of the creek like nothing more than trash. When Sir John, Sir William's son, came through during the Burning of the Valleys, he sought revenge, to destroy, to take what was his. He and his assorted Loyalists burned, maimed, killed. Lodowick Putman, an officer in the Tryon County Militia, and his son, Aaron were murdered. Our good friends, people who sat at our table!"

In my mind, I saw the paper I had written in college, sharing in detail about all of the losses we had experienced in and around Johnstown. I had presented it to the class, fired up, dramatic in my delivery. The passion I felt then was only a candle compared to the inferno that consumed me now. What had been snippets of facts, unearthed in old history books, felt all too real now, piercing me, cutting deep. "I have lost much, Benjamin! Good friends...security...my innocence... and my dreams of dancing." *Or living happily ever after with the man I love.*

I turned away and my shoulders began to shake as the sobs finally let loose. The cries I had been holding in night after night and day by day, weighed down by the burden I carried, broke the bonds of my self-restraint and I gave in without shame.

A strong hand rested on my shoulder...and then the other. Benjamin turned me to look at him. He cupped my face and his thumbs wiped away my tears. "Forgive me, Charlotte. I know that many have lost much, more than I have. My bitterness knows no bounds at times. Nothing pains me more than to think of good people like yourself and William being hurt by this blasted war. It all has to count for something." His forehead dropped to mine and he closed his eyes.

We were still, the wind wrapping itself around us, the sound of our breathing loud in my ears. Benjamin slowly lifted his head and offered me a smile colored with sadness. He took my hand, bowed over it, and dusted my fingers with a kiss. "My lady, I may not be a prince, but I am a man. May I have this dance?"

I raised my head and met his eyes. If I stared hard enough, looked closely enough, I could see my reflection burning bright in his gaze. I took his hand, his other settling on my waist, and we began to sway. Round and round, on a carpet of autumn's finery, with the last of the leaves drifting around us on the air. I felt as if I danced on air. So many times I had lost myself to the moment when the prince danced with the princess in childhood movies and later in books. That was nothing to dancing with Benjamin.

*I could have danced all night...I could have danced all night...and still have begged for more. I could have spread my wings and done a thousand things I've never done before...*Yes. This was what Eliza Doolittle had been talking about in "My Fair Lady." I didn't ever want to stop and held on with a sort of desperation. I wanted to stay in the here and now. Forget about what was to come. Benjamin was in my arms. He was mine and I was his.

All too soon, our feet ceased to move, the ball of fire in the sky dropping into the trees. My Patriot took hold of the nape of my neck and set his lips on mine with the greatest tenderness. "Thank you for the dance, my lady. I will never forget it."

"Neither will I." I whispered huskily and rested my head on his chest, calmed by the lullaby of his heart. I might not be able to change history, but I could build memories and give him the gift of my love, a love I hoped was strong enough to break the barriers of time.

We made our way home slowly, neither one of us in a hurry, neither one of us wanting the moment to end but darkness was coming. William would worry. The first stars were making sparks in the sky as we turned down our lane. A light gleamed in the window and my forefather stood on the porch, waiting. Catching sight of us, he raised his hand in greeting and went inside.

As I mounted the steps, Benjamin squeezed my hand, making me stop. He stood below me on the bottom step, looking up. Behind him, he was framed by the light of the moon, his dark silhouette frozen before me, but I could see his eyes gleaming and the line of his mouth drawn tight. I thought maybe his leg was aching again, but his words proved otherwise as he raised a hand and set it on my cheek. "Charlotte, don't ever stop dreaming. You carry a light inside of you that burns so bright it blinds me. The thought of anything snuffing it out is more than I can bear."

I set my hands on his shoulders and kissed him until we were both breathless. "I won't, Benjamin. I will dream every day and night. Every dream will begin and end with you."

*MY AGITATION CONTINUED TO GROW.* My nights were sleepless, staring dry-eyed at Benjamin or the ceiling, ticking off the days. Only a little more than a week until the Battle of Johnstown and I was haunted by a grave marker with a date that could not be erased from my mind.

139

I couldn't sit still, cleaning everything outside and in, wearing a tread in the floor with my walking back and forth. I'd been short with Benjamin, wounding him with my tongue. His hurt look may have prompted William, always an observant one, to speak up. "Young ones, I think you need to get out of this house. I suspect you are feeling as if the walls are closing in around you. Why don't you accompany me to the smithy? It will be like old time's sake for you, Charlotte, and a learning experience for you, Benjamin. After all, you will need a trade when this war is over and it *will* soon be over. I feel it in my bones. Would you care to try your hand as a blacksmith?"

Benjamin's eyes lit at the prospect. Working with William was a great honor, not to mention it would bring him a step closer to making me his own. "I know it will be more than my hand. I will need every ounce of strength in my arms and my back. One cannot help but notice the evidence of your hard work, sir. I would be greatly honored to begin an apprenticeship with you. I have been chomping at the bit to find some way to repay you for all of your kindness."

William laid a hand on his shoulder. "Lad, I do not expect any kind of compensation other than your friendship and your obvious care for my Charlotte. If we're all in agreement, we had best be off." Without further comment, the men put on their coats and I tied my cloak around my neck. Benjamin went on ahead to get Raven and Bonnie ready, returning with both horses saddled. William mounted Raven. Benjamin climbed on to Bonnie with only a twinge of discomfort in his face as weight was placed on his leg. He extended a hand to me and pulled me up, settling me in front of him.

A slow, steady pace and we soon arrived at the smithy. William gave Benjamin a heavy apron and fired up the forge until it felt like we had stepped on to the surface of the sun. I perched on a stool in the corner and fanned myself with my bonnet, longing for a cool drink or the refreshing touch of my Patriot's hand on mine.

My forefather gestured to the wall and all of his tools, carefully arranged on hooks or on his workbench. "Here are all of the things that are necessary for my trade. You will need to be skilled in using the forge as you heat the iron without scalding yourself. The anvil will be your best friend as you beat at different pieces with your hammer." He handed the tool in question to Benjamin and the Patriot nearly dropped it, his look of surprise comical.

William laughed heartily. "Yes, it is heavy. That over there is the fuller, used to pound grooves into your creations. The mandrel, that hornlike tool, will help you to shape each piece. You'll also need to know how to use those grabbers when you are taking red hot metal straight out of the forge. The claws are used to hold it in place while you are wielding the hammer."

Benjamin eyed each tool and picked them up, familiarizing himself with them. He asked thoughtful questions and surveyed projects in various states of completion with a keen eye. The Patriot snatched my forefather's arm and rolled up the sleeve, revealing his many scars. "No, your work is definitely not easy, so I'd surmised all along. You bear the badge of your efforts in your scars. I am fully prepared and willing to gain some of my own at your side."

As the day went on, I could only marvel at the beauty of Benjamin Willson, his tall, straight body, his limp nearly gone, tendrils of hair clinging to his face and neck. My hair was curling up at the humidity and I brushed a strand from my eyes only to catch my Patriot's idiotic grin. He burnt himself on a horseshoe, cursing and pressing the offended hand to his mouth. I went to him and cooled his hand with a dousing of cold water. Benjamin repaid me with a kiss.

Many townspeople visited during the day, Talmadge Edwards, Nicholas Stoner, and Richard Dodge to name a few. Militia members and civilians alike proved to be regulars. They shared any recent tidbits on the war front, talked of daily news, and brought work to my forefather. The projects varied, from anchors for fishing, to nails, hooks, anvils, hoops, hammer heads, and wheel barrows. In modern-day America, you would go to Home Depot or Lowe's. In colonial times, you would see the likes of my forefather.

William was gracious to each man who set foot inside his smithy, putting down his work to offer his undivided attention, offering refreshments in the form of water or a bit of whiskey. Most took the whiskey before moving on. As I watched each exchange, including my forefather's undeniable skill and wealth of knowledge, my respect and admiration grew for a man who instilled the same in everyone who called him friend.

The hours stretched on and yet William was tireless, my Patriot doing his best to keep up. Benjamin was leaning against the wall, massaging his bad leg with the base of his palm. My forefather stopped what he was doing and took the young man by the arm. "All right then, that's enough for one day. I can't have you overdoing it and causing a setback. It's time you accompany my blessing home. I will follow as soon as I can."

"Thank you, sir. I find your work to be fascinating. I want nothing more than to learn as much as I possibly can. I can only hope that I can be half as talented as you." We said our farewells and mounted Bonnie, waiting for us at a hitching post outside. Benjamin needed a moment once in the saddle, massaging his leg while his breath hissed between his teeth. He did not complain but I knew that he was sore. I was grateful we didn't have to walk.

The wind was blowing strong enough to set my cloak to fluttering around me, making me shiver as the leaves whipped around us in miniature cyclones. Benjamin wrapped an arm around me, holding me close, his heat welcome. The solid wall of his body was even more inviting. All I wanted to do was turn to face him, to run my hands up and down his chest, to kiss him senseless.

My Patriot was battling tensions of his own making. His muscles were tight and hard as I pressed against him, his breathing ragged. Finally, he pulled Bonnie to a stop by the rock where we had rested the first time we traveled to Johnstown together. He dismounted, taking care to land on his right leg, and reached up for me. His hands took hold of my waist and brought me to the ground with ease. I had no doubt that Benjamin could rise to the challenge of being a blacksmith.

His fingers threaded through mine as he led me to the stone and gestured for me to sit. "I simply cannot stand it. I cannot wait another minute." He slowly knelt on one knee and the heat surged from my chest, flooding my face. I pressed my hands to my cheeks. They were on fire. When had this time-honored tradition for proposals begun?

He reached in his pocket and pulled something out, setting it in my palm and closing my fingers around it. It was round, smooth, and warm. "Charlotte, I know that we have known each other only a short time, but it feels like a lifetime. I do not have much to offer you, but one day I will give you much more. Right now I can give you this ring, forged in your father's shop with my own hands. I promise to give you my strength, my body as your shield, and all the love that my heart can hold. Will you take me as your husband when the war is over and be forever mine?"

I looked in his coffee eyes and could see his heart and soul shining back at me. I opened my hand and a small band of iron sat in the center of my palm. With fingers that shook, I took it and slid it on my ring finger of my left hand. I could not manage to make my tongue work as my eyes clouded over with tears.

Benjamin pulled me to his chest. "Does this mean you accept?" His joy was barely contained, raining down on the both of us.

I started to laugh and cry at the same time as I pulled his face down for a kiss, my hands embedded in the dark strands of his hair. "Yes, a thousand times yes! If I could marry you this instant, I would!"

His lips met mine and hope for the future shimmered brightly, rising up between us, casting the rest of the world aside. As the wind buffeted us against each other, driving us closer together, and the leaves drifted by our feet, I waited. *Now. It is time for me to leave. Right now!*

Nothing happened, except for a passion that only grew stronger, strong enough to make us cling to each other, our hands wandering and leaving the flames dancing through my veins. My heart began to trip and Benjamin's answered, thrumming against my ear as I leaned against his chest. We were still standing there, oblivious of anything else, when hoof beats approached and the sun nearly dipped below the horizon.

William reined in, his smile wide enough to split his face. "Enjoying ourselves, are we young ones? Did you lose your way?"

Benjamin wrapped an arm around my waist and led me to my forefather. He offered the older man his hand. "If you approve, your daughter has agreed to be my wife."

"Why do you think I taught you how to make a ring?!" I held up my hand to reveal his handiwork and William let out a great whoop. He leaned forward and accepted my Patriot's hand, shaking it so hard the arm could have dislocated at the socket. He took my hand next and kissed my fingers. "This is what I have hoped and prayed would come to pass between the two of you. This is cause for a celebration!"

With that, we mounted and accompanied my forefather the rest of the way home. Benjamin stayed with William in the stable to take care of the animals while I went inside to prepare dinner. I stopped at the small table and rested my hands on its smooth surface. Bowing my head, I said a prayer of my own. *Please Lord, bless us all. Protect them if you can. I beg you. Spare my Benjamin. Spare them both.*

We lingered over our meal, William breaking out a new bottle of whiskey, only adding to our celebratory mood. I kept rolling the ring on my finger in the same way that Benjamin often fiddled with his musket ball. He grabbed my hand and snatched a kiss, casting aside propriety and all sense of reserve. My laughter spilled over, my cup full.

"You and Charlotte have my complete blessing to begin your married life here after this dreadful conflict is over. Such a promising prospect gives me reason to smile and makes hope burn brighter in my heart. You will complete your apprenticeship with me and have a home of your own one day. Until then, our home is yours, young Benjamin." My forefather touched his mug of whiskey to his future son-in-law's, then mine, in a toast and benediction.

"It already has been, sir. You do not know how many times I have wanted to hit my knees in gratitude for whatever brought us together and brought me here." Benjamin's gaze met mine and I was a bonfire, rising higher. If he were to touch me in that instant, my love would become a wildfire, obliterating us both.

A loud knock sounded at the door. William rose to answer and Jacob Cooper entered, bringing tension, his dark companion, with him. Benjamin rose to his feet and approached to form a small circle of men. I had the irrational urge to charge our visitor and push him out the door before he could speak.

"I am sorry to disturb your meal, William, Benjamin." He nodded in recognition of the young Patriot, his gaze meeting mine for only an instant. This was not a social call. "The militia has been called up again. Informants have reports of at least 700 on the move, Redcoats, Loyalists, Indians, under Ross and Butler. Willett is attempting to muster as many men as possible. He hopes to take them by surprise and intercept them before they wreak any more havoc on us." Jacob was breathing hard, his eyes flashing with barely contained fury. He was fired up, ready to lay it all on the line in the name of liberty.

As the men discussed joining the rest in two days' time, my body turned to stone. My stomach clenched so hard I thought I might lose my meal. I covered my mouth, my hand forming a fist in my skirt. I wanted to hit something, anything.

So, it would end like this. This life I'd fallen into, that had become mine, had begun to unravel at the seams. The echoes of the Battle of Johnstown rang in my ears and fear breathed down my neck, ready to plunge its teeth in my heart. I wanted to scream at them, to tell them that none of them should go. The battle would soon be in our own backyard if they wanted to meet it head on. Better yet, they could all stay home because Britain would raise the white flag of surrender on October 19th in Yorktown, Virginia when 8000 troops would be brought to their knees, effectively ending the conflict.

I sat, stock still, and said nothing. If I spoke, my warnings would fall on deaf ears just like Cassandra out of Ancient Greek mythology. They would not believe a word I said. Even if they did, their unwavering patriotic spirit would spur them on to fight. None of the men in this room were cowards. None of them would back down while others might fall.

A few more minutes of discussion and Jacob left. Silence fell over the room, all joy snuffed out like a candle. Benjamin and my forefather turned to look at me and I could not bear it. I stood so quickly, the bench tipped over and crashed to the floor. Covering my mouth to hold back my sobs, I ran past them and out the door. Straight to the barn and Bonnie's stall. She was lying down in the sweet smelling hay. I dropped beside her and buried my head in her neck. Whatever was I supposed to do? How could I watch them go and be left behind, trapped in this time, alone?"

The barn door opened and closed with a loud creak, a gust of wind blasting through and making me shiver. I did not budge.

The door to the stall shifted and someone knelt in the hay beside me. Strong hands took my shoulders. "Charlotte, do not take this so hard. We will go and return to you. With all that is holy, I promise you that there will be a future for us."

*You lie and you don't even know it.* I let Benjamin take me in his arms. His hand came up to stroke my hair and all the while, I held on to the ring that he'd forged with his own, two hands, with his heart. I turned it round and round, relishing its warmth and smoothness. If only I could make him stay, change what was to come.

We sat there together for some time until I had no more tears to cry, the warmth and peacefulness of the barn a balm to my ragged soul. I knew that the hurting would only get worse, but I could not tell Benjamin, could not plant the seed of doom with death as its harvest.

He bent down and kissed my cheek. "Let's go back to the house and keep your father company. It pains him deeply each time he has to leave you and he is worried about you. We must give him whatever we can to bolster his confidence and bring him peace."

"You're right, of course. I am being selfish." Nothing could be further from the truth. I wanted to spare him, all of them. If only I had the power to tell every member of the Tryon County Militia that they should all stay snug in their beds until word came making America's victory official. There was only one problem. The enemy would come on, leaving destruction in its wake for they knew nothing of the surrender either. "It is you and William, all of those who fight, who pay the highest cost."

Benjamin stood and pulled me up on shaky feet. He tucked me in against him and set his chin on my hair. "Sweet Charlotte, I know that you pay a price that is just as high, waiting here, worrying, keeping the home fires burning, picking up the pieces. Don't ever estimate the role of a woman at wartime."

His voice cracked and his pain made me conquer my own. I squeezed his hand and we walked together to the house, creating a lifeline at our touch. Inside, William sat before the fire, elbows on his knees, his head in his hands. He looked completely dejected, a sight I had not seen since I had arrived in this troublesome time, not even when we nearly lost Benjamin. It tore at my heart.

I rushed to his side and knelt beside him, resting my head on his leg. "Papa, do not look so downhearted. All will be well, I am sure of it. You came back to me before. You *will* come home again with Benjamin at your side." I fervently prayed my words would be true, that the future could be changed. After all, I did not intend to change anything monumental in the grand scheme of things. I only wanted to hold two lives in my hands, nothing more.

My forefather placed his hand on the crown of my head. I felt it tremble and the fissures in my heart grew wider. Much more and it would shatter. "My blessing, I pray that you are right. I wish that this cup could be passed from young Benjamin and I, but we have no choice. Know that I will pray for you every day that I am gone. I hate to leave you, daughter. Each time, it tears me in two and half of me is left behind with you. If only we need never part." Emotion cut off his words and he bowed over me, wrapping his arms tightly around my shoulders.

The man that so strongly reminded me of my father had nearly reached his breaking point. My Patriot was not far behind with a hand pressed to my forefather's shoulder as he stood behind him. I made myself a vow. If it was in my power, William Ross would not be forced to leave me behind.

# Chapter 11

*NONE OF US SLEPT WELL THAT NIGHT, IF AT ALL.* William did not snore, tossing to and fro often on his pallet on the floor. Benjamin could not settle either, the bed creaking with each movement, his covers rustling. When I closed my eyes, I was overcome with visions. Of a field of grass and trees, one I passed many times in the 21st country, a place that would soon be riddled with bodies. Benjamin's. Perhaps William's and Jacob Cooper's, and others who had become familiar faces, friends even since I walked in Charlotte Elizabeth Ross the First's shoes.

I yanked my thoughts away from the upcoming confrontation, only to picture that I was standing inside a giant hourglass. The sands of time were pouring down over my head, so fast and so strong they threatened to drown me. I beat at the walls, pounding until my hands were bruised and bloodied, screaming. If only I could make it shatter and freeze us in this instant.

When I opened my eyes, I turned and found Benjamin staring at me which such intensity, it was as if an invisible cord spanned the room, connecting us. I was aware of each rise and fall of his chest, each time he blinked, the way the moonlight made him look like a statue. A chill ran through me and I wanted nothing more than to cross the room, slip under the covers, make him move. To touch me, kiss me, hold me, warm me as my body slowly turned to ice.

William rose well before the dawn, giving up all pretenses of rest. Usually light of heart, on any other morning his steps would be quick. He would even whistle or hum. Today, my forefather's shoulders were hunched and his feet dragged. He was not eager for the task before him. Did a premonition of approaching doom darken his optimistic spirit?

Unwilling to send him off in such a dejected mood, I got out of bed and prepared his breakfast. I set a cup of coffee in his hand as he sat before the hearth and pressed a kiss to his cheek. "Good morning, Papa."

His hand caught mine and held it for a moment. "You are the good in it, my blessing. Because of you, I can put one foot in front of the other today. You...and Benjamin give me a reason to have hope." He nodded to our Patriot as the young man sat in a chair beside him. Both stared into the flames. There was no lively banter or earnest conversation on this dark

154

morning. Both were lost in their own thoughts. Impending war made men pensive as they mulled over their lives and worry gnawed at them, buffeted by faith. Love. Hope.

All too soon, William set his mug on the table and headed to the door. This would be the last morning that we could pretend there was any sense of normalcy for tomorrow my men would join the militia. It did not matter that I had only lived in this this time, this home, and this skin for barely two months. William and Benjamin had moved into my heart and belonged to me. The sorrow I felt was all too real.

"I must go to town today to tie up some loose ends, attend to business matters. I leave you two to each other on this day." William's eyes were sad, the gray storm clouds brewing.

I went to him and hugged him as hard as I could. My forefather held my face in his hands, kissed my forehead, my cheeks, and my mouth as he had many times before but on this morning, there was an overwhelming sadness. "You have always been, and always will be my greatest blessing." Choked with emotion, he left, neither one of us able to say more.

I stood in the open doorway, the wind whipping my dress around me, and watched him go. I was very close to losing control completely as I turned back and busied myself with breakfast preparations. Benjamin had no appetite, although he made an attempt to eat some of the meal I had prepared. I just picked at my plate.

At loose ends, I made coffee and handed him a cup. My hand was shaking so hard as I tried to drink my own that the hot brew spilled over the side, scalding my hand. I cried out and dropped the mug, the tears finally letting loose.

Benjamin was at my side in an instant, down on his knees, snatching my hand in his. He grazed the red skin with his lips, his thumb turning the ring he had made for me round and round. Finally, come undone, I dropped beside him, threw my arms around his neck and sobbed, "Please, Benjamin! If you love me at all, don't go!"

He spoke softly and stroked my hair as if gentling a horse, his hand pressing my head to his chest. "Charlotte, don't you understand? It is because I love you that I must go. I am fighting to give you a better place to live, for your freedom, and to protect you from Britain's tyranny. Besides, if I do not take up this sword, the cause could be lost or someone else might pay the ultimate sacrifice. I could not stomach that, sitting back and letting others pay the price for my liberty. I could not let your father go without me at his side. I owe him too much. I know William feels just as strongly, Charlotte, if not more so. He wants to give us every possible advantage."

Benjamin held me for a long time, rocking back and forth with my head pressed to his chest. The steady thrumming of his heart was a comfort, hypnotic even. Sit here long enough and I could almost fool myself into believing that he would never leave me.

"What can I do to console you, Charlotte, to help you take heart?" His voice cracked. So much pain caused by this war and shared by too many. He pressed his finger beneath my chin and raised it until I could look into his eyes. They were searching and dark with a sorrow of his own. The last thing I wanted to do was burden him more as his departure neared.

I gathered my courage and spoke, even though the words made my pulse start to race and I clutched at my stomach to still the butterflies swarming in a frenzy. "Let me know you completely, every part of you. Let me give the gift of my body to you before you leave so that you can carry the seal of my love with you."

He stood abruptly and backed away, alarm and longing tugging at his features. "Charlotte, no! I cannot ask this of you. You must wait until we are united in marriage. That is the right and honorable thing to do." His jaw clenched, his hands forming fists, a study in tension.

I approached him and hooked my hands around his neck. "If you can take the risk of laying down your life for this cause, this gift I give to you is the least I can do. No one knows what tomorrow will bring, but we have right now. Do not throw this back in my face. I give myself willingly and will not accept no for an answer." There was steel in my tongue as I lifted my chin and faced him head on. He would know my intentions were sincere and dead serious.

His eyes closed and he swallowed, pressing his forehead against mine. His fingers

157

wrapped round my upper arms and a shudder ran through him. I had the feeling he was dangling by a thin thread. Benjamin stepped back and held out his hand. I latched on and he led me out into a day of brilliant sunshine that was blinding, although the air was cold enough to make me shiver. He sheltered me with his arm around my shoulders and led me to the barn. We could not do what we were about to do in William Ross' home.

We walked to the back of the barn where a pile of clean straw would form our bed. Bonnie whickered as we passed, Belle's tail swishing to and from as they munched on oats in their stalls. Benjamin knelt down and I went with him, the two of us staring at each other, holding on by both hands. The pulse in his neck was all a flutter. Swiftly, his finger came up and grazed me at the base of my throat, coming to rest there. I felt the humming flurry that accompanied each pump of my heart. I closed my eyes and my lips parted. I couldn't get enough air.

"Charlotte..."He spoke roughly, his hand shifting to cup my cheek. The need and the wanting blazed in his eyes. Get lost in that dark gaze long enough and I would liquefy. "My life has been shredded by this war. I have never had the opportunity to make love to a woman..."

I silenced him, setting my finger on his lips. "Then we will be each other's first."

He pulled me in, cradling my head. "You *will* be my last." His mouth took mine even as his words sent an icy chill running through my body as I envisioned that cold, white stone centuries away. I held on with all of my strength and kissed him hard, seeking warmth and reassurance, in denial of whatever was to come. We had right now.

Eventually, we were forced to breathe. Benjamin smelled like hay and the sunshine that was clinging to William's cotton shirt, dried in the open air. His hair gleamed in the shaft of sunlight streaming through the small window, clubbed in a neat tail at the base of his neck. I knew that if I buried my face in those dark strands, I would smell my homemade soap. He made me dizzy.

I rested my hands on his chest to steady myself and pressed my forehead against his collarbone where it fit so perfectly. His fingers skimmed over my shoulders, leaving a trail of warmth before moving to my cheek. My face tilted up toward his, a flower reaching for the sun. Now. It had to be now and I knew that Benjamin, ever the gentleman, would not make the first move.

My heart was skittering out of control as my fingers moved to the buttons of his shirt, shaking so that I thought I would pop them clean off. One by one, I moved downward until I revealed his chest. Impulsively, I darted in and kissed him over his breastbone.

His breath caught and his hands grabbed hold of my hips. "God but I do love you, Charlotte Ross."

His eyes were a glittering brown like the great buck in the woods, a flush rising up his face, and he began to gasp. I took the next step and set my fingers on my collar. Within a minute's time, my dress was undone, revealing my simple undergarment. In one fluid movement, I pulled my dress over my head and I was bathed in sunshine.

"I love you too and that is why I'm giving myself to my promised one. There can be no other. There is no sense in waiting when we already belong to each other. The rest is just a ceremony. We are married in our hearts. Please, Benjamin. Do not waste these precious moments we have. All too soon, they will be gone." I implored him with my eyes, with my words, with my hands held out to him, palm up in supplication.

After an instant of hesitation, his hands began with my hair, setting it free, the curls tumbling down over my shoulders. Next, his nimble fingers roamed, lighting a fire everywhere they touched. My neck. My collarbone. Cataloging each and every rib. Back up to my shoulders and my shift was sliding down, forming a puddle of fabric at my waist.

"I would go to the ends of the Earth to be with you." My words drifted on the air, forming a chain between us.

He grabbed hold, threading his hands in my hair, and drew me in for the hungry kiss of a ravenous man. "I would break the bonds of time for you." His lips took mine roughly and my hands learned the map of his strong, firm body. The ridges of muscle were solid beneath his clothing. Unable to wait any longer, I reached up and yanked his shirt down.

160

Benjamin laid on the straw and then he was pressing me down next, sliding the lightweight fabric past my hips, to my ankles, until there was nothing except my bare skin. He knelt beside me and his eyes shone brightly; the tears were not far from the surface. "You are too beautiful, more than I could ever deserve."

Boldly, I set my hands on his breeches and began to ease them down to his knees. He closed his eyes as I sucked in a deep breath. "You are a marvel yourself."

His sweet smile slowly took shape, one I would remember for the rest of my days. He lay down beside me, our bodies pressed together, skin flaming. His hand massaged the nape of my neck and his lips met mine once more. "Charlotte, it's time we finally become fully acquainted." Benjamin drew me into his arms and I closed my eyes as an explosion of reds popped behind my eyelids. The fireworks on the fourth of July couldn't hold a candle to my Patriot.

*HE DRIFTED OFF*, his body finally going limp in a bed of straw, dusted in sunbeams, the pain and sorrow wiped from his face. Younger. At peace. This was the way I wanted to remember him.

I lay beside him, unable to find relief in sleep. My thoughts were a dove battering itself against its cage, feathers raining down, desperate for an escape. There had to be some way that I could protect William and Benjamin, that I could keep this separation from happening. Finally, an idea was formed. They said that necessity was the mother of invention...the same could be said of inspiration.

I dressed hastily and covered him with my cloak, braiding my hair swiftly and twisting it to form a bun. I brushed at the hay and dust on my clothes before making for the door. Bonnie snorted in greeting. I gave her a fleeting pat, made sure to include Belle, and streaked outside. The barn door closed quietly behind me. I dashed down our lane and continued at a run until I made it to the Andrews' home, a quarter mile past ours. I was breathless, holding onto a stitch in my side when Abigail answered the door.

"Charlotte, what's wrong? Come inside and sit. You look like the devil himself has been on your tail." She grabbed my hand and tried to draw me in, but I stood firm.

"Please. I can only stay a moment and I don't want to bother your mother." Abigail's father was answering the militia's call as well, casting a shadow of gloom over the Andrews' home. My friend's eyes were red and puffy. She had been crying. I threw my arms around her and hugged her fiercely. "I'm sorry to bother you. I know you have enough on your plate, but I don't have anywhere else to turn."

I began to shake, unable to stop, my body at odds with my mind. So much was happening, so much was weighing on me, I thought I would go crazy. Abigail backed away. One look at my face and her eyes widened in alarm. "*What's* wrong, Charlotte? Tell me, please!"

The words spilled from my lips in a mad rush of trepidation. "I'm going after them, my father and Benjamin, tomorrow. Don't ask me how. I simply must go. Will you take care of Belle and Bonnie while I am gone?" The men would be riding together on Raven, leaving Bonnie for my use, but the beloved mare could not accompany me. I would not put her at risk.

Abigail wrapped her arms around me and clung so tightly I couldn't breathe. "I beg you, don't go, Charlotte. Stay here with us so you won't be alone. We will hope and pray together for everyone's safe return."

Accepting would be so easy, but I had already made my decision. "I can't let them go, Abigail. I can't let *Benjamin* go. He is my everything and I must follow."

My friend began to cry again, this time for me. "I am afraid for you. I love you."

I stepped forward and kissed her cheek. "I feel the same. Your love for me will be the beacon that brings me home." The tears were streaming down her cheeks as I hurried home, her handkerchief raised in farewell. I turned back for one last look before leaving her lane and blew her a kiss.

When I returned to the barn, Benjamin continued to sleep soundly. I eased myself down beside him and placed one hand on his hip, the other on my belly. I closed my eyes and concentrated intensely on the intricate wonder that was the human body, focusing on his seed and mine. If only I could force them to be united.

His thumb brushed my cheekbone and I gazed at him. "I dreamt that you left me and I was all alone. I couldn't find my way to you, couldn't find my way home. It was as if I was in a great white room, wandering aimlessly, waiting for you."

Fear and pain colored his words. I snatched his hand and kissed it before resting his palm on my heart. "I am here, always here, only a beat away."

He tucked me in under his chin and made a haven out of his body. We remained that way until hoof beats sounded in the distance. Benjamin shot to his feet and dressed hastily with my help. His eyebrows shot up when he realized I was already completely dressed, but he did not say a word. We were standing by Bonnie's stall, stroking her neck when the barn door opened. William had come home early, his duties in town attended to, eager to steal a little more time with me.

After a poor attempt at a cheerful greeting, we went inside together, my forefather hooking his arms around two sets of shoulders. Benjamin and I avoided eye contact, but I saw the crimson stains on his cheeks, the straw in his hair. My cheeks burned as well. I went to the kitchen area and poured coffee, giving the soup over the fire a stir. We would have an early dinner. The morning would come all too soon and the men would need to get their rest, *if* they could rest.

I was carrying a cup to William when he motioned for me to wait and went to the bed. A package was lying there, wrapped in brown paper. He handed it to Benjamin. "Go on now. Open it." My forefather sank into his chair and accepted his coffee. His gray eyes were heavy with emotion, his mouth drawn tight.

My Patriot slowly undid the paper to reveal a jacket, the dark blue of the militia with red trim and shining buttons, USA etched artfully into each one. Beneath it was a Brown Bess. He stared at William, at a complete loss for words.

"Grannie Brown sent those for you. They belonged to her grandson, Nathaniel Brown. He did not survive the Battle of Oriskany, but his uniform and musket, left behind in his tent, did." My forefather stepped forward, set his hands on Benjamin's head, and kissed him on the forehead. "Grannie Brown sends you that as well, her blessings and a prayer for you—that you will come home safe."

I turned around, unable to bear looking at them a minute longer. The sob was rising up and I couldn't let it loose, couldn't cause them any more pain. I rushed outside, all the way to the barn, straight to Bonnie once again. I could find some sweet comfort with the sweet mare.

I wrapped my arms around her warm, sturdy neck and buried my face in her mane. I let the tears come, let the cries rise up. Smothered in her hair, against her body, tucked away in the barn, no one would hear.

The door creaked behind me and footsteps approached, Benjamin come to calm me as he had the night before. "I knew I would find you here again, Charlotte. Please do not carry on so. Come in. We do not know when we will sit at the table together again. Let us share each other's company while we can. You grieve because of our parting, but we are still here. Do not waste this moment."

Benjamin's voice was heavy but his touch was light. I swabbed at my cheeks with the sleeve of my dress, accepted his kiss on my cheek, and gave one in return. A deep breath later I was able to go back. William was in his chair by the hearth, but he rose to his feet when we entered, crossed the room, and picked me up as if I was a child once more.

He settled in the chair and tucked my head under his chin. "I know you are too old for this, Charlotte, but let me cradle you like I did so many times when you were little. Let me keep you safe while I can and pray that I will do so again."

My cheeks were wet, the tears running down freely once again, but there was no stopping them. William glanced up and reached for Benjamin. "You too, my son. Come sit here with us. Let us be a family."

Benjamin sat in front of my forefather's chair and pressed his back against William's knees, as if he was a boy once more. The older man's hand rested on the younger man's head and we formed a circle of love.

Eventually, we ate dinner, a dark contrast from the joyous occasion the previous evening. Tonight felt like a funeral as we all pushed the food around on our plates, our conversation dying before it began. I plunged into the chore of cleaning up, anything to occupy myself, while Benjamin and William packed for the next day. I could not watch them.

The dishes slipped from my hands and I scrambled to pick them up. A hand settled on my shoulder. "Charlotte, come sit. You have done enough."

Benjamin stood beside me, his head tilted, his eyes warm enough to make me want to crawl in and stay there forever. My gaze swept over him and I pressed my hand to my mouth. He was wearing the jacket from Grannie Brown, so handsome he stole my breath away. When I could speak, I pressed my palm to his cheek. "You are the spirit of patriotism. Liberty lives in you."

He bent to me and kissed me tenderly, until my legs went limp, my hands pinned between us, and I could feel the hammering of his heart as the blood rushed to my head, making me lightheaded. "My Lord, Charlotte, but you are so beautiful. You are the reason we go to fight, that we will continue to fight to the last breath. You are my home. *You* are the spirit of America."

I buried my head in his chest, letting the tears soak into his jacket. Each one was a prayer that he would be safe. That he would come back to me.

We went to bed early only to pass a dreadful night. I felt like I was trapped in an endless night, lying in the darkness, in a state of terror. At the same time, each hour went by too fast. All three of us shifted to and fro, the snap and crackle of the fireplace unable to hide our agitation. My eyes were burning, dry from staring at the ceiling...or Benjamin until we could no longer bear it and had to stop looking.

All too soon, the light began to change, the darkness fading away. I wanted to take it in my hands to wrap around us like a cloak, sheltering my men. Keeping them safe. I pulled the blanket over my head, fists forming at my sides, and willed the morning to never come.

I could hear them readying themselves, speaking in hushed tones. I lay still, imagining this was all a dream, that none of this was happening. If I plugged my ears and hummed to myself like I did when I was a little girl, I could make the monster—war—go away.

Being real life, all too real, I could not ignore Benjamin and William. I slipped out of bed and wrapped my robe around myself, flinching at the chill of the floorboards beneath my feet. I went to the hearth and began to prepare them coffee and something to eat during the first leg of their journey.

William approached and stroked my hair, giving my braid a gentle tug. "We tried not to wake you, my blessing."

I knew my eyes and nose had to be red from my crying during the night, but I pasted on a poor excuse of a smile. "I could not in good conscience send you off without your breakfast."

I went about my business, Benjamin and I barely acknowledging each other. Our hearts were too sore. If I didn't busy myself, if I stopped and looked in his eyes, I would break down and throw myself at his feet. I would grab hold of his legs and grovel, begging him to stay.

In a blink, it was time. William turned to me, his eyes bright, and pulled me to his chest, kissing the crown of my head. "I have said it before and I say it again. You were my greatest blessing the first day you were placed in my hands and every day of your life since. You will be my greatest blessing until the last day that I live. I will carry your love with me. By the grace of God, it will keep me safe and bring me home."

"I love you, Papa. More than I can say. Be safe. I will pray for you every day." I held on tight, burying my head in his jacket. His hand rested on my hair and I felt it tremble.

For a moment, he could not speak. My forefather cleared his throat. "I will give you two privacy to take your leave." He stepped out the door and my heart ached for this man who was so like my father that they could have been brothers.

Footsteps approached behind me, slow and steady. Strong, callused hands rested on my shoulders. I could feel Benjamin's breath on neck and I shivered as the whispers of liberty swirled in my mind. *Now! Take me back now. Don't make me say goodbye! Don't make me watch him die!*

"Everything your father said...I feel the same. You are my heart. I love you, Charlotte. God willing, I will come back to you and we will build a life together." He turned me to face him and I saw myself in his eyes, saw the love, the pain, the yearning.

I swallowed a sob and flung my arms around him. "I love you, Benjamin. I want nothing more than to be yours."

He held me and a shudder ran through him. Benjamin cupped my face in his palms and whispered. "Kiss me. Let me carry your love as a torch to light my way and lead me back to your waiting arms."

We kissed until I went weak in the knees. I didn't want the moment to end, but he pulled away, turned, and stepped through the door. I followed him and stood in the door frame, waving my hand, the tears coming unbidden as William and Benjamin, my men, mounted Raven and rode out to the end of the lane. My Patriot looked back once...and gave me one last smile. My heart cracked. As I listened to the thunder of the blood in my ears and dragged in an unsteady breath, I expected it to burst into a thousand pieces, leaving me in a heap on the doorstep of the Ross homestead.

# Chapter 12

*I REMAINED IN THE DOORWAY* in the faint light of pre-dawn, that moment when the whole world seemed to be holding its breath, waiting for the day to begin. I did not breathe, my hand a white flag of surrender, giving up my men...but I *could not* let them go. There was no time for grief, no time to waste.

As soon as they were out of my sight, I stepped inside, shut the door, and pressed my back against it. I closed my eyes, one hand clenched on my fluttering stomach, and steeled myself for the plan I was about to put into motion. My resolve became hard as granite. I could not stop time. I did not know what would become of William, if I could save Benjamin or not. I only knew that I must go after them.

To do so, I would borrow a page from Deborah Sampson's book. I slipped Benjamin's

171

ring off my finger and kissed the warm band of metal before setting it on my bedside table, my wish for a bright future. I would not risk losing that precious keepsake. Next, I opened William's chest and pulled out breeches, a cotton shirt, and the brown jacket that Benjamin wore to dinner at Richard Dodge's house. I went to the kitchen area and found a long strip of a rag. With shaking hands, I yanked my dress and underclothes off, binding my breasts with the piece of cloth, pulling it as tight as I could bear. I wished Abigail was there to help me, but I'd already put enough of a burden on her. I would not make her carry this secret.

In only a matter of minutes, I was dressed. I had to get a piece of twine to tie my breeches around my waist so they would not fall down. My own shoes would have to do; they were a plain, serviceable brown and could pass muster. With the shirt loosely tucked in and the jacket, I felt fairly secure that my chest was hidden. I left my hair for last.

I found two strips of leather and tied one just below the nape of my neck. With shaking hands, I hastily formed a thick braid of my hair, tying it off at the end. I took up the scissors, squeezed my eyes shut, and swiftly cut off the braid, just above the first strip of leather, leaving enough to tie back in a short tail. Stuffing the rope of hair in my pocket, I clapped a tricorne hat on my head. A hasty foray in the kitchen and I had a sack of apples, bread, and cheese on my shoulder. I grabbed the Brown Bess off the hooks over the hearth. Ready. At last.

Two steps toward the door and I stopped as if roots had sprung out of my feet. The place that had become mine for only two months was pulling at me. My eyes stung as I surveyed the cozy living space. I had the sinking feeling that I would not be back. With a deep breath, I stepped outside and went to the barn to say goodbye to Belle and Bonnie. I could not help but cry as I kissed them both and pressed my face to the horse's warm neck. I would miss both of these peaceful, sweet animals. I would miss all of it. Most of all, I would miss a reason to stay here. Finally, I forced myself to walk away. If I didn't go now, I'd never catch up with them.

The sun burst over the horizon as I followed William and Benjamin's hoof prints. The day was cold enough to make me wish I had my cloak. I shivered in my coat, the musket heavy on my shoulder, making it ache. I grimaced and shifted the Brown Bess to the other side. A picture of Benjamin filled my mind, the glaring hole in his leg when he arrived, the hideous scar he'd bear for the rest of his life. If he could carry his burdens, I could carry this musket.

I'd been trudging along for at least a half hour or so, kicking up dust that coated my pants and shoes, when the steady rhythm of hoof beats approached. I moved off to the side of the road and glanced up at the rider about to pass by. It was a man with an all too familiar gaze of a brilliant green and a head of tousled sandy hair poking out from under his cap. Talmadge Edwards! I sucked in hard, pulled my hat over my eyes, and stared at the ground. If he

173

discovered my plan before I really began, I didn't know what I'd do.

He slowed to a stop and eyed me closely, the low rumble of his voice rolling over me. "Going to join the militia, are you now? You're a runt of a lad. If we didn't need you, I would send you on home to tend to those you've left behind. The sorry truth of the matter is we need every able-bodied man, or nearly a man, that we can spare. You might as well ride with me. I've a late start, but we'll catch up with the others soon."

Talmadge reached out a hand and easily pulled me up behind him. "Your hands are like ice, lad. Reach in and grab a pair of gloves out of my saddle bag. You're shivering too. The sun will warm you soon enough."

I pulled the hand-crafted works of art on to my hands and instantly appreciated them. "They're nice sir." I spoke in as low of a voice as I could manage. Between the gloves, the horse beneath me, and the older man's body heat, I began to thaw. The fine quivering that had been running through me since my men left faded away.

"I made them. With the grace of God, they'll be my livelihood...if I live to see the end of this war." Talmadge's words took on a serious tone. The Revolution had a way of dampening the spirits of even the most optimistic souls.

"I think you will, sir." I murmured the words that I knew to be true in my heart, written in the history of my town, posted on a marker on the side of the road for all to see.

174

The older man chuckled softly and patted my leg. "Aye, you have to have hope, don't you, lad? That's what this whole endeavor has been all about. Hope as we face the lion in its den. If we are lucky, if we are blessed, we will bring it to its knees and young ones like you will have a better place to live in a land that belongs to you."

We rode on in silence, the sun beating down on my head and making the sweat bead up beneath my hat. At least an hour of riding later, we approached a small gathering of men milling about, making camp in a thick stand of trees, secluded enough to have an advantage over the enemy with the element of surprise. If possible, the militia men would lie in wait and intercept the Loyalists, hoping to create a blockade that would protect Johnstown. My heart thudded painfully, my stomach twisting. I knew better.

"Talmadge, who have you rounded up from under a rock? Is it one of the fairy folk?" William asked cheerfully enough, his good nature not allowing him to be any other way for long as I slid to the ground and was joined by my good Samaritan.

"I found the lad on my way here. I knew we could use an extra set of eyes and hands so I offered him a ride. I don't even know his name." His eyes widened as he clapped me on the back. "I didn't even introduce myself. Forgive me my poor manners, boy. My mind is cluttered with more than it can hold. I'm Talmadge Edwards and this is William Ross."

Benjamin approached at that moment, making the heat flare in my cheeks. I ducked my head as Talmadge rattled on and another set of shoes came into my line of sight. "This is Benjamin Willson. Who might we have the pleasure of adding to our fine company as we prepare to fight?"

"I'm Charlie Ross." I mumbled the first name that came to mind. Benjamin leaned in close and cursed under his breath.

William's eyebrows shot up and he grabbed my arm, his fingers forming a clamp around my upper arm. He gave me a little shake. "Charlie?! Why this is my cousin Charles' boy from Currytown." I had to give him credit. The man didn't miss a beat with that sharp wit of his. "Whatever brings you here, lad?"

There was steel adding an edge to my forefather's words, a tone I had never heard that gentle soul use before. He was furious, his eyes snapping, struggling to maintain a façade of control. I licked lips that had gone dry and told him hoarsely. "Papa was wounded and couldn't fight. When he heard of trouble coming your way, he sent me in his place."

Benjamin had started to pace, strung tighter than a native's bow. William's nostrils flared and he gave a jerk of his head. "Is that so? Come in the tent I share with Benjamin. We have much catching up to do. Thank you for getting him here safely, Talmadge."

My forefather turned and walked beneath the cover of the trees with great strides, making it hard to keep up, even with his hand still gripping my arm securely. I wasn't going anywhere but where he willed me to go. I tripped and stumbled. Benjamin took hold of my other arm none too gently, creating the guise of being supportive. The two of them were more like jailors as they ushered me into the tent and closed the flaps.

William grabbed hold of both of my arms and shook me so hard my hat dropped to the floor. "For the love of God, Charlotte, what are you doing here?"

If he was angry, Benjamin looked like Vesuvius about to erupt, but desperation made me raise my chin, set my shoulders, and look my forefather in the eye. "I will not sit alone at home, worry gnawing a hole in my stomach, waiting to hear word of you or have someone bring your coats and your guns to my doorstep. I won't go home with my tail between my legs either." I hissed the words between my teeth, practically a whisper. This conversation was for our ears alone.

The thunderheads gathered in William's eyes as he whipped around and raked a hand through his hair. Benjamin grabbed me by my shoulders. "This is madness, Charlotte. You cannot do this!"

The tears sprang to my eyes and my voice shook, overcome by the rush of my emotions. "If you two are willing to fight and risk sacrificing your lives, I can be by your side. My love for the both of you is just as big as yours. I *will not* leave. Cast me out and I'll hide in the brush, following you every step of the way."

Benjamin cursed again, his forehead creased with worry. He turned to my father and

177

threw his hands in the air. "What will we do with her?"

William's breath came out in a rush. He set his hands on his hips and glared at the ground, working through his inner turmoil. When his gaze meant mine, calm was restored, but there was a sadness that nearly flattened me. "You remind me very much of your dear mother, my blessing. When I tried to leave her home in Britain to get established, she'd hear nothing of the sort. Thank God she didn't listen to me otherwise I would never have had you."

He gathered me into his arms and rested his chin on my hair. The thump of his heart in my ear was soothing, a sound I had heard many times when his great grandson many times over comforted me through the years. "I know that it must be hard waiting at home. It has always been very trying to me whenever I've had to leave, thinking about you, wondering if you are all right." William swallowed hard and cupped my face in his hands. "But this, Charlotte? Now I must worry every minute that you are with us that I will pay the ultimate price and lose you. That is a cost I could not bear."

Benjamin set his hand on my forefather's shoulder. "Sir, I promise you. With every drop of my blood, with every bone in my body, with every breath that I take, I will be her shield."

William's eyes gleamed brightly as he eyed the young militia man. A curt nod and he pulled us both in for a hug. "That will have to suffice. God save us all. Now, we'd best go out and join the others."

He went out first while I settled my hat on my head. Benjamin went before me, only to turn back and clamp his mouth on mine. "I *will* keep you safe, Charlotte, but you must listen to what I say. I know the ways of war. You do not."

I did not argue. There was no need to upset him more than he already was. I followed him out of the tent. Men were gathering wood, building a fire, and preparing their tents. Some were gathered around maps, discussing strategy. Others were sent on ahead to be on the lookout. As one party set out, I saw a copper head gleaming in the sun, a familiar set to the man's shoulders, his bold stride. *Jacob Cooper*! I would definitely have to do everything possible to avoid him.

Benjamin kept me by his side, with William on our tail. We were sent off into the forest to look for any signs of the Redcoats and a good place to depart at a moment's notice if there came a need. After trudging along for hours, the branches whipping at my face and a chill setting in my bones, I began to understand that a soldier's life was even harder than I thought. The telling silence of my men, their disapproval clear as crystal, didn't make it any easier.

By the time we rejoined the others, the sun was a ball of fire on the edge of the horizon and men had settled on the ground around several fires, eating the food they'd packed from home. William gestured to a fire near our tent when a commotion stole our attention.

A new group of militia men approached, numbering twenty or so. Their dark-haired leader dismounted and approached us, his position obvious in his full uniform, his proud bearing, and his tidy appearance. Most of the others wore frayed, soiled uniforms or their everyday garb this late in the war. He stopped in front of my forefather and gave him a hearty pat on the back. "William, good to see you, my friend."

My ancestor gestured to a log that had been set before the fire as a seat and we all settled ourselves. "James, the pleasure is mine. You are looking well. Young ones, this is James Livingston. James, this is Charlie Ross, my cousin's son, and Benjamin Willson, a Patriot from Boston. How did you manage to get caught up with our small band of men? I heard you had retired."

"I couldn't resist, my friend. When word came my way that Ross and Butler were trying to stir up trouble again, I had to do my part." His mouth turned up in a grin, the fire reflected in his dark eyes, as he held his hands up to the flames.

My hands balled into fists and I had to bite my lip to keep quiet. One more notable from the Colonial Cemetery was in our midst. Not only would Colonel James Livingston be buried in Johnstown, he would forever be remembered for his vital role in revealing Benedict Arnold's betrayal. If not for this man sitting at our fire, the history books might tell a much different story and a different flag could be flying over the land.

Beside me, Benjamin's jaw had dropped and he nearly tripped over his tongue in his haste to speak. "I have heard of you, sir. You were at Verplanck's Point, down on the Hudson. You forced the Vulture to turn back and when you did, you caught that bastard, John Andre. Only then did the world know that Benedict Arnold was a wolf in sheep's clothing. You turned the tides of war in our favor then. We are forever in your debt, sir."

Colonel Livingston bowed his head in humble acknowledgement. "Thank you for your kind words, lad. I was simply doing my job. It was more luck than anything else, but I am grateful we were there to intercept those blasted papers."

William clapped him on the back. "Our gratitude knows no bounds. Share a bottle of homemade whiskey with us, my friend. It is quite good and will help you to stave off the cold."

The temperature had dropped considerably, making a fine, continuous ripple run through my body. From time to time, I caught Benjamin glancing at me out of the corner of his eye; he shivered as well. I wanted nothing more than to seek the warmth of his arms. When I had first hatched this plan, I had not thought about how hard it would be to sit at his side, unable to touch him, to even hold his hand.

A few rounds of the stoneware jug and we all had a fire in our bellies, took our fill of the rations we had packed, and enjoyed a round of storytelling, interspersed with moments of total levity as the older men discussed intelligence that had been gathered and potential outcomes in the near future. Feeling like I was listening to probability problems in math and none to heartened by their wishful predictions, I claimed I was tired and went to my tent.

Benjamin followed. He exercised restraint, showing considerable strength of will when he grazed my mouth with a kiss, and lay down on the opposite side of the tent, ensuring William would see no impropriety when he entered a few minutes later. With a quiet good night and a kiss on the top of my head, the lamp was doused. We were all covered by a blanket of darkness.

The sounds outside our tent faded, the flicker of the fires dying out as all of the flames were smothered. My forefather's quiet snores rose up, but I could hear Benjamin breathing in our close quarters. Listening to him, craving his arms around me, to have the wall of his body at my side, lying still was one of the hardest things I had ever done. I did not sleep that night.

Come morning, I found out what war was all about. Walking and waiting. We packed up and moved on. Benjamin and I went on foot, joining the majority of the militia, while William and a few others scouted ahead on horseback. From that point on, we forged ahead, hoping to intercept the war party coming our way. Often, we seemed to take two steps forward and three steps back as we retreated and took cover, holding steady when word came that men were approaching, only to discover another band of Patriots come to join our cause.

One week. Five Days. Three days until the Battle of Johnstown would be fought, or at least the date when the battle was *supposed* to happen. Hope and terror were making my heart run a marathon. In only a matter of days, the winner of the race would be revealed. How I dreaded that day.

My feet and my legs hurt. My shoulders ached as I switched the Brown Bess from one side to the other. My face was scratched from branches slapping me every time we were forced to move into the heavy undergrowth of the forest. Only Benjamin's steadfast presence at my side, his encouraging smile, and his strong hand to help me up when I fell, kept me going. As October 25 drew closer, I felt like I was preparing to meet the executioner.

My stomach was in knots and my food would not settle. We'd run out of fresh provisions by the third day and were getting by with fire cake, a simple, tasteless cake of flour and water. Each morning, I lost my breakfast almost as quickly as I ate it. Today, I barely made it away from our fire before I began to wretch.

I stood, hunched over, lightheaded as my stomach rebelled. The queasiness took my breath away and I couldn't find my balance. Swiping a hand across my mouth, I slipped away from our group and stumbled to the nearby creek, holding on to trees from time to time. I was still dizzy.

I didn't feel like myself. My inner voice laughed bitterly at that one. *You aren't yourself.* At this point, I wasn't sure where the past left off and the future began. I hadn't felt right for the past few days. I was so tired I wanted to lie down at the side of the road and go to sleep. My breasts were tender and my lower back ached. Once I lost my morning meal each day, a vague sense of nausea remained throughout the day and cramps, similar to those I felt during my period, were a constant companion. As I knelt to scoop some water into my hands to wash the terrible taste from my mouth, it was the last thought that almost made me topple into the creek.

I splashed my face with the icy water, took a sip, and sat down hard, feeling like I'd just been run over by a freight train. The cramps...I'd only experienced that feeling with my period, but my period was overdue. I'd never been late a day in my life. As I pressed my hands to my stomach, my mind raced, a hamster running itself ragged in a wheel. *Could I be....No! It's impossible to know so soon!*

My mental voice was laughing itself silly, in complete hysterics. Why should I question an instant pregnancy what with everything else that had happened to me? I closed my eyes and breathed out slowly, then in. Once. Twice. Three times. Finally, I found the strength to get to my feet and attempted to push this latest shocker to the back of my mind. Even if I was pregnant, there wasn't a thing I could do about it.

I turned to find Benjamin waiting for me, leaning against a tree. There were shadows in his dark eyes, his mouth turned down. As I approached, he reached out and took my arm. "Charlotte, are you well?"

I laughed shakily and gave him a shrug. "I guess being a soldier doesn't agree with me."

A spasm of grief passed over his face and he tugged me into his arms, roughly kissing me on the top of the head. "You shouldn't *be* a soldier."

I was very still. "Neither should you, but we are making the best of it and cannot ever forget why. We'd best get back before someone comes looking for us or sees us behaving in such an affectionate manner."

"I want nothing more than to give you all of my affections and lose myself in your arms." He bent to steal one swift kiss, squeezed my hand, and broke away. Each time he let go, I felt as if my heart was tearing apart at the seams.

# Chapter 13

*TWO DAYS UNTIL THE BATTLE.* Cornwallis had surrendered four days ago and I wanted to stomp my feet, tear at my hair, and scream bloody murder until everyone listened to me, until every man went back home to their mothers, wives, and children. Instead, I remained tight-lipped and marched woodenly with a ragtag company of men ranging from age 12 to 62. They were weary, worn, and fed up with war. They were also anxious, never knowing what they would meet around the next bend, when the war would come crashing into to them. We continued to march away from Johnstown and with each step we took, the hands of the clock ticking closer to October 25th, hope became a bonfire in my heart.

"Take cover! Take cover now! A regiment of British troops and Loyalists is coming this way, not even a half hour's ride away!" A messenger came flying down the path in the woods on horseback, his eyes wild, his clothes streaked with mud, his face bloodied from branches that tore at his skin. He couldn't have been sixteen.

Shots rang out and there was shouting up ahead, too close for comfort. This was it. The beginning of the end. My stomach plunged and a sour taste rose up in my mouth. I swallowed hard. I *would not* throw up on Benjamin's boots.

He turned to me, stark horror making his eyes nearly black and he grabbed hold of me by the shoulders, his grip as strong as a vice. "For the love of God, run and conceal yourself, Charlie. Your *father* would not forgive me if anything happened to you. Don't come out until I come for you!" William was somewhere up ahead and panic paralyzed me. What if something happened to that dear man? What if I never had the chance to speak to him again?

Around us was chaos, men calling to one another, shouting out rapid-fire plans, forming strategies, and fading into the woods until only Benjamin and I remained. He shook me hard enough to make my teeth clack together then pulled me in close, sealing his mouth over mine. The crackle of musket fire sounded, getting closer, and now there were screams of agony. "Go, Charlotte! Now! I must go see if I can help. Your father may need me."

It took everything I had to do as he said. While Benjamin headed into the fray, I did the opposite, breaking off of the path, straight into the heavy undergrowth of the forest.

Tears sprang to my eyes, blinding me. My breath came in sobs as I plunged through the thick pines, branches slapping me and snatching at my clothes. I hit a steep slope, twisted my ankle on a root, and pitched forward. I tumbled down like Jack and Jill, landing in a heap at the bottom.

The wind knocked out of me, I lay still, fighting to draw breath and calm the racing of my heart. My ankle throbbed fiercely, but that was nothing compared to the pain that clouded my mind. *God, keep them safe. Please, God. I beg You.* The prayer repeated over and over again in my mind. If I lost Benjamin and William, I lost my compass to the past. I would be cut adrift with no one to call my own.

"Charlie!" A voice called from the top of the hill, pulling me into a sitting position. My spirits lifted, expecting Benjamin, when a man of a smaller, burly build scrambled my way, the sunlight gleaming off of his fiery hair. Jacob Cooper.

I glanced around me frantically and lunged for my tricorne hat, slapping it on my head and pulling it down to shield my face.

Jacob was fighting for breath when he finally reached me, bent over, gripping a stitch in his side. "Sweet Jesus, I thought I'd never find you. Benjamin sent me. When he told you to conceal yourself, I don't think he wanted you to fall off of the face of the Earth. You wouldn't believe how worried he is about you, since you're such a little tyke and green around the ears. Willson's seen a lot more than me, more than anyone should see. That and your being William's nephew are part of the reason he's keeping such a close eye on you." His breath came out in a great rush and he straightened. "Lord, but I did run fast. By the way, I'm Jacob Cooper. I've seen you at a distance, but have been too busy to introduce myself."

He offered me his hand in greeting and to help me to my feet. His blue eyes held warmth even with fatigue and strain tugging at his face. I took a firm hold of him and stood quickly. One step forward and my ankle nearly gave out. I yelped, making a most un-masculine sound.

Jacob wrapped an arm around my waist to support me and brushed against my slightly protruding breasts. He froze, his eyes springing wide. His hand came up, as if in slow motion, slid my hat off, and pressed firmly beneath my chin. I was forced to look him in the eye.

He went white and cursed softly. "Charlotte?! What are you doing here? Are you out of your mind? You should be safe at home!" He shook with barely unleashed anger.

I bit my lip and my eyes started to sting. "I had to come! They are all that I have, Jacob! I couldn't sit there in good conscience while they were out risking their lives. I just couldn't! I need William. I need Benjamin because..."

"Because you love him and he loves you. I could see that the night the two of you came to Dodge's. Your bodies were practically humming each time you looked at each other." He eyed me closely and gave a sharp nod. "Well, we'd best get you back to him, but I don't think that carrying you will look good. Sit down." Jacob tore a strip off of his shirt and bound it around my ankle. He was gentle, but firm. "Okay. Give it a go now."

I stood cautiously and stepped forward. I felt a twinge of pain, but the ankle held. "I'm all right. Thank you." I reached out and touched his cheek. "I know you wish things were different between us, Jacob. I'm sorry."

He kissed my hand like he did at Richard Dodge's and pressed my palm to his heart. "Your friendship will have to be enough, sweet Charlotte."

We worked our way slowly up hill, his shoulder a godsend. By the time we reached the top, the both of us were panting. "Why didn't Benjamin come?"

Jacob was uneasy, his eyes troubled. My hand gripped his arm hard, my fingers digging in. "Tell me!"

"It's your father. He's been wounded." That had me moving forward faster, almost at a run, the pain making me cry out. I didn't know when William died. What if?

The young militia man caught my arm and helped me along. "Now don't look that way! A musket ball just grazed his arm, but Benjamin refused to leave him while someone tended to William's wound. Your young man is quite loyal." We continued on, Jacob squeezing my hand. "He's a good man, Charlotte. I wish you only blessings."

We reached a small clearing, a scattering of dead in red coats on the fringe. William sat on a rock, swaying slightly while Benjamin held him steady. Both men were pale, covered in blood and dirt, much like the day Benjamin first arrived at the Ross homestead. Talmadge Edwards was binding my forefather's upper left arm, pulling the bandage tight, making what little color was left spill from the wounded man's face.

"Papa!" I cried out, running forward to him, not caring about the charade or anything else. Fortunately, no one else was near. The rest had continued on...toward Johnstown.

Talmadge did not seem to be surprised in the least, a hint of a grin tugging at his mouth before he turned back to his old friend. "I always did think your daughter was a remarkable woman, but then *you* are a remarkable man." I had the feeling that he suspected all along.

I knelt by William and rested a hand on his knee. He drew me in close and kissed the crown of my head. Relief made his body go loose. I saw it mirrored on Benjamin's face as he turned away and swiped an arm across his eyes.

"My blessing. You are all right." He offered his hand to Jacob. "Thank you for bringing her back safe to me. I see our secret is out."

Benjamin grabbed my rescuer's shoulder. "How can I repay you?"

"Take care of her." Jacob told him gruffly and stepped back. My Patriot pulled me into his arms and set about kissing me senseless. I could taste his desperation, his fear, his overpowering love, all the feelings that I had been drowning in for days. I sagged against him for only an instant. William groaned behind us as he unsteadily rose to his feet. Talmadge snatched at him before he fell, Benjamin taking hold of his other side and brushing his injured arm, making him cry out.

I stepped up to my forefather, my chin raised, and grabbed hold of the lapels of his jacket. "You can't fight like this, Papa. You must go back home and rest, heal. You will only be a risk to yourself and others."

"Listen to him, sir. Go back to the house on Raven." The horse was tied to a tree nearby, grazing in the weeds at the side of the path. "Charlotte and I will join you as soon as we are able. We'll be slower on foot." Benjamin took hold of his good shoulder. "Please, William. After all you did for me, do this for us."

Talmadge put an arm around his friend's waist for support. "I will go with him and care for him until you get home."

William's jaw clenched, but he sighed heavily. "I'm obviously outvoted...and you're right. I would not even be able to hold my musket." He reached out with his good arm and pulled Benjamin in first, kissing him on the forehead, saving me for last. "My blessing, be safe. My love goes with you both."

I nodded and bit the inside of my cheek. "You too, Papa. I love you." I waited until he was mounted with Talmadge's help. A wave and the men were off.

Jacob extended his hand to the both of us. "Some of our company went the other way. I'm going to see if they need my help. God keep you both." With that, he sprinted off in the opposite direction. I wanted nothing more than to take Benjamin's hand and follow his lead.

Benjamin squeezed my shoulder. "Let's go, Charlotte. It was only a small band of men that clashed with us earlier, just a skirmish. Word has it there is a much larger group headed this way." *700 or so*, my all too keen memory reminded me.

I glanced up and saw there were lines etched around his mouth, his eyes clouded with weariness. He was limping slightly, the strain too much on his leg. I took his hand and we began to walk toward the last place on God's green earth that I wanted to go.

We'd gone about a half hour when Benjamin cursed and pulled me into a thick stand of evergreens. His hands skimmed up my sides, to my face, and threaded through my hair, touching me like a man touched a woman for the first time since I'd joined the militia. I put my hands around his neck and opened myself to a desperate kiss. "I was so afraid I'd lose you." The words caught in my throat and almost made me choke.

Benjamin took my hand and pressed it to his chest. I could feel the hammering of his heart. "I was terrified that I would never see you again. I need you by my side, Charlotte, always."

I kissed him once more. "I will be, right now, and forever in your heart."

We stood there, sharing the same air, our foreheads pressed together. Only the sound of a commotion, the distant rumble of many feet approaching, forced us to break apart and move on. As we began to run, my heart went out of control. They were coming, right on our tails, the messengers of war breathing down our necks!

Moving at quite a clip, venturing on a trail that cut through the woods, we soon broke out into a field and horror made me want to drop to the ground, press my body over Benjamin's to hide us both, to run away and never look back. This...this was the place where the marker stood in the twenty-first century, labeling the site of the Battle of Johnstown. A battle that was one of the last in the American Revolution, it came six days to late. Unnecessary. No one knew that the war was already over.

Behind us, the boom and clamor of the muskets began again, many more, even a cannon in the distance. Ahead of us, Patriots streamed from the cover of the trees. There was screaming, shouting, and grunts, cursing, crying as clouds of smoke rose up in the distance. Closer. They were coming closer.

"You must go to safety!" Benjamin stopped and turned to me, yanking a button loose from his uniform with one swift tug. "Charlotte, this is all I have to give you, this and the promise that I *will* find you. I keep my promises." He pressed the button into my palm, the letters *USA* digging into my skin.

I dug in my jacket and pulled out my braid that I had carried since I became a soldier.

195

I stuffed it in his pocket. "Keep that with the musket ball in your pocket to protect you." I kissed him fiercely and grabbed his hand, laying it on my stomach. "I give you one more gift. I am carrying your baby."

His eyes lit, the soft brown of melted chocolate, the tears rising up and overflowing. He held on for a moment more and I could feel him trembling. He raised his hands to cup my face and set his lips on mine. "Let me stamp your face on my heart. You give me more joy than I have ever known. Now please, Charlotte. I beg you. As the mother of my child, I need you to run now. Run and don't turn back. As soon as I can, I will come to you. Go now if you love me."

My heart ripped down the middle, a sob rising up, a raw, terrible sound. "I love you more than you know." One more kiss and I clung to him as hard as I could. I pressed my head to his chest and listened to the music of his heartbeat one last time and turned away. I began to run, stumbling, weaving, unable to see through my tears, holding on tightly to his button as if for life itself. I clung to his words even tighter.

My lungs were burning, there was a stitch in my side, and my stomach was in knots. Behind me, the sounds of war crashed in my ears and the weapons of war crashed in on our men.

I made it to the trees and turned back for what I knew would be my final glimpse of my Patriot. Behind him, a large group of men in the hundreds came on, inexorable. Benjamin stood firm, turning my way to catch sight of me, to be sure I was out of harm's way. He raised his hand to me when musket fire exploded nearby and a crimson flower bloomed on his chest, staining his white shirt. As if in slow motion, his arm fell first and then his body toppled to the ground in an untidy sprawl. A familiar figure approached him, John Little, gripping his own arm where a musket ball had hit home. He struggled to reach my Patriot and knelt by his side, his face twisted with pain and sorrow.

"Benjamin! No!" I headed back on the field, intent on reaching him, to hold him until the end, to go with him, when Jacob Cooper streaked toward me and grabbed my arm.

"Get out of here, Charlotte! He died for you. Do not let his death be in vain!" He glared at me, fire and grief twisting his face. Not even pausing for my response, Jacob started dragging me along into the woods. We went about twenty feet when he kissed me roughly, a slight grin lighting his eyes. "Forgive me. In case I die, I had to taste your lips at least once. Now run, run like hell is nipping at your heels!" With that, he gave me a forceful push and turned back to the battlefield.

"God be with you, Jacob!" I shouted. I stood there until I could no longer see the fire of his hair burning in the forest. *Benjamin. Benjamin is dead.* Those cold, lonesome words hollowed me out and the sadness rushed in with a force that was strong enough to sweep me off my feet. I began to run again, my Patriot's button a tangible link to his heart, but I didn't care where I went, and it felt like the fires of hell were blazing through my veins, the pain of

Benjamin's loss singeing me, about to consume me.

I crashed through the trees, splashed into a creek and fell down, cutting my knees and palms on the sharp rocks, but I would not let go of his button. Drenched and freezing, I crawled out on onto the shore, panting and sobbing, struggling to breathe. The clash of war crowded in on me and drove me to my feet, making me scramble up a steep slope, pulling on roots, breaking my nails trying to find something to hold on to. I made it to the top and found myself at Sir William's estate. The sight of it made me sick and I dropped to my knees, retching until my stomach was empty. "Oh, Benjamin," I wailed. "Why did you let me find you only to be taken away?"

I had no answers, only a button to bolster my courage as musket fire, the crunch of boots on the dead leaves, and voices gone hoarse with yelling proved the enemy was closing the gap. I was up and on the run once more, down the long lane, on into town, the church a beacon, all the way to the cemetery. I threw myself on to the ground in the spot where my journey began, where a cold, white stone would soon find a home, keeping watch over bones that I held dear. I dug my hands into the dirt, laid my cheek on the dry, dead grass, and wept until I knew no more. A clap of thunder sounded overhead and the skies opened up. Heaven was crying with me.

# Chapter 14

*I WAS COLD AND SOMETHING SCRATCHED* at my cheek. Someone was shaking my shoulder gently. "Hey? Are you all right? That guy can put you to sleep. I think even the ghosts have taken to their beds by now." In the background, the steady drone of Maynard Hughes' voice continued. The tall, dark figure of a man stood over me, shielded by clouds that covered the moon. The leaves shook and the bare branches rattled while the wind made a low, eerie moan. I sat up slowly and found myself lying in front of Benjamin Willson's grave marker. *Dear Benjamin.* I had to bite my lip to keep from crying out and laid a trembling hand on the stone. *Here. It all starts...and ends...here.*

The clouds shifted, allowing the moonlight to stream into the cemetery, illuminating the darkness and my good Samaritan frowned.

"You've got a bump on your forehead. Are you sure you're all right?"

"I'm...I'm clumsy. I must have fallen." That was it. That explained the whole thing, the jaunt through time, the elaborate memories and experiences. A simple bump on the head. I was giddy with relief, even as a wave of disorientation clouded my mind, making me question what was real and what wasn't.

I reached up to touch my head only to feel something small, round, and warm cradled in the palm of my hand. I did not need to look to know that the letters *USA* were being traced into my skin, like a tattoo, and the pain of loss nearly flattened me, sending me into a tailspin. The button...Benjamin's button...was all too real and had managed to cross over with me, bringing his heart with it.

I started to sway and the stranger took my hand. "Maybe I ought to call an ambulance or something." At his touch, a sizzle of recognition shot up my arm, the same sensation I'd felt on that first night that a militia man from Boston stumbled into the Ross homestead. *It's you*, it said with a jab to the gut.

I sucked in deeply and glanced up to study him, just as the clouds parted again. It was déjà vu all over as I looked at eyes that were as rich and warm as chocolate, concern forming a crease in the middle of his forehead. Brown hair tumbled in a carefree manner into his face. His mouth turned up in a sweet grin and I couldn't breathe. Give him long hair, a Brown Bess, and clothes of the time period and my Patriot would stand before me. "Benjamin?" I asked faintly.

He helped me to my feet and stood frozen for an instant, his hand gripping mine. Nervous laughter bubbled up and his grip loosened, but he did not let go. "It's just Ben, actually." He pretended to tip a hat with a flourish and a bow. "Ben Wilson at your service, mam. How did you know?"

My legs nearly buckled and black fuzziness crept over my field of vision. I would have fallen if he didn't step in and wrap an arm around my waist. "I guess you look like a Ben." The words came out in a whisper and I sagged against him.

"Whoa. I think you should get your head checked out. Why don't I go get you some help?" He was poised to sprint off, bring back the cavalry.

I forced myself to laugh. "I told you I was clumsy. I must have tripped on something. I'm Charlotte Ross."

His face went blank, his head tilted as he stared at me intently. I could see my reflection in his pupils. What did he see? The wind kicked up at that moment and drove me against him. Ben visibly shook himself and took my hand. "Well, Charlotte Ross, it's a pleasure to meet you. It's my duty as your rescuer to make sure you really are okay. How about a cup of coffee in the café? Extra cream, extra sugar, just a dash of coffee, right?"

For an instant, my nails dug into his skin and I had to force myself to ease up. The words...

they were so similar to what my Patriot had to say, that first morning I cared for him. They nearly made my knees cave and I wanted to weep. At the same time, I felt an instant connection with the man beside me. If I had my way, I'd never let go of him. Was it Ben or by some miracle could this man be my Benjamin?

He paused to look down at me and his hand came up to cup my cheek, his thumb grazing my skin, leaving intense heat like a brand. I closed my eyes and my breath caught, my heart fluttering. I almost pressed my head against his chest. Ben pulled back and I felt like a lifeline had been cut off. "Sorry. I don't know why I did that. I feel like...like we've met before." I nodded, my mouth gone dry, and clutched Benjamin's button. I slipped it in my pocket and felt it pressing against my skin. I could swear it burned.

We stood there, frozen in place, staring into each other's eyes. For an instant, I could hear the whispers of liberty on the wind and the moonlight seemed brighter than the sun. Something pushed at me, made me falter, and Ben caught me. I held on for a heartbeat, mumbled I was all right...and let go.

We walked a short distance, just around the block, to the Livingston Café, a place dating back to the fifties and lovingly preserved. Ben led me to a booth in the corner, making sure I was settled and comfortable before sitting down across from me. Our conversation went in fits and spurts until the waitress arrived. While the stranger who was not such a stranger put in an order for two mocha lattes, I studied him carefully in the bright light of the restaurant.

The color of his eyes and hair were the same, although the hair was shorter, brushing his collar, getting a bit shaggy around the edges. His face was not quite as chiseled; war, deprivation, desperation, and despair had probably not been a part of his life. As for the rest, the cut of his chin, the broad shoulders, and the height, they were all the same. Staring closely at him, I could not help but think of those final minutes with Benjamin. The tears rose up and I stared down at my hands, shredding a napkin to bits, all the while aware of the button sat in my pocket. I plunged my hand in and pressed it to my palm.

Ben reached across and his fingers pressed on mine. "I really think I should take you to the emergency room to get your head checked. You're white as can be and you're trembling."

I shook my head and swiped at my eyes. "I'm just embarrassed. I can't believe you found me on the ground like that."

Our coffees arrived at that moment, giving me an excuse to be quiet. We both sipped at our cups, the steam rising up to our faces. Ben's hand was resting on the table. I wanted to slip my hand into his and never let go. The waitress returned with the bill. My rescuer hardly acknowledged it, simply dug out his wallet and handed her his credit card before she left. Less than five minutes later, she was back with a slip for him to sign.

Ben signed and leaned back in his seat, watching me. With his attention, the heat rose up in my face and I pressed one hand to my cheeks. He chuckled and leaned forward to push a stray curl behind my ear. "Sit tight. I need to use the restroom."

While he was gone, the waitress dropped off his credit card and receipt. I reached out with trembling fingers to spin the card around. *Ben Wilson.* What were the odds? The same last name, a different spelling. Shakily, I picked up my cup and took a great gulp, scalding my tongue. He might not be my Patriot, but the two men were so alike, they could have been brothers.

*WE STOOD ON THE SIDEWALK,* buffeted by the wind. I was shivering from more than the bite in the air. I suspected I was in shock. "Thank you for the coffee, Benja...Ben. I think I'll head home now. The ghost walk has lost its thrill tonight. Have a good night." I turned to go.

He caught my arm and his words were terse. "If you think I'm going to let you go by yourself, you're crazy. The next thing you know, you'll get dizzy, fall, and be a heap at the side of the road. I won't feel right until I see you home safely. Lead the way."

Ben gestured for me to go first. Seeing no way out of it, I set off, past Sir William's grave, past the Colonial Cemetery that made me shudder, past the Drumm House, and the courthouse...all those familiar places that had been landmarks all of my life. *Or lives.*

We took our time, walking slowly. My hands were thrust in my pockets. In one, I still clasped the button, turned it round and round. Ben kept close, but did not talk, perhaps sensing my strange mood. With each step that we took, the feeling of déjà vu became so strong that I felt like I was walking in quicksand, being tugged back through the years. In my mind, I saw a dirt road...scattered homes...trees...fields, where sidewalks, a cluster of houses, street lights, and power lines now stood.

I remembered. Walking with Benjamin when he insisted upon accompanying me to the market place. He wasn't well enough, not nearly strong enough, limping heavily at my side with the cane that William gave him. I saw him grin and bear it because that's what Benjamin did. I felt the warmth of the sun on my head and dark dress, the way he made me feel safe, holding my hand. I felt the lightness in my heart every time he slid a glance my way and his mouth curled up at the corners. I remembered counting every step along the way, trying to make them last so I could spend more time with him...until we reached a long lane that ended...at the Ross Homestead.

I came to a stop with a lurch, staring at the fieldstone foundation of my cottage...the foundation that dated back to the Revolution...and a house, although rebuilt, that was very similar to the home that became mine in 1781. In my mind's eye I saw the tidy, little cottage, the barn out back, the corral, and animals. The vision was so strong I had to shake my head, blink hard, look again. Ben, watching me waver, grabbed hold of me and my body went loose.

"Charlotte! Are you all right?" His eyes were wide with fright, his arms like bands of steel. All I wanted to do was bury my head in his chest, to make this all go away, to believe he was mine.

Instead, I drew myself up and pulled out an attempt at a grin. "Yes, yes of course. I'm just going to go in and lie down, maybe put some ice on my forehead. Thank you for walking me home." I glanced down the road and the way we came only to call out with dismay. "Now you have to walk all the way back!"

He smiled, a smile so heartbreakingly familiar that I almost broke down and sobbed. "It's okay, really. It's a fine night. I can use the fresh air and exercise." A line formed between his eyes and he took my hand. "I know that I'm a stranger and this is going to sound crazy, but I feel like I know you. Would you like me to come in and sit with you for a while, just to be sure you really are okay?"

"No, that's not necessary. I've kept you long enough. I'm fine, really." I gave him assurances. In truth, I was falling apart. I held tight to his hand. In my other hand, I held onto the button as I straddled a tightrope between the past and present. My heart began to skip and I had the insane urge to kiss him until we both fought for air. Finding it hard to breathe, I closed my eyes for an instant. When I opened them, Ben Wilson was gazing intently at me. His head tilted and in an unexpected move that somehow felt completely right, he brushed my cheek with a kiss.

"Good night then, Charlotte. Can I...Would it be all right if I come back to see you again sometime?" His smile had slipped away and there was a yearning in his face that tugged at my heart, made my gut clench, came too close to begging him to stay.

I nodded. "Yes, I'd like that, Ben. Thank you again for being my knight in shining armor." I stepped up onto my porch and held on to the post, pressing my face against the cold wood, holding on tight because nothing else was keeping me on my feet. I fought the stinging in my eyes as my hair whipped around my face and my fingers tightened around the button in my hand.

Ben went off into the distance with long, sure strides. As he walked away, the shadows gathered around his dark coat, the wind tangled his hair, and for an instant, I could swear it was my Patriot...or the ghostly figure that entangled me smack dab in the middle of this strange web of events in the first place. He turned one last time and raised his hand in farewell. I returned the gesture and continued to keep watch until I couldn't see him anymore.

I held onto the post a few minutes longer, gathering my strength, and latched on to my doorknob. I leaned my head against the sturdy wood and fumbled in my pocket, found my key exactly where I put it...233 years ago...or just a few hours ago? I was so confused.

I shut the door and locked it with hands that shook. On wobbly legs, I weaved through the house, to the bedroom, and dropped on my bed. I lay there, curled in a ball, and sobs took hold of me, wracking my body, making the bed shake. My comforter and pillow was wet with my tears and I could hardly see straight when I finally pulled myself up and turned on a light. I was afraid I was going out of my mind.

I bit my lip and looked down at my hand, letting my fingers unfold like the petals of a flower opening to the sun. In the middle of my palm was a small, brass button, the only thing that convinced me that I was not completely unhinged.

*USA* was proudly etched on its face, the same button I had admired the first time my Patriot wore Nathaniel Brown's jacket, the same button he tore off from that jacket when we said goodbye. I raised it to my lips and kissed it while my heart ached so badly I thought it couldn't beat anymore. *Benjamin, you said you would find me.*

I squeezed my eyes shut and closed my hand again, comforted by the warmth of the smooth, round memento. In my mind, an image of the man in the cemetery tonight flickered, merging with the ghostly figure that led me on my journey, and Benjamin Willson. *Ben Wilson.* I heard his voice in a low whisper. I'd never believed in reincarnation before, thought it was nothing but a sham. Now I wasn't so sure. Maybe

208

my Patriot was trying to make good on his promise. At the moment, maybes weren't good enough.

My head pounded, battered with all of the thoughts, memories, and pictures that kept crashing into each other like a ship on a storm-tossed sea. Unable to handle anything more, I kicked off my sneakers, stripped down, and threw my clothes in an uncharacteristic heap, the jeans, sweater, and jacket I had worn when I was the only Charlotte Ross I had ever known. Now there were two wrangling inside of me.

I pulled my favorite pair of flannel pajamas out of my dresser, still half expecting to find a long white nightgown in a chest at the foot of the bed. My pj's were so worn that the original pattern had faded and was no longer recognizable. They'd seen me through many a tough night and personal crisis. They usually made me feel better, but as I lay in the darkness in my bed, staring up at the ceiling in a house that was painfully silent, I was beyond the power of pajamas.

The grief! I'd never felt a hurt like this before, like my heart had been ripped from my body and crushed before my eyes. I was tangled up in conflicting emotions—confusion, disbelief, and shock, but above all it was the overpowering loss that pinned me down to the center of the bed. I wasn't sure I could ever get up. I wanted to go back, so ironic when at first I wanted nothing more than the present, but going back was pointless. Benjamin was dead.

209

I stared out the window. The moon was shining brightly, illuminating the trees that had shed most of their leaves outside my window, their skeletal branches reaching like imploring hands to the sky, but I could only see those final minutes with Benjamin. I felt the burn of his kiss on my mouth, the scrape of his stubble against my cheek, the warmth of the metal button in my palm. I heard the crack of the muskets, heard the ragged screams of the men fighting, saw the bloom of blood over my Patriot's heart.

A part of me longed to return to the cemetery. To lie down, cling to that cold, white stone. To never get up again. Only one candle of hope flickered in my heart and its name was Ben. My kind Samaritan had helped me up, kept watch over me, walked by my side. I couldn't believe that his timely arrival was purely coincidental.

As exhaustion finally won out, I began to drift off and slid into dreams that began with Benjamin...in the cottage, in the meadow, by the creek, dancing at Sir William's, lying in each other's arms in the barn, clinging to each other on the battlefield...and then they became entwined with Ben. His uncanny resemblance to my Patriot started the stirrings in my gut. My blood began to rush through my veins even at the most casual touch of his hand with an intensity that was enough to bring me to my knees. Staring in his eyes, I felt like I was lost and didn't want to be found.

I awoke a quivering, sniffling mess, the tears streaming down my face, my heart breaking all over again. I was filled with such longing that I didn't trust what I would do if Ben Wilson showed up at my door again. I'd probably throw myself at him.

Unable to still my mind, I finally turned to my last resort and grabbed a bottle of wine I had been saving for a special occasion. I poured one glass, then two, gulping down the sweet vintage until my head was swimming and the room was spinning. I tumbled into bed and reached out, resting my hand on the button on my nightstand. A twig of worry poked at the back of my mind...something important, something I should remember, but it snapped under the weight of my exhaustion. I closed my eyes and my brain crashed to a halt. Fade to black.

# Chapter 15

*"MY BABY!" I CRIED OUT SO LOUDLY,* it pulled me from my sleep. I sat up in the faint light of pre-dawn, snagged in the covers, one hand grasping my stomach while the other snatched up the button. Caught in the wreckage of grief and the transition of time, I'd completely forgotten. Our baby.

I sprang out of bed and began to pace, frantic, panting for breath. At the same time, my head felt like it was about to fall off of my shoulders. I wasn't used to drinking. I pressed both hands to my midsection and pressed hard, half-expecting to feel a slight swelling, a tiny mound that would hint at a budding, new life growing inside of me.

Craziness! It was pure craziness! I knew there couldn't be a baby inside of me. The evidence was plain to see in the flow of my menstrual cycle when I rushed to the bathroom, overcome by cramps. As I sat in the bathroom, bent over at the waist, Benjamin's button pressed to my lips, I shut my eyes. I attempted to stop the cyclone of my thoughts, to make sense of the kaleidoscope of memories. I *couldn't* be pregnant. *I* hadn't actually gone anywhere, had I? Yet the button was still in my hand...

On my feet again, I went from one end of my little cottage to the other, back and forth. I thought back to how my body had felt when I was Charlotte the First, ran my hands over my breasts, skimmed my fingers over my midsection. No. *I* did not feel pregnant. The urgent question in my mind now was what happened to Charlotte after the Battle of Johnstown? Was I right? Did she carry Benjamin's child and his future? I sat down on the edge of the bed, gripped my knees, and rocked back and forth. How could I find out?

*The Ross Family Tree!* My father had shown it to me countless times over the years, rolled it out for school projects, been absolutely obsessed as he worked tirelessly to fill in as many gaps as possible. I clearly remembered William, Mary, and Charlotte, 1760, because my father had told me time and again, tapping their names on the page, *"Here's the seed that was planted here in the colonies, the beginnings of our family line in Johnstown, traced back as far as I could possibly go."*

My father never did find out what came before and I didn't pay attention to the rest. I didn't care to know...until now. *Dad! Dad can bring me our family tree!*

I couldn't call him, not yet. I had to wait until my heart stopped galloping out of control, until I could catch my breath. I took a shower, scalding my skin with the steaming water, singed my tongue with hot tea, and couldn't eat or I would throw up. My stomach was rolling and my head throbbed. I sat down in a large, stuffed chair in my living room, tucked my legs beneath me, and wrapped up in a blanket. I closed my eyes and formed a nest in my hands for my button, praying fervently, although I wasn't sure what I was praying for. Answers? Peace? Benjamin?

At eight o'clock, I picked up the phone and dialed Dad's cell. His voice mail picked up; he was teaching a class. At the sound of his voice, my hand began to shake and the tears slid down my face. To hear his voice again, that beloved sound that I had heard all my life, one that called to mind William Ross. They sounded practically identical.

At the beep, I rallied to pull myself together. "Dad, hi! I was wondering. I'm doing a little research. Could you bring the Ross Family Tree after school? I'll even cook you some dinner, okay? Mom will be at her painting class tonight, right? Let me know if you can't. Hope to see you later. Love ya!" I attempted to sound breezy, casual. I probably sounded strung out.

I swiped at my eyes and cleared my throat as I called into work next. My girls, Erin and Trish, could handle the store without me. One thing was certain. I was not fit to go in or face the public. I claimed I was sick and wasn't lying. I was heartsick.

I went back to bed, my mind running ragged, and slept in fits. At 4 o'clock, I woke with a jolt and threw back the covers. My father would be coming soon. *Get it together, Charlotte!* My mental voice grabbed me in a steel-like grip and gave me a hard shake.

I dressed in jeans and a loose, flannel shirt, pulling my hair up in a ponytail to get it out of my face. I slipped the button in my pocket, feeling the need to keep it close at all times. Whenever I touched it, I felt like Benjamin was with me. I poked around in my refrigerator, stuck some marinated chicken breasts in the oven, and tossed a salad. That would have to be good enough. If I had any culinary skills, they were lost in the shuffle of confusion right now.

While I waited for my father's arrival, I walked through the rooms of the house that had been mine for two years, reacquainting myself. With every step, images of another cottage and time filled my mind. Another home that had been mine, a home that I believed stood here on this foundation.

I picked up random keepsakes. A piece of pottery dating back to the 1700's. A family heirloom of a quilt, passed down through the generations. A bonnet hanging on a hook on the wall, one that I could've worn. As I stood still and stared at the prints, the grave rubbings, and photos of Revolutionary landmarks, I finally understood what drove me to collect so many reminders of that time. It wasn't just because the love of history ran in my blood. *My* history ran in my blood.

I was setting the table and pouring wine when there was a rap on my door and a deep voice called out, "Is there a Charlotte Ross in the house?"

I had just enough time to rearrange my face when my father stepped into the kitchen. One look at that man I knew so well, so like William, someone I missed terribly and had come to love, and I flung myself in Dad's arms. I fought not to cry.

"Charlotte, a daughter that is such a blessing like you should not look so sad. What's wrong?" He took my face in his palms and pressed a kiss to the top of my head. His words and his actions were so similar, I felt a stab of longing for William...and yet he was here, in my father. That made the dam break.

The tears started and I wasn't sure I could turn off the tap. My father rocked me and whispered comforting words. I clung to him, my anchor that kept me from drowning, until the knots inside of me slowly became untangled. A hand gently lifted my chin. "Honey, you know you can talk to me. Tell me what's bothering you."

I stared into calm, gray eyes that could soothe the most ruffled spirits, and a sandy head of hair with only a few strands of white. In Martin Ross' face, I saw the past and the present combined, two strong men coming together, and I was overcome with a love so strong, I could barely speak. "I'm okay. It's just that time of the month, you know?"

He raised his hands in the air. "Say no more. After all those years in a household of women, those words instill terror." Dad grinned and inhaled deeply through his nose. "Mmm. Something smells really good. What's for dinner?"

"Chicken a'la Charlotte. Come sit and I'll bring you something to drink." I poured a glass of wine for myself and grabbed a beer—Sam Adams, of course—for Dad. I carried them out to the living room where he sat on the couch. I handed over his bottle and gave him a peck on the cheek before I resumed my spot in my favorite chair. "How was school today?"

He took a long swallow and leaned back, rubbing at his eyes. "Long. I'm wading through about a hundred essays right now. I could go blind." His characteristic good humor won out as his smile grew, excitement building with it. "It's worth it, though. I've got some brilliant students this year. How was your ghost walk?"

*Do I have a ghost story for you!* It hit me like a punch in the gut. I'd had the experience of a lifetime...several lifetimes...and I couldn't say a word. Not to the Daughters of the American Revolution. Not to our town historian. Definitely not to my parents. They'd send me for psychiatric evaluation, think I'd gone off the deep end. I brushed my hand over the button in my pocket, reassuring myself that it was still there, that it was real.

218

My father cleared his throat. "Charlotte? Are you sure you're all right? You're never at a loss for words and you look so down, not your usual sunny self." He leaned toward me and set a hand on my knee. "Plus you're a thousand miles away. What's going on?"

*Try a few hundred years away.* I bit my lip; otherwise, I'd spill the whole story and be on my way to a padded room. I shook my head and fought the burning at the back of my eyes. Damn the catch in my voice! "I'm just tired, Daddy. The walk was a bust. Maynard put us all to sleep with his stories and then I didn't sleep well. I'm a little off today." *Way off and I don't even know for sure who I am, where the Charlotte I was leaves off, where the Charlotte I've always been begins.*

My father didn't even hesitate. He took the wine glass from my hand, shifted me over in the oversized chair, and gathered me into his lap, forming a cradle with his arms. With his chin on my head and my ear against his chest, I felt like I'd found a safe haven for the first time...really since this whole crazy stint with time travel began. His own voice was hoarse with emotion when he spoke. "You're never too old to sit in my lap, never too old for some comfort from your father. Rest your head a bit, ease your worries. Soon enough, you'll calm the troubled waters and find yourself again."

He hummed softly and slowly, I relaxed, letting him carry me back to my childhood, letting his strong arms carry the load on my mind for a little while. William Ross had done well; the best of that man lived on in the man

219

who held me now. I sighed and told him softly, "I love you, Daddy."

"Right back at ya, kiddo. Now, what do you say to dinner? It smells out of this world and I am starving. I forgot lunch today." His stomach rumbled loudly at that moment, making us both laugh. I stood up and lent him a hand to pull him to his feet. My father wrapped an arm around my shoulders and kissed me on the top of the head on our way to the kitchen. I couldn't help but wonder how many traits our forefather had instilled in the Ross sons and daughters who would come after him.

We wandered back to the kitchen and made a team effort, setting the table, serving the food, pouring drinks. Dad turned on the radio to an old-time station and the soothing sounds of Glenn Miller filled the room. As we sat and ate, my father told me humorous stories from his classes that made me forget everything else for a while. The longer we sat together, the more relaxed and at home I felt, like I was where I belonged and in my own skin again.

Dad cleared when we were done, filled the sink, and plunged into washing while I did the drying, as was our usual routine. As we rubbed shoulders, I slid a glance his way time and again. Love, strong enough to make me weep if I let it, grabbed hold and wrapped me up tight. I hadn't realized how much I missed Martin Ross until now.

"Well, sweetheart, I'd best be getting home. Mom will be back soon and I promised I'd have dinner ready for her. I think there's a hot pocket in the freezer." My father winked and dried his hands on a dish towel. He bent over me and kissed the crown of my head. "Thanks for a delicious meal."

"Thanks for the company. I really needed some Dad time tonight." I started to head to the door then held up a finger. "Hold on." I foraged in the fridge and brought out a plastic container. "Leftovers?"

"I always knew you were my greatest blessing." He pulled me in for a hug without a clue about the power of his words, how they made my heart ache.

We walked to the door, his arm around my waist, my head on his shoulder. My father turned to leave then tapped himself on the forehead. "I almost forgot." So had I.

He reached into the inside of his tweed jacket, so typical of my image of a scholar, the standard in his closet all of my life. A rolled up paper was tucked in the inside pocket. "I even had it laminated. I'm really happy to see you interested in our family tree, Charlotte. You can learn a lot from our history."

*You have no idea.* I stood on tiptoe to give him a kiss and a fierce hug. "Thanks, Daddy. Get going now before Mom beats you home and thinks you forgot about her...again." He often got sidetracked, distracted by his trips through old books, videos, and piles of artifacts. If someone didn't make him come up to the surface, Martin Ross could be buried in yesteryear for days.

"Goodnight, sweet Charlotte. Come by for dinner soon. Mom misses you. I think she misses me too!" With a wave, he was off.

I stood in the doorway, the rolled paper clutched to my chest, holding on so tightly, you'd think I was worried someone would snatch it out of my hand. I was afraid to look at it, afraid not to look. I waited until I could no longer see my father, closed the door, and locked it. I did not want to be disturbed. I turned off the outside light and leaned against the sturdy oak. *Breathe in. Breathe out.* I had to bolster my courage, reach past my racing heart to my churning stomach and find it.

I went through the rest of the house and shut off all the lights except for a dim light over the sink in case I was restless in the night...which was likely. At the moment, I doubted I would ever sleep easy again.

I set the document on my comforter, washed up, and pulled on my pajamas. Finally, unable to put off the confirmation or disproof of my theory a minute longer, I sat in the middle of the bed. I grabbed Benjamin's button off of the nightstand, set it to my lips, and whispered a prayer. *Please, God.* I wasn't sure what I was asking for.

Slowly, I unrolled the paper and spread it out on the bed. At the top, I could easily find the first dates, those I had memorized because Dad pounded them into my brain—our beginnings in America. *William and Mary Ross, gave birth to Charlotte Elizabeth Ross, 1760.* I wondered where they lived before they settled in the Ross

Homestead in 1764. *On the ground where your house stands right now.*

I ran a finger down the page and found the answer to the burning question that had ignited since I first awoke. *Charlotte Ross Cooper and Jacob Cooper, gave birth to Benjamin Willson Cooper, 1782.*

I covered the page with my hand and the tears were falling down, splashing on the lamination. "I told you, Benjamin," I whispered. I knew without a doubt that Benjamin Willson Cooper was not Jacob Cooper's son, but I cast up a prayer of gratitude and blessing for that young militia man. For standing by her. For marrying her. He'd always loved Charlotte the First and proved to be a good man. I had firsthand knowledge of his sterling character. I would never forget the day in the forest when Jacob came to my rescue or when he sent me off of the battlefield to keep me safe.

Now the next pressing question and mystery to be solved. Was Ben the descendent of Benjamin Willson? I followed Charlotte's line and the further I went down the page, trailing my fingers across what looked like an intricately tangled web, the faster my heart began to beat, thudding painfully in my chest until I hit a dead end in 1865. My father had added a notation in his tiny, neat handwriting: *Records destroyed in a fire. Trail has been lost.*

At a loss, I turned to William's line next and was relieved to see that he married again in 1785 and had a son, giving birth to a long line of Ross men that led to my father, Martin William

Ross. Because of that great man, I could lay my finger on my name, Charlotte Elizabeth Ross. *The Second.*

I set my family tree on my night stand and flipped Benjamin's button in my hand, over and over while I stared off into nothingness. I'd found some answers, but would have to dig deeper into the past.

*Dig!* Unable to still my mind just yet, there was something else I had to do. I sprang out of bed, slipped into a coat, and grabbed a flashlight. Outside, I found a shovel in the shed and began to circle round my cottage. I had no idea what I hoped to unearth as I studied the foundation of my house, one that looked remarkably similar to the one that supported the Ross Home. It had faded over time and there were spots that had crumbled after exposure to the elements, but otherwise the workmanship looked like the same fieldstones that I had seen over 200 years before.

Thankful for a brightly lit night with a full moon, I studied the stones closely. On occasion, I used the shovel to dig at a spot concealed by the leaves. I panned the flashlight back and forth, going several circuits around when the wind picked up debris and scattered it, clearing my view. My flashlight caught something etched in one of the stones. I dropped down on my knees, heedless of the damp grass or any mud. On all fours next, I moved in as close as possible and pointed my light at ground level. Writing stared back at me. *WR 1764.*

I dropped the flashlight, shaking so hard I couldn't hold on to anything for the moment, including my sanity. All these years, I'd been drawn to this house, stopping when I went for a walk, pulling the car over, admiring it from afar until the day the "For Rent to Own" sign went up and I snagged the place without giving it a second thought. The first day I walked in, it whispered *Home*. If I was honest with myself, I'd heard it talking to me long before. This place was my place and now I knew why. I believed this was the Ross Homestead without a doubt. I'd have to see if I could get more concrete evidence or confirmation.

I slipped my cell from my back pocket and snapped a few pictures. I nearly dropped my phone and had to rub my palms on my legs. My heart couldn't take anymore. The search for answers could keep until morning. If I didn't head in now, my neighbors would think I was harboring a dreadful secret.

The wind was making a mournful sound as I hurried back inside. I wanted to plug my ears and forget everything until tomorrow. I washed my hands, changed my muddied clothes, and climbed back into bed once more. When I turned out the light, the button was illuminated by the moon's glow. Somehow the sight gave me a little sliver of peace. I set my hand on it as my mind became fuzzy. As I slipped into a state of unconsciousness, I heard a baby's cry.

*My screams shattered the darkness, making my throat raw, shredding my voice as I* leaned forward. "Now, Charlotte! Push with all of your might!"

Jacob Cooper was hoarse from shouting, stationed at the foot of the bed. My muscles strained, my knuckles gone white, as I pulled as hard as I possibly could on the strips of rag tied to the headboard. My entire body was in knots, my teeth gritted together, my breath coming out in a hiss as I pushed from somewhere deep inside of me. The rags began to rip, my body tearing as a great, warm gush poured out and I felt a pain like nothing I'd ever felt before in my life. I didn't mind. At least it swallowed the pain in my heart for a little while.

A high-pitched wailing filled the room as the first tendrils of morning reached through my window, igniting the fiery strands of Jacob's hair. Drenched with nearly as much sweat as I was, his curls were damp, pasted to his forehead, face, and neck. His shirt was stained with perspiration and smears of blood as he snipped at the umbilical cord with trembling hands, gathered the baby in a blanket, and approached the head of the bed. There was a smile and light in his clear, blue eyes, yet he was drawn, with lines of exhaustion written on his face. Delivering a baby was hard work for the mother and the coach.

"What do you want to call your son?" He asked quietly as the warm bundle was placed in my arms.

The sun touched my little one and the dark swirls of hair clinging to his face. His mouth scrunched up, his tiny fists in balls as he readied to wail. I set him on my breast and he latched on, *suckling hungrily, appeased for the moment. The love, tangled with sorrow, wrapped tightly around my heart and the tears splashed down on his cheek. "Benjamin." Even the name hurt to say and I knew that this child would give me a lifetime of pleasure made bittersweet by the pain, a price I was willing to pay. After all, his father had sacrificed his life to give us ours.*

*Jacob laid a hand on my head, the other on the baby's. "Benjamin Willson Cooper, welcome to the world. I will protect you, care for you, and love you until the day that I die."*

*I reached blindly for him and he snatched my hand, kissing my fingers. "You have my promise to do the same for you, Charlotte. I know that I can never replace Benjamin, nor would I try. I know you may never come to love me, although you care for me. Know that my love is strong enough for the both of us."*

*The sun blazed in his eyes and branded my skin as the room flooded with light, bonding the three of us together in a tight-knit circle. A breath of warm air pressed against my cheek like a kiss and the baby's blanket shifted. I was flooded with an overpowering wave of love as a strong wind blew past us in a room with no open windows. "Go with God, Benjamin," I whispered as Jacob sat beside the bed and leaned his head against my knuckles.*

I awoke with my face and pillow wet from my tears. I half expected my breasts to feel full, my body wracked with the lingering pain of childbirth, while I held a warm, soft weight against my chest. Instead, there was nothing but

227

emptiness. In my body. In my arms. In my heart. In my soul.

# Chapter 16

*I DREW A DEEP BREATH* and the pain came rushing in, making me long for the numbness from only a moment before. I curled into a ball, head to my knees, arms hugging my legs, and tried to get back to my dream...or the distant past and one of the brief respites I had when Benjamin held me in his arms. I tried to imagine he was with me now, entangled in my bedding, his legs entwined with mine, his heart thundering in my ear. I listened for the sound of his breathing, waited for his reassuring touch as his fingers skimmed over my body and threaded in my hair. I waited for his lips to take mine and consume me until I knew no more.

Nothing happened. I could not go back...and even if I did, *he* would be gone. I did not want to relive the days leading up to the Battle of Johnstown. I could not bear to lose my

Patriot again. I was still bound up in a web of grief when the pale wash of dawn crept into my room. I climbed out of bed on legs that trembled and took a shower. I made the water as hot as I possibly could, nearly unbearable, trying to wash away this heavy sadness and bring myself back to the present. To be in the here and now in a time and town that had been mine for 22 years, but now made me feel completely out of place. *I understand what it is to be a stranger in a strange land.*

The sobs rose up, shaking me to the core, and I pressed my head to the wall as the water poured down on my head. No one could hear me. My fists banged against the tile, bruising my knuckles, making the hurt bloom. I didn't care.

I cried until I was an empty shell and there was nothing left...until the water ran cold and I was shivering so hard, my teeth chattered. I stepped out of the tub, towel-dried my hair, and put on a heavy robe. My feet left a trail of wet footprints through the house as I put on the tea kettle. I stood in the kitchen, waiting, gripping the counter until the pot's shrieking broke the silence. A few minutes more and I carried the steaming cup to the living room. I sat down in my chair, feet tucked beneath me, and sipped at the hot, sweet brew. It burnt my mouth and the tears sprang up again, running down my cheeks, mingling with my tea and making me taste salt.

I sat there crying as the walls went from a pale white to purple, then pink. Finally, the full morning light filled the room, announcing the new day. A bird trilled outside my window, singing of the promises that were in store. I only felt a heavy weight of grief pressing down on me. I finally understood what true depression was, made worse by the fact that I could not share my sorrow with anyone.

The cup was empty and I was sitting in the same position, growing stiff when my alarm sounded from the bedroom. I *had* to go into work today. Keep calling in and there would be questions, well-wishers at my doorstep, prying eyes. The people who loved me would want answers and I could not tell them *anything*. I could only say I was sick, but being sick at heart wouldn't cut it for long.

Somehow, I dredged up the energy to stand, to go back to my bedroom, to lay clothes on my bed. I stood there, staring at them, and the faucet began running again. My jaw clamped shut to hold back the urge to wail and I swiped at my cheeks angrily. No. This would not do. I saw the button sitting on the bed stand and picked it up, kissing it, pressing it to my heart, curling my fingers tightly around it. *Benjamin, I miss you.*

There was no answer, only the sound of my ragged breathing and my sniffles. My heart ached with every beat, but I couldn't stay home forever, stuck in the past. I had to act, to go on a scavenger hunt and find remnants from the Ross family and the days leading up to the Battle of Johnstown, something to prove that I wasn't crazy. I needed to know that I really had seen what I had seen...that I wasn't delusional...or suffering from a brain tumor. I pressed a hand to my forehead as a major headache threatened to bloom and I began to hyperventilate. Only the button could calm me. *This is real, tangible proof of Benjamin's love. He gave it to you. Hold on.*

I went through the motions of getting dressed. I chose comfortable clothes, jeans with worn spots that were soft on my skin and loose— no girl in her right mind really liked tight jeans—and a big, baggy sweater. I stuck my button in my pocket. Otherwise, the thought of leaving it behind gave me a panic attack. A few more deep breaths and I could finish getting ready to meet the day.

A quick sweep of a brush through my hair, my curls tumbling down over my shoulders, and a dab of makeup would have to be enough to make me look human. I slipped on my tall, brown boots with a flat heel and shrugged into my coat, intent on taking a vigorous journey on foot the several blocks to work. Fresh air might clear out the cobwebs that were clouding my mind from a few centuries ago.

I stepped out on to my porch, the door clicking shut behind me, and couldn't move. Ben Wilson sat on the top step, a Dunkin Donut bag in his hand. He wore a navy pea coat, jeans, and hikers. His dark hair was tousled in disarray around his face, falling into eyes as warm as a doe's and his crooked smile touched my heart. If I closed my eyes, I saw my Benjamin in his blue uniform from Grannie Brown. "Good morning," the words slipped out faintly.

In one fluid movement, he was on his feet, holding out the donuts. "Hi. I come bearing gifts.

I thought you might be hungry." He attempted to speak lightly, but there were shadows crowding in. "I...I don't know how to explain it, but I just had to see you. I couldn't stop thinking about you, worrying about you. I'm not a stalker or anything. I just wanted to know that you were all right. You were pretty shaken up the other night."

I nodded and gestured to the steps. Together, we began to walk and I felt as if my other half was at my side, completing me. Ben held the bag open and I rummaged inside, pulling out a Boston Crème of all things, savoring the greasy, sugary treat. *When all else fails, feed your sweet tooth.* I dusted off my good manners and attempted a smile. "Thank you. This is perfect. I'm fine, really, but I appreciate your checking in on me."

We walked at an easy pace. It was early and there was no hurry with little traffic off the main thoroughfare. The birds were singing, the squirrels scurrying about while the leaves drifted by. It looked like a completely normal day, but inside I was topsy-turvy, a royal mess.

I shivered and Ben caught me in the act. He thrust his hands in his pockets. "It's a bit nippy. Do you walk *every* day?"

"If it's decent out. I break out the car if there's snow, rain, or it's frigid. This is my exercise regimen. I'm not one for the gym and DVDs." I fished in my pocket for the button and held on tight, praying to God...and Benjamin...for guidance.

Ben's gaze slid over my body and his mouth turned up in appreciation. "It's working." A few more steps and he inched closer, entwined his fingers with mine, and that instant sense of connection knit us more closely together. "You know, I've never seen hair quite like yours, like wild grasses or wheat gone gold in the sun...and your eyes are making it hard to swallow or remember how to breathe. They're sweet as honey dripping from a spoon into the hot tea that my mother made for me when I was sick." His words trailed off and he cursed quietly under his breath. "Not too romantic, is it?"

I gave his hand a squeeze. "I think it's beautiful." The words were just as romantic this time around as they had been the first time Benjamin Willson tried to capture me in words.

We reached the corner of Main Street and I gestured to the right. "I'm on this block, three doors down. The Colonial Book Nook. That's my baby."

A fire of enthusiasm was kindled in his eyes. "Oh, a Colonial buff are you? I'm hooked on that time period too, especially the American Revolution. I can't get enough of it, read everything I can get my hands on and soak it up like a sponge."

I felt unsteady. Another coincidence and thing we had in common. I was sure it wasn't by chance. "Me too. You'll have to come in the shop some time. I've built quite a collection about the time period and our local history." An awkward silence fell between us, the two of us standing close enough to touch, both of us reluctant to leave. I made the first move. "I've got to go now. Where are you off to?"

"Oh, I have to check on a customer in town, a few blocks over. I might as well walk over there now since I'm this close. My truck's across the street in the public lot, but I'm not ready to sit still yet. The guy has an iron gate from the Revolutionary era that needs repair. I work with metal, do welding. Think of me as a modern day blacksmith. This will be right up my alley."

A blacksmith. What Benjamin would have been. If he had lived. I thought the earth would open up and swallow me whole. Somehow, I managed to keep a smile plastered on my face, to stay on my feet, to keep a polite distance from the man beside me when all I wanted to do was grab his jacket, shake him, yell, *"It's me, Benjamin! It's me!"*

Ben went still, staring at me. He visibly shook himself and laughed softly. "Well, I'd best go. Do you think...could I give you my phone number? You could give me a call sometime, *if* you want to. Maybe we could have coffee, when you're really with it, and you could decide if you really want to spend time with me." His lip turned up at the corner and yearning made his eyes go dark. He had no clue of his effect on me. I longed to be with him with every fiber of my body and didn't even question it. Since the first time I laid eyes on Benjamin Willson, I didn't question anything about him. Ghost, past generation, or reincarnation.

"Sure. I'd like that." We took out our phones and exchanged numbers. "You can call me too. Any time. I do want to see you again." I took myself by surprise then, rising up on tiptoe and setting my hands on his shoulders in order to kiss him swiftly on the cheek.

Crimson stains flared up in his face and his eyes glittered. Ben appeared to be having a hard time breathing and was a tad wobbly on his feet. "Good. All right. Okay," he murmured shakily. "I'll see you around then."

He turned to go, then spun back around and took me in his arms, his mouth coming down to form a seal on mine. The sunlight was warm on my back, the late October air cool on my skin, and his hands were a tether when my spirit wanted to soar. Somewhere deep inside me, a humming began, making a beautiful music.

Ben's breath came out in a sigh and he stepped back. "I'm sorry. It had to be done." With that, he walked away, his cheerful whistle drifting back to me.

I could do nothing except watch him until he was gone. Finally, I made myself turn in the opposite direction. I had work to do as well.

Thankfully, I was the first one in. I locked the door behind me, went straight to my office, and fired up the computer. I logged on to findmyancestors.com, paid the fee without hesitation, and started plugging in information about William Ross and his offspring. As for Charlotte Ross Cooper, there was nothing past 1865. I soon discovered my father was extremely thorough; he'd managed to find more information than a database that specialized in genealogies.

I tried Ben Wilson next, but there were at least a hundred Ben Wilsons, not to mention I knew nothing specific about the man in order to pinpoint his family line. I would have to be patient, see if he could give me something to go on to try and find out more about his background, see if our paths crossed in the past.

I read voraciously, any scrap related to local history, my town's connections to the American Revolution, the Battle of Johnstown and its aftermath. Sources were sparse when it came to this tiny patch in the Revolutionary quilt. While it was important to us and especially me at this moment, Johnstown did not play a monumental role in the grand scheme of things. If only Charlotte Ross the First had left a journal. All I had was a family tree, a button, a picture of my cottage's foundation, and a gut feeling. Not enough. Not nearly enough.

I hungered for more than my tangible evidence and my imaginings, memories, visions—whatever they were. Not so much for confirmation of what I knew in my heart to be true, but to touch my past again and be carried back to that tumultuous time.

I was staring out the window, resisting the urge to tear out my hair, when the bell sounded and chatter rang out from the next room. Footsteps approached and I attempted to pull myself together, pushing my hair out of my face and flipping my notebook shut. Otherwise, any onlooker would see *Charlotte loves Benjamin* and *Mrs. Charlotte Elizabeth Willson* written over and over again.

"Well, look who the cat dragged in." Trish was a larger than life kind of woman who did everything in a big way. She wore high heels, giant earrings, and piled her auburn hair up in a style that was a throwback to the eighties. She also had a heart that was big enough for my troubles and arms strong enough to hold me up when I was about to fall. Like now. "Oh, honey. You should *not* be here."

She bustled over and gave me a hug before leaning back to look me in the eye, her hazel gaze penetrating and all-knowing. Trish Jenkins often gave the impression that she was staring into a crystal ball and could make accurate predictions. I didn't want her to see beneath the surface of my mind right now. Otherwise, she'd be stepping into a scary place.

"I'm all right, really. I've just been working on a new project and you know how I go overboard, stay up too late until my eyes are ready to fall out and my head is spinning. Add my period on top and I'm a real treat." I leaned against her sturdy shoulder for an instant, just long enough to find my equilibrium. Like Abigail Andrews in the past, she was a thick and thin friend I could count on.

"I know just what the doctor ordered." Trish hurried out and returned with a steaming cup of coffee and a turnover. "I even doctored it, made you a cup of my famous coffee extraordinaire. Extra sugar, extra whip cream, and an extra dollop of chocolate. Drink that, eat that, and don't leave this office until you are ready to go home...which I suggest is early. Erin and I have got this." One more hug and she was back on the floor.

"Thanks, sweetie," I called after her and buried my face in the cup. Unbelievably enough, sugar and chocolate did make a dent in my discouragement, helping me to dredge up enough energy to go back to my search. I scoured databases, looking for more facts about the Battle of Johnstown, property deeds dating back to Colonial days, and other people whose lives had become entwined with mine during my adventure. Meanwhile the angle of the sun dropped in the sky, my eyes became dry from staring at the screen, and I wasn't getting anywhere.

At some point after one, Erin Matthews rapped on my door and poked her head in. She was a pixie of a girl, petite, with tattoos up and down her arms, a spiked, white-blonde cap of hair, and blue eyes that bordered on violet. She took one look at me and wagged a finger. "Trish was right. You should be at home. You're whiter than these walls, your eyes have lost their sparkle, and you've got smudges as big as my finger under each one. You are going to take a break now and eat Millie's homemade, chicken noodle soup. Got it?"

She flitted to my side, gave me a peck on the cheek, and slipped out, leaving the soup behind. I ate about half when the grief, never too far away, rose up and nearly choked me.

*Benjamin, what do I do? How do I find my way back to you?*

I laid my head on my desk and wracked my brain for answers. Finally, inspiration struck. *Maynard Hughes!* A gold mine of information, the town historian had forgotten more than I had ever learned about Johnstown's colorful history. If he didn't have the information I needed, the man would find it. There was nothing he loved more than a challenge. I picked up the phone and dialed, my heart falling when it rang and rang. I was about to hang up when his voice cheerfully answered. "Maynard Hughes, town historian. How can I help you?"

He sounded distracted. I'd probably just forced him to emerge from an excursion into the past as he scoured a mountain of historical documents. "Maynard, it's Charlotte. Listen, I'm working on a new book and need some more information about Johnstown, dating back to the beginning. I've also got some questions about the Ross family history that you might be able to help with. I know you did wonders for Dad."

The older man chuckled on the other line, a warm sound that was a balm to my sore heart. "Any time for you, Charlotte, any time. Come on in after work and you will have my undivided attention."

"Thanks, Maynard. See you in a little while." I hung up and turned off my computer. Time to make some effort to be a shopkeeper and show a little courtesy for my girls. I made small talk, attempted to focus on their latest news, and helped a few customers. When business dropped off in the late afternoon, I sent them off early, as was my habit, locking up at five.

Taking a deep breath for fortification, I crossed the street, walked past the courthouse—*Sir William's courthouse*—and mounted the steps at the Johnstown Historical Society, giving a nod to the benevolent lion statues that stood guard. When I was little, I used to sit on them and hug their manes. This building was one of my favorite places in the world. It unlocked the door to bygone days. Hopefully, some of mine would be unearthed. One more deep breath and I rang the bell, arranging my face in what I hoped was a normal expression.

"Charlotte, my dear! Come in, come in! The tea is brewing, cookies are on the table, and I've dug out several resources already. Let's get started." He reminded me of my grandfather, or Mr. Rogers, with his sweater, loafers, reading glasses on a chain on his neck, and snowy hair. He took my hand and shivered, giving me a closer inspection. "Your hands are like ice and you do not look like yourself. What's wrong?"

"Nothing, really. I just need to find out more about my history and the Battle of Johnstown for a project I've just started. You know how I am when I get the bug." I settled in at the table in what must have been a dining room to get down to work, taking comfort in the cozy setting and warm welcome.

Maynard's hair gleamed in the lamplight as his face was wreathed in a smile. He was in his glory. "Oh, yes! The bug of discovery is a wondrous thing. You can blame your father for instilling it in you. That man is insatiable, more so than me. When it comes to our local history, particularly the Revolutionary period, Martin has catalogued more information in that amazing brain of his than this entire building holds."

He set a steaming cup of tea before me and slid a plate of cookies across the table. "Go on now. They're Thin Mints, your favorite. I've kept some in the freezer ever since the Girl Scouts came around, just in case you dropped by." Maynard was more like family to me. He kissed the crown of my head and sat down with his own cup of tea.

Sitting in the familiar room, listening to the soothing notes of a Frank Sinatra song in the background, the knot in my stomach began to unwind. As I began to sift through documents and artifacts, I felt completely at home. I'd been a fixture in this place, accompanying my father many times since I was a toddler. We'd spent many happy hours here, devoted to the past.

I'd been skimming over the piles, flicking through this book and that, when Maynard cleared his throat. "So, do you have anything specific in mind that you are looking for?"

Startled, I nearly knocked over my tea cup. I was so jumpy. His eyebrows raised, but he did not make a remark. I dug my phone out of my pocket. "Well, for starters, I found this marking on the foundation of my home and I think my cottage sits on the site of none other than the original Ross family homestead. Can you help me to prove it?"

He peered at my phone closely and his eyes lit up with excitement. "Oh, my! Charlotte, what a find! I do have land deeds and maps of the town layout soon after Sir William established his settlement. They're locked away, but I'll start rummaging." Maynard slapped a palm on his knee. "Simply amazing! You must send me a copy of that picture, my dear! To think you've been living there all this time. What are the odds? Your father will be thrilled. Now, what else do you need?"

This was harder. I had to clamp down on the tears. "Do you have a list of all of the casualties from the Battle of Johnstown?"

Moving rather swiftly for a man of over seventy, Maynard was on his feet, grinning broadly. "Do I ever! I have quite a comprehensive list you know, considering record keeping was not the best back then." He rifled through a filing cabinet in the corner and pulled a stack of papers out with a flourish. "Hmm. Here you go." His fingernail tapped the top page. "12 lost, 24 wounded. We even had 5 that were captured if you can imagine that. Everything is meticulously documented right here."

I could picture all of it too clearly. I'd been there, heard the blasts of the muskets, seen the clouds of smoke, listened to the gut-wrenching screams, watched the man I love fall. I had to struggle to keep my hands from trembling as I touched the page. *Be still, my heart.*

I ran my finger down the column and my eyes filled with tears. Some of the names now had faces as well, many of them sitting at

Richard Dodge's table that night at dinner, others marching with me as the militia made its way through the woods to attempt to head off the enemy at the pass. They had failed on their initial attempt, but our brave Patriots would prove victorious in the end.

Thank the Lord, William Ross and Jacob Cooper were absent from the list; they had been spared, as I already knew. My hand grew still when I discovered the name that mattered most and I nearly broke down. *Benjamin Willson.* He *had* been there...and I was with him until the end when I gave him my heart.

What good was my gift without him? It ached, the longing for the man and love I lost on that lonely field. I bowed my head and pressed my face to my hands, unable to contain my tears.

Alarmed, Maynard set a hand on my shoulder. "My dear Charlotte, what is troubling you? You are usually as steady as the sun and as cheerful. Please tell me what has made you so upset."

It was so tempting to tell him everything, to let it all spill out like a purge, but I was afraid he'd laugh or question my sanity. He wouldn't be the only one. There was one other reason I held my tongue. My feelings for Benjamin, the entire experience, and the memories were precious. Mine. If I was going to share all of it with anyone, only one man came to mind from long ago. A bold Patriot that might be here again.

I swabbed at my cheeks with a handkerchief provided by the ever resourceful historian. "I'm sorry. I always get sentimental about all of this. I think your ghost walk got to me."

Maynard sat beside me and gathered up his papers. "I can really spin a yarn and talk your ear off. I like to think I get the Colonial spirits stirring every year around the anniversary of the battle."

My hands were clenched in my lap; I'd pulled out the button and held on tight. My old friend may have set off more than he knew. I'd always thought I'd walked with ghosts. Now I felt like one was inside of me.

I cleared my throat. Unable to resist, one finger grazed my Patriot's name. "This Benjamin Willson. I...I just noticed his grave marker for the first time a few days ago. The stone looks like it is brand new. I don't know why I didn't see it before."

My old friend grabbed my arm. "Oh, that is another cause for excitement. A mysterious benefactor had it erected in the place of his old marker that had been wiped bare by time. I'd really like to find out who is responsible. We need more people like that to preserve the past."

We talked for a few more minutes when I begged off with exhaustion. It wasn't a lie. I thanked Maynard and slipped out for the night. Shivers ran through me, brought on by a chill that was a combination of the weather and my recent discoveries, forcing me to flip up my collar. I stuck my hands in my pockets, set to launch into a brisk walk home. I wished I'd brought my trusty, red mini cooper.

Something made me glance in the direction of the Colonial Cemetery. Once a friend, a comfort, and a place of curiosity, that graveyard now filled me with dread. I fought down the urge to start shaking, to flee, even as the hair on the back of my neck sprang up thinking about the night the cemetery took over my life.

Intent on resolutely putting it behind me, I was about to turn toward home when I was pulled up short by the sight of a man heading out of the gates of the burial ground. Tall. With broad shoulders. Dark hair fluttering in the wind. For one second, I thought it was my Benjamin, back from the dead. My feet remained firmly planted. Nothing could make me go back to that place, not even to meet him halfway.

Ben Wilson approached me and the déjà vu was so strong, it could have been the night of the ghost walk all over again. He raised a hand in greeting even as his face became clouded the closer he came to me. "Hi. What brings you here?" I asked.

A smile chased away the shadows and he shrugged. "I don't know really. For some reason, my truck turned this way on my way home from work and the cemetery pulled me in. I go there a lot. No idea why, although I do love all things related to history." He glanced up at the building behind me. "I see you've been hunting in the past yourself. I've been meaning to check this place out. Maybe I can find out why the cemetery grabs me every time."

"I know what you mean about that graveyard. I used to go there almost every day. I even have some rubbings hanging up on my wall. If I was out for a walk, or for my lunch break on a nice day, I'd head in there. It's a peaceful place."

*At least, it used to be.* If I set foot in that cemetery now, it would only lead me to one place. Benjamin Willson's grave. Going there would be like ripping the bandage off a deep wound. If I broke down, gave in and let his stone draw me in, I would bleed out.

Ben stood, studying me, his hands thrust in his pockets. Mine were hidden as well, concealing the fact that my fingers were working the button over and over again. Any time I felt agitated, which was most of the time since my return to the present, the keepsake soothed me, making me feel closer to my Patriot.

I glanced down at my feet, my teeth clamping down on my lips. I felt like I was on an emotional roller coaster, plunging up and down by the minute. After attempting to unearth more proof from my past, the sinking feeling that I was mentally imbalanced and going down in quicksand was hard to shake.

Maybe I really had gone round the bend. The tears threatened to rise up, close to the surface ever since the impending doom of Benjamin's death had hung over me like a dark cloud. Desperately, I closed my fingers in a fist around my button.

"Hey," Ben said softly, cupping my chin in his palm, forcing me to look up. My vision blurred, the waterworks about to turn on. "Hey. You look so sad. What's wrong, Charlotte? How can I help?"

Any other man, especially a man I had just met, would run in the opposite direction as fast as his feet could carry him. Not Ben Wilson. He stood his ground...like another man I had come to know very well. I shook my head, took a shaky breath. "It's nothing, really. Sometimes when I go digging through history at the historical society, it hits me hard, the sense of loss. You probably think I'm ridiculous."

"Not at all. When I read about the Revolution, everything is so real to me and I get really worked up. It's like I was there." My inner voice shouted, "*You were!*"

We stood staring at each other. It was easy to become frozen, to lose track of time and place when I was with him. Finally, Ben broke the silence. "You are shaking and it's getting pretty cold out here. I know you don't have your car. Would you like a ride?"

At that moment, with that man, I'd go anywhere he asked. Away from my home and family. Into the middle of a war. On to a battlefield. Across two centuries. I'd done it before.

# Chapter 17

*BEN POINTED TOWARD THE PUBLIC LOT* and we walked in that direction. His hand came out and I accepted, my palm nestled in his, that sense of belonging singing in my veins. He made my heart beat faster, made me fight to catch my breath, made my head start to spin. I closed my eyes a moment, tried to settle myself. *Act normal, Charlotte. Ben still doesn't know who he is, even if you do. Besides, you could be wrong.* The warmth of the button in my other hand said otherwise...and another voice, one that I longed to hear, rang out clear as bell. *You're not. Trust yourself. You've always walked in the right direction before.*

We came to a stop in front of a large, black Chevy, a mighty steed of a truck all decked out in chrome. Ben walked to the passenger side, opened the door, and gave me a hand up.

249

Chivalry was very much alive. When it came to this man, it didn't surprise me.

He went around to his side, climbed in, and fired up the engine. As he drove to the rode, his signal on, his hand caught mine again. "Would you like to come over for dinner? You seem lonesome tonight and to be honest, I don't want to go to an empty house right now. I haven't killed anyone with my cooking. I promise."

He tilted his head and gave me an imploring grin that was impossible to resist, especially when his hair tumbled into his chocolate eyes and he looked so like Benjamin that I melted. "Okay. Sounds good." Funny. I wasn't even questioning going for a ride with this man I hardly knew. *Because you know him better than he knows himself.*

We went down Pleasant Avenue, to O'Neil, then Johnson Avenue, roads I'd traveled countless times in my life. I didn't really pay attention. What with the Ben sitting so close beside me, I was trying not to hyperventilate, cry, or climb into his lap and beg him to remember me.

We passed a stone monument with revolutionary soldiers on a plaque and then a historical marker caught my peripheral vision. There were photos of both hanging in my living room. They highlighted the date and the details, in simple, unemotional terms, about the Battle of Johnstown, but they turned me into a wreck.

One glimpse of that innocent field, covered with weeds, tall grasses, and dead leaves, a tree scattered here and there, and I saw enemy forces in red coats crushing the grass beneath their boots. I saw Patriots falling to the ground. I saw my Benjamin, his shirt stained crimson, the color and life bleeding from his face. My stomach rolled and I thought I would be sick. I breathed in deeply through my nose and kept my mouth clamped shut.

I resolutely kept my eyes on the opposite side of the road, fighting to put the battle behind me, until Ben turned left just past the field where the battle took place. I looked straight ahead as we rolled up a hill, to a small log cabin nestled in a stand of trees, graced with a wraparound porch. If I stood on it, I would have a clear view of the field below, of the place where my Patriot took his last breath. What could have possibly drawn him to live here of all places, so close to the place where we lost each other? I wrapped my arms around myself, trying to keep it together. None of it made sense to me.

Ben pulled up in front of a garage that matched the house, cut the engine, and got out. He walked around and opened my door, helping me down and we walked to his porch. I kept my eyes forward, even as the wind sighed in the trees and seemed to be calling for me to turn around, look back. I wondered what would happen if I walked on that field again. Would time suck me up, chew on me, and spit me out next to Benjamin's broken body? I wasn't about to find out. We reached the steps and Ben gestured for me to go first.

At the top, I felt obliged to turn around, make nice. He stood beside me, his hands thrust in his back pockets as the breeze kicked up and whipped his hair around his face. *Charlotte.* The word seemed to be whispered on the wind, making me tremble. I forced myself to ignore it.

Shutting out the field below, I focused on my host. "This is a beautiful place. I'd no idea you lived here. I've been curious ever since I saw the construction team roll in and the real estate sign come down. How did you find out about it?"

He laughed, yet looked a bit uncomfortable, a feeling I understood well ever since my life had spiraled out of control with an innocent stroll into a cemetery. *Curiosity really can kill a cat.*

"Well, it's really strange actually. My parents died in a car crash about two years ago. They were the only family I had and I didn't have any reason to stay in Boston anymore, no ties, too many bad memories." The word Boston sent a jolt through me that stopped my heart. It was a moment before it started up again. He didn't seem to notice as I struggled to breathe, his eyes gone dark with grief, battling his own demons.

"So anyway, there I was, alone, pretty tore up, at a complete loss about what to do next with my life. I'd just finished college and I needed to move forward, but didn't know how. One morning, about a week after the funeral, I just got in my truck and started driving. I was up before dawn and I drove for hours, with no destination in mind, just decided I'd go wherever the whim took me. I didn't turn on the GPS or bring a map. Next thing you know, I'm driving through the Adirondacks for the first time in my life."

He stopped, collecting himself as his eyes glistened and he stared down at his feet for a moment. "God, I love this place! My parents..." His voice broke and he took a breath. "They would have loved it too. The mountains, the trees, the trails. I actually got out and went on a hike on Kane Mountain. Went all the way to the top, to the old ranger cabin and the fire tower, climbed it, dangled my legs over the side, stared out all around at the lakes, the land...and let the place work on me. My face was wet and I cried harder than I ever did in my life until I was ready to get down, get back on the road."

Ben stared over my head, into a night sky lit up by an explosion of stars. Outside of town, away from the street lights, I could see so much more clearly, feel like I could reach up, catch one in my hands. One particularly bright star blazed hot enough to mesmerize me. *A wishing star.* I stared at it, hard, and wished harder than I ever had in all of my life, all of my birthday candles, eyelashes, and dandelions combined. Wished for everything to make sense. For the man beside me to be the key that would unlock the door.

A blink, my eyes stinging, and I forced myself to concentrate on the steady stream of his words, to try and understand how the currents in the ocean of his life had brought him here. "It was near sunset when I happened to turn on to Johnson Avenue...and I saw the marker for the battlefield. Something made me pull over, get out, walk the field, when all of a sudden, people were running about, wearing Colonial clothes, some in red coats, some in blue. Muskets were going off, there was smoke and shouting. Then they took to the woods, ended their reenactment at Sir William Johnson's. Stunned at first, I let my feet take me where they would, straight to the real estate sign right here and I thought, 'This is it. The place I have to live.' I figured it would be like my very own ranger station, a little private patch on earth. The guy who built it never moved in. He put it on the market as soon as it was done and there was something about it that said home to me, that I belonged, gave me some peace. My inheritance was enough to own it, free and clear. I snapped it up the next day, packed my stuff, and left Boston behind. I never looked back. Does that sound crazy?"

I wanted to smooth the line between his eyes, rest my palm on his cheek to calm the rough waters just under the surface. With my world turned upside down recently, making me question everything I had accepted as the norm, I understood how it felt to be on board a rocking boat, ready to spill overboard with any sudden moves. I shook my head and laid a hand on his arm. "Not at all. I was drawn to my house in the same way and other places around here too."

*Two years ago.* Another strange coincidence... or not a coincidence at all, that we would both be drawn to the homes that would become ours at the same time. That we would both be led to places that were tied to our Colonial past.

We stood still, staring into each other's eyes and I thought Ben would kiss me again, hoped that he would. Maybe a good, long kiss would shake off the dust of the present, clear his head, show him where we came from. If he took me in his arms, held on tight, would we both go back to yesteryear...before disaster struck?

Ben cleared his throat and smiled. "Well, I'm glad I'm not the only one who feels a connection to this place. Now, I guess dinner isn't going to cook itself. Come on in and I'll put something together."

Once inside, he hung my coat and his on a coat rack by the door. "Would you like some tea?" At my nod, Ben gave a wave. "Take a tour of the place. I'll catch up with you in a few."

I began to poke around and had to struggle to keep my jaw from hitting the floor. The layout reminded me of my place...or the Ross Homestead. The furniture was simple, wooden, and could have come from Colonial days. A flag with thirteen stars in a circle, the original flag of the United States, hung on the wall. A stoneware pitcher and mugs, identical to those that sat in the tiny kitchen area of William Ross' home, dressed the mantel. A musket and pistols were proudly displayed on hooks. Many other pieces from the Revolution, including the Declaration of Independence and a series of prints that depicted highlights from the war, open to close, went from room to room in a décor that was so similar to my own. Choices made by a kindred soul that walked in the past. Or was he from the past, like me?

I stopped in his loft bedroom last, a spacious room with a high ceiling, a balcony overlooking the living room, and an attached bath. A flag print quilt dressed the bed. Beside it was a small nightstand with a dish...something shiny and metal gleamed in the center, drawing me closer.

I crossed the room and peered closely to discover a small, metal ball, scuffed and worn. Something made me touch it and the image of Benjamin, rolling his musket ball in his palm, clinging to it while the pain ripped through him as I tended him, was a jab to the gut. So strong that I had to grip the table or my legs would give out.

I saw his face twisted in agony. Smelled the wood smoke, blood, stench of infection, fear. The whiskey on his breath, on my hands, on his wound as I fought to save his life. Heard his screams rip through the night, making his throat raw, tearing at my heart. Felt his fingers gripping my arm, strong enough to crush my bones, as his muscles strained and nearly burst the seams of his shirt, making him shake, the pain was so fierce.

Ben's footsteps sounded on the stairs, giving me enough time to steady myself and back away, to yank myself back to the present. I turned and gave him a slip of a grin. "Your home is beautiful. I love how you've decorated. Simple, full of the past, like my place. Where did you find the musket ball?"

I tried to sound off-the-cuff. All the while, my heart was tripping, the air squeezed from my lungs. The echoes of Benjamin's screams still rang in my ears and I could feel his hot, sweaty hand clutching mine, holding on with all of his tenacity as he fought to survive.

Ben crossed over and picked up the ball, letting it roll in his palm. His eyes darkened and his mouth tightened. For an instant, he went someplace else, far away...or long ago, until he remembered that someone else was in the room. "It's strange. I was walking one day right after I moved in. I was scoping out the grounds and something made me head out into the field below. It had rained really hard the night before and the ground was soggy. My boot was stuck in the mud. When I bent down to free my foot, I saw something shining in the sunlight. There was that musket ball, turned up in the soil. Who knows how long it's been there or where it came from? Probably from one of the reenactments, you know? Once I picked it up, I couldn't put it down. I had to bring it inside, polish it, put it by my bed. When I can't sleep or something is bothering me, I hold it and let it roll across my palm."

His story spurred me to reach in my pocket and pull out my button. "I feel the same way about this. I found it the other night...in the cemetery." That was only a tiny, white lie. The button had been given to me in 1781 and carried back with me to the graveyard, God only knew how.

Ben stood so close, his breath kissed my skin. He studied the button, then looked up in my eyes, and became trapped there. A heartbeat.

Another, and his voice was low, striking a cord deep within that made my stomach tighten. "May I?" His hand reached for mine and I swallowed hard. I nodded.

He picked up the button...and his breath came out in a rush. His eyes shut and he pressed a palm to his forehead. "Whoa. I feel...dizzy."

Alarmed, I took back the button and shoved it in my pocket before ducking under his arm, giving him a shoulder to lean on. I led him to the bed and eased him down, sitting beside him with his arm around my shoulders. It felt right. The perfect fit.

"Are you all right?" I asked anxiously. I waited, my hand on his knee.

Ben opened his eyes and found his crooked grin. He set his hand on mine and our fingers entwined. "I'm good. Must be hungrier than I thought. Come on downstairs. Our tea is getting cold." I offered him a hand up and he threaded his fingers through mine, only to pull me in and set his lips on mine. "Sorry. Something about you makes me want to kiss you."

A giggle rose up, a bubble of happiness ready to set loose. "I don't mind. You're pretty kissable yourself." He grinned and set the musket ball back in its dish.

Hand in hand, we walked downstairs, and I sat at a table that looked like the table that William Ross had built. When I complimented it, and the simple, sturdy benches, Ben's cheeks flushed at the praise. "I built them." I shouldn't have been surprised. My ancestor had left a major mark on both of us.

My host carried two, steaming mugs to the table, along with a plate of cookies and I fought the urge to laugh. This would be my second helping of sweets before dinner. We talked about our childhood, our growing up years, college, our tongues loose as the conversation flowed easily, the way it would between two people who had known each other for many years. *Try centuries.*

A timer dinged and Ben was up in a flash. "That's my culinary delight. Sit tight." I ignored him, clearing the table and trailing behind him. A bottle of wine sat on the counter, along with a tossed salad. Ben popped the microwave open to pull out a cloth pouch.

"What have you got in there?" I asked, making him jump. On my sock feet, he didn't even hear me coming.

"Potatoes. They come out just like they've been baked in the oven for an hour. I'm good at finding shortcuts. What are you doing out here? I told you to sit. You're my guest." He gestured to the dining area and turned to the stove, oven mitt in hand. A tray with sizzling steaks was pulled from the broiler. He crumbled cheese and dried onions on top, then glanced over his shoulder. His grin bloomed, making me want to kiss the corner of his mouth. "What are you still doing here?"

In answer, I took the platter of steaks and salad bowl out to the table, returning for settings. We worked together like a team, like two parts of one whole that belonged together...because we did. He just didn't know it

259

yet. Ben poured the wine and passed the plates of food. Light from the lamp over our heads glanced off of the wine in my glass, turned it to a gleaming ruby, and the scene shifted.

I was in a meadow with Benjamin. The sunlight was warm on my hair, the scent of fresh grass and autumn leaves sweet as I filled my lungs with fresh air, filling my eyes with the sight of my Patriot. He sat beside me, his leg stretched out before him, the color coming back to his cheeks and lines of pain fading. We'd survived the Redcoats' attack, Benjamin's life had been spared from the deadly infection, and he was on the mend. For the moment, hope was shining bright and our love was budding, soon to be in full bloom. Benjamin took my hand in his, drew me into the shelter of his arms, and his eyes were bright enough to eclipse the sun.

"Charlotte? Charlotte, are you all right?" Ben's voice seemed to come from far away, as if through a tunnel and *SNAP!* I was back. He stared at me intently, poised to act. To catch me if I fainted dead away. To call 911 if I was having a stroke.

I started to chew my first bite of steak and gave him a big smile. "You are an amazing cook! You've tantalized my taste buds!"

He laughed. "Don't get too excited. It's the only thing I can make. Everything else is boiled, toasted, frozen, or microwaved. I'm really good at running through a drive through too. Not much sense in cooking when…"

"You only cook for one." I looked into his eyes, felt like I was slipping away again, and gulped at my wine to try and find some balance.

Ben's hand found mine. "Exactly." The silence fell around us and he was up, on his feet, crossing over to my chair. He set his hands on my shoulders and kissed me the way I'd longed to be kissed ever since I was a little girl and first saw Disney movies.

I didn't know how it happened, but I was in his arms. We moved to the living room, wrapped around each other, and sat on the couch in front of the fireplace. Everything else faded into the background. There was only this man, his fingers threaded in my hair, his breath kissing my skin, his heart thudding madly against mine. I pressed myself closer, trying to become one, to be part of the fabric that was Ben Wilson and pick up the thread that would lead us back to my Patriot.

When I thought my heart would explode and I couldn't breathe, he pulled back and pressed a hand to my cheek. His voice was hoarse when he spoke. "I know this is short notice...and we hardly know each other...but, what are you doing for Halloween?" Ben sounded like he'd run a marathon. Perhaps he had. Finding his way through the maze of two centuries was hard work. Hopefully I would have the stamina to keep up. Time to dust off my running shoes.

# Chapter 18

*ALL HALLOW'S EVE.* The night that the spirits were supposed to walk. This holiday used to rank right up there with Christmas for me, until the night a ghost walk became extremely personal. I wasn't ready for any more spiritual encounters. Ben had invited me to a costume dance at Sir William Johnson's of all places. I'd accepted, but now I was uneasy. What if time shifted once again, especially with the both of us there at the same time on such a momentous occasion? I held on to Benjamin's button and prayed for the strength to remain in the present...to keep the both of us in the present.

*Now I know how Cinderella felt on the way to the ball.* I stood in front of the mirror in my bedroom and stared at my reflection. In the blink of an eye, I expected to be transformed into someone else or transported back in time again as a young woman from Colonial days looked back at me. She was a woman I had come to know very well. I'd lived in her skin and walked in her shoes two centuries ago for two months.

I pressed a hand to my stomach and inhaled deeply through my nose, letting the air hiss out between my teeth. Repeated the ritual twice more, trying to still the mad frenzy that was my pounding heart. The last time I had danced with a man, it had been in the arms of my Patriot, at the same place I would be headed tonight. I wondered if the stars would be in alignment or if we were tempting fate?

My hair was pulled back in a neat bun at the back of my head with tendrils of curls around my face, mimicking the style that ladies of the Revolutionary era would have worn, that *I* had worn during my brief stint as Charlotte Elizabeth Ross the First.

The dress was a vision in pale rose, the color of sunrise giving birth to a new day, of the beginnings of a young girl's blush after her first kiss, of the promise I had felt fluttering in my heart the first time Benjamin Willson held my hand. I'd found a vintage shop in Saratoga, another hot spot for all things related to the Revolution, had actually felt as if someone pressed a finger in my back and pointed me in the right direction.

The gown looked just like the one Abigal and I had admired in the shop window of *The Needle and Thread*. With a heavy, hooded cloak in a rich, deep plum to go with it and a string of pearls on my neck, I looked the part of a lady of high society, someone who would have attended Sir William's gatherings.

I closed my eyes and imagined I was with Benjamin at Johnson Hall, swaying round and round in his arms, the scent of autumn filling my lungs while the leaves skittered by my feet. I was overcome with a rush of longing to freeze time, yet our love story had come to an end like Cinderella's night at the ball. Or had it?

A loud rapping sounded at the door and the first notes of *Someday My Prince Will Come* drifted through my mind. Maybe Benjamin had come back for me after all. I answered and had to prop myself against the jamb. Otherwise, my legs would not hold and I wondered if I'd gone completely white. I felt like I'd just lost every drop of blood in my body.

Ben stood on my porch, decked out in the Revolutionary finery of a militia man which he wore exceedingly well. "You look...amazing," I whispered. *Resplendent.* My runaway train of thought began constructing a list of adjectives that would do him justice. None of them were good enough.

His dark hair was brushed until it shone, slicked back, and neatly tied with a ribbon at the nape of his neck, forming a short tail. His jacket was a royal blue, long and cut to fit his lean body like the coat that Grannie Brown had passed on to Benjamin. Brass buttons winked at me in the dying light as the day came to a close. I studied them closely and was relieved to find that they were bare, without writing, and none were missing. An irrational part of me thought it really was my Patriot's coat. White breeches and black shoes completed the ensemble to create a breathtaking picture.

For an instant, I had double vision and saw Benjamin standing by Ben's side. Both were tall, making me look up. Both were broad of back, their shoulders set, their heads held high. Ready to take whatever life threw at them, head on. Strong enough to carry their burdens and mine. They made my stomach twist into knots as my heart began to thump erratically.

Ben was at a loss for words, his body gone still, as he gazed intently at me. His hand seemed to float through the air and skimmed over my hair before resting on my cheek. "You are the most beautiful thing I've ever seen." His mouth came down to take mine and my breath came out in a rush, my knees gone weak. His arms cradled me and he whispered huskily, "Sorry. I don't know what comes over me whenever I see you. You're just *too* beautiful."

My skin grew hot at his touch and a flush rose up in his face, painting his cheeks until they were scarlet. He offered me his hand and actually kissed my fingers before cupping my palm in his. We walked down the steps, both of us shy all of the sudden, mesmerized by each other.

The drive to Johnson Hall was all too short and it became harder to breathe with each passing minute. Imagine if I'd had to wear a corset! Sweat popped out on my forehead and my stomach clenched as we rolled down the lane, closer to the grand estate, beautifully restored as a museum, the grounds neatly kept. Ben's truck slowed to a stop and he was at my side in a flash, opening the door and helping me down.

He smiled eagerly and took my hand. "This is incredible! Look at this place! I bet this is what it was like in its glory days."

As I walked by his side, I held on tightly, my other hand clutching my handbag. I could feel the reassuring outline of my button. Ben was right. The estate was dazzling, every window ablaze from the glow of chandeliers, the shrubs dressed with strings of white lights that made them look like something out of a fairy tale. Festive ribbons of black and orange dressed the house itself and trees, but the most fascinating sight was all of the people in period dress. For this one night, it truly did look like Sir William Johnson's had come back to life.

A horse and carriage was giving rides around the circular drive in front of the main entrance. People were chatting and laughing in small groups, their breath forming clouds around them in the chill. As we approached the steps, the carriage stopped and the passengers dismounted. Ben bowed low. "My lady, care for a ride?"

The driver introduced herself as Tara. She was a dark-haired woman with short hair, a long, flowing coat, and a wide-brimmed hat, the picture of elegance, grinning openly at my handsome companion. Any woman would fall under his spell.

I accepted his hand for a boost and climbed in, Ben following. We started off at a sedate pace and I closed my eyes. If I wished hard enough, perhaps the ride wouldn't end. The clip-clop of the horse's hooves was hypnotic. I imagined it to be in time with the beat of my heart. I truly did feel like Cinderella at the ball or Sleeping Beauty, caught in a dream. I wondered if I would ever wake up.

When I looked up at the man beside me, his eyes were somewhere far away. Ben was drifting. I wondered where his mind carried him. Or when.

I laughed nervously and gave him a slip of a grin. "I expected you to dress as George Washington tonight."

His mouth became a grim line and he stared off into distance. "George Washington was a man beyond measure, larger than life..." He tilted his head my way, focused on me once more. "Or so I've heard. I didn't think I could pull him off, that anyone could. So I picked an ordinary man."

We came to a stop and he jumped down, light on his feet. Ben placed his hands at my waist and set me on the ground. My heart went into overdrive. "You're anything but ordinary," I told him softly.

Hand in hand, we made our way inside. Champagne was flowing while cake and other bite-sized desserts were served on platters. Elegance was in order for the evening, down to the string quartet playing in the great entrance way. The costumes were a delight, ranging from a blacksmith to a militia man to Betsy Ross, and all of the founding fathers. Several Sir Williams roamed the premises and I had the insane urge to call out, *Will the real Sir William Johnson please stand up?*

"Who do you suppose that ample, white-haired, white capped woman is supposed to be?" Ben asked as he handed me a glass of champagne and we stood in a corner, sipping and eying the other guests with curiosity.

I giggled. "Why, she's one of my favorite dress-up subjects for my presentations in school when I was growing up. I almost chose that costume myself for tonight. If you had been George Washington, she would be the love of your life, dear Martha. Don't you recognize her?"

He took my empty glass and set it on a tray, along with his own, freeing his hands to cup by face. "Yes, I do." He gazed into my eyes and I didn't think Ben was talking about Washington's wife. "Would you like to dance?"

I nodded and allowed him to lead me to the middle of the hallway to join in with the rest of the party goers. Each floor of the hall had ample hallways. While the rooms were cordoned off, carefully preserved to allow visitors to envision how the place might have looked when Sir William was alive, there was still enough room in the passages to hold a ball. Ben set one hand on my waist, his other taking my hand and began to dance me around the room. I felt as if I was waltzing on air.

Somewhere, far away, the sweet sound of a violin played pure, high notes and dresses swished along the floor around me. There was a river of conversation, laughter, heels tapping on the tiles, but nothing else mattered. I was with Ben and we were dancing in the place that Benjamin never had a chance to dance, where Charlotte the First had dreamed of dancing like Cinderella, but had been left standing outside, because they belonged to a different class of people with a different set of loyalties.

Ben stepped in closer, his forehead grazing mine. His strong arms were wrapped around me, sharing the shelter of his body. I set my head on his chest and his voice dropped down low. "You've had your dance after all, Charlotte. I told you never to give up on your dreams."

Startled, I looked up and he kissed me, holding on until the music stopped, and the dancers drifted away, leaving the two of us in each other's arms, under a chandelier. "What did you say?"

He tilted his head and stared into my eyes, a line creasing the middle of his forehead. "I...I don't remember."

His words, his expression, his selective memory made me dizzy. I had to cover. "Ben," I murmured, my voice faint. "I think...I think I need some fresh air. I'm feeling a little...overheated."

That was an understatement. The heat had come up in a rush and my blood was thrumming in my veins. I wanted to go douse my head under a faucet. Ben was flushed and breathing hard, his hair damp at his temples.

His tongue darted out to lick his lip and I thought I'd liquefy like the Wicked Witch of the West, right there, at his feet. "Come on."

We made for the back exit when he pulled me into a room to the left, one that had no barriers and housed displays about the estate's history, as well as that of Johnstown. No one else was there, the perfect opportunity for Ben to press me up against a wall. His hands started at my hips, went up my bodice, then roamed to my arms. I tipped my chin as a soft moan escaped from somewhere deep down in the pit of my stomach. He lodged his fingers in my hair and I was a goner, sealing his lips with mine.

I ran my fingers up his jacket and grabbed hold of his firm shoulders, fighting to keep my head above water, otherwise I would drown in him. We didn't stop until another couple stepped in, only to back out in a fit of giggles.

Overcome with laughter ourselves, we forced ourselves to separate, still linked by our hands. We began to walk around the perimeter of the room, feigning interest in the exhibits when all the while, I was completely attuned to Ben and the flutter of his pulse at the base of his throat. His hand came out to rest on mine and I closed my eyes. *God help me.*

"God help me." The words were spoken in a tortured whisper beside me, echoing my thoughts. My eyes snapped open and I found my partner gone rigid, whiter than the walls, staring at a painting before him. Fearful, I forced myself to look at a local artist's rendition of... the Battle of Johnstown.

"I...I need to get out of here. I feel like...like I can't breathe." I had to strain to hear

271

him. I didn't question him. I took his hand and his fingers closed around mine, almost crushing the bones with the force of his grip. I drew him out the nearest exit. He dropped on the top step. "I'm lightheaded."

"Put your head between your knees. That's it. Now breathe." I pressed my hand to the nape of his neck and began to stroke his hair.

He shuddered, turned, and instinctively, I gathered him into my arms. "Will you just hold me? Somehow, having you near me makes it better." We sat there drawing heat from each other as the cold air kissed our skin, nipped at our ears, slipped down our necks. Ben drew in a shaky breath and set his chin on the nest of my curls. "I'm sorry. I don't know what came over me. I'm okay. I'm okay now."

He pressed his palms into his knees, his muscles straining against his coat, his whole body taught. I thought he would drive his hands through to the ground. When I laid my hand on his shoulder, I could feel the fine ripples of his shivering still running through him.

"Are you all right?" At his nod, I shifted and took his hand, threading my fingers with his, needing the link with him as much as he needed a connection with me. "What happened to you in there?"

He studied the view before us as clouds rolled in overhead, weighing down the sky and the wind moaned in the trees. In my mind, I saw a sun-kissed, autumn afternoon, unkempt grounds, and an estate that appeared to me abandoned. That day, Sir William's had been lonesome, tugging at my heart even if his side was the wrong side. Right now, the place felt wrong again.

"I can't really explain it. I saw flashes of images. Heard people shouting, screaming. Smelled smoke. There was gunfire. Chaos, unbearable pain...and then it was gone." Ben's jaw clenched and he closed his eyes. When he met my gaze again, they were nearly black with confusion. "Do you mind if we go home?"

"Not at all." I led the way to the front door, Ben trailing close behind me, and grabbed my cloak off of the hooks by the entrance. He helped me to put it on, wrapped an arm around my waist, and we crossed the grounds to the parking lot. I had the impression I was supporting him instead of the other way around.

He started the truck and pulled out fast, peeling the tires in his haste to get away, as if the hounds of hell were close on our tails. Casting a sideways glance his way, seeing the way he gripped the steering wheel with his arms and face gone tight, I thought the comparison fitting. The demons of the past were creeping up on Ben and he didn't understand one bit of it. For some reason, there was no road map to help my Patriot make his way to the present.

Ben was painfully quiet on the five minute ride to my house. Ever the gentleman, he made sure to come around. Help me out. Walk me to the door when I had the feeling all he wanted to do was retreat and lick his wounds. A clap of thunder sounded, making us both jump.

273

He failed miserably at a pitiful attempt at a smile and bent to gently kiss me. "Good night, Charlotte. Thank you for a wonderful night. I'm sorry for cutting it short with my meltdown or whatever it was. You probably want to sign me up for a psychiatrist."

"It's okay, really. Remember you're talking to someone who has been an emotional basket case since you met me. I can't believe you haven't run away. I had a good time. Go home and try to get some rest. Things always look better in the morning." I gave him a hug and pressed my cheek to his chest. His heart was a trip hammer.

I stood and watched him walk to the truck before stepping inside. I leaned against the door, wondering what Ben would see next and how painful it would be. *His* reawakening of the past was not coming easy.

Lightning tore across the sky and the heavens opened, dumping a torrent of rain. Another blast of thunder, like the bang of a gigantic drum, and a pounding on my door made my pulse race. I opened the door to find Ben standing there, breathless and drenched, his hair plastered to his face. "Charlotte, I'm so confused. Lately, ever since that night that I stumbled into you in the cemetery, I feel this overpowering sense of déjà vu. Sometimes, I don't know if it's the past or the present. I feel like I can't eat...or sleep...or breathe—unless I'm with you and I just met you! And tonight...what I saw, what I felt."

He reached out, his hand catching the door jamb and his knuckles were white from holding on so tight. "I can't be alone, not tonight."

I pulled him inside. "Then stay with me."

He was shaking. I pulled off his coat and hung it up while Ben stood still as a statue, his teeth starting to chatter. I took his hand and led him to the living room where I wrapped him in a blanket on the back of the couch and made him sit. His hands circled round and round, one traveling to his pocket to rub at something round protruding out of it. *The musket ball?*

"Can I just stay on your couch? I won't take advantage, I won't be a bother. I promise and I..."

I caught his hand, felt his tension. "Keep your promises. Of course you can stay, but you don't need to sleep on the couch. We are two, responsible adults. We can behave ourselves." *At least I will try. Scout's honor.*

He would not back down, insisting on the couch. I found some flannel pajama bottoms and a t-shirt my dad had left behind when my parents spent the night one New Year's Eve to break in my new place. A pillow off my bed and an extra quilt were all Ben wanted for bedding. He didn't want anything to eat, nothing to drink, had nothing more to say, drained by his experience at Johnson Hall.

I leaned over him and kissed him lightly on the forehead, the way William had so many times when he greeted me or said goodbye. "Try and get some sleep. 'Night, Benja...'Night, Ben."

He caught my hand and pulled me down to his level, burying his face in my hair before giving me a kiss that tasted of desperation. "Thank you, Charlotte. Good night."

I was a good girl. I locked up, turned off the lights, changed my clothes and climbed into bed. Somehow, I managed to stay in my room, to keep my hands off him, a truly difficult thing when I knew the man I had loved for over two hundred years was lying in the next room.

The rain drummed on the roof and pinged on the windows, eventually lulling me off to sleep when another crash of thunder sent me flying out of my bed. Waiting for my heart to still, I gazed out the window into a storm tossed night, illuminated by a brilliant streak of lightning that nearly blinded me. From the next room, there was only silence. What if he was gone? What if the past sucked him back, leaving me no way to go with him?

Panicked, I padded out on my bare feet to check on Ben and the rush of relief made me grab hold of the back of the sofa. He was sprawled out, one arm and one leg hanging over the edge of the couch. Sleep took away the crease between his eyes, the tightness around his mouth, made him seem younger.

The longer I watched him sleep, his resemblance so strong to Benjamin, the more he called to mind the many nights I had sat and watched my Patriot sleep. I nearly drowned in the wash of memories from a past that felt like yesterday, not 233 years ago, more real than today or the rest of my life in the 21st century.

I sat down in my arm chair, my legs tucked under me, and simply stared at the man in my living room. I was positive Ben Wilson was my Benjamin, come back through the ages, who knew how many times in his quest to make good on his promise. I wanted to hold on to him, to touch him, to run my fingers through his hair. I felt like my Benjamin was here, that he'd parted the veil of time, defied death, and I had to latch on with every ounce of my strength.

"No!" The silence was shattered by his shout, his voice ragged as he scrambled into a sitting position and tossed his blankets aside. Ben propped his elbows on his knees and buried his hands in his hair, pulling so hard I feared he'd tear it out.

I went to him and picked up the blanket, wrapping us both in a warm cocoon. He was quaking and his skin was like ice. "Ben, I'm here. What's wrong?"

"Just...just stay with me. Hold me. Keep the nightmares away." I didn't hesitate to wrap my arms and legs around him, to make myself his safety net...like that afternoon when the fever raged through my Benjamin, burning him up from the inside out. Gradually, Ben's breathing eased and the trembling stopped. I ran my fingers through his hair until his eyes drooped shut. His body went loose.

He slumped on to the couch and I lay down beside him, spoon style. I didn't let go until dawn tiptoed in, bringing with it a glorious sunrise and a new day, banishing the storm. When Ben awoke, we were nose to nose. His lip quirked up at the corner and his lips brushed my cheek. "Good morning, beautiful."

"It's good because of you." I rested my head on his chest and gave thanks that Ben made it through the night and we were both still here.

*"I'M GOOD, THANKS."* He waved me off as I tried to top off his coffee. Ben sat at the table, holding his mug, staring into it. Bathed in sunlight, he was drawn from lack of sleep and whatever visions tormented him the night before. At Sir William's. In his dreams. He was too quiet, his eyes filled with shadows, as if his light has been snuffed out.

I sat down across from him and slipped his cup out of lifeless fingers, took his hands in mine, pressed my button into his palm. A ripple ran through him, making him quake. "I want you to have this." *Remember!*

Perhaps the button would help Ben to find his way back to Benjamin, help us to close the gap between the past and the present. After all, *he* was the rightful owner. "No, I can't. This is yours. Besides," he patted his pocket and I saw the small, round bulge rising up. "I've got my musket ball."

He tried to give back the button, but I closed his fingers around it, grazed them with a kiss. "That means it's mine to give. Accept my gift. That button helped me when I felt lost. Maybe it can do the same for you."

His hand tightened on it and he pressed his forehead to mine. "Ever since my parents

278

died, I've felt like I was cast adrift...until now. When I'm with you, you're my compass and I can find my way home. That's why my nightmare, last night, was so terrifying."

He swallowed hard. "I couldn't find you! We were on a field, crushed by a heavy fog or smoke and you were running away from me. I tried to follow you, but it was as if my feet were stuck in quicksand and this excruciating pain shot through my chest. I thought I was having a heart attack. When I woke up, I actually had to make sure my heart was still beating...then you took my hand and I knew I was alive."

"Anytime you have trouble finding your way, I am here for you. I'm not going anywhere." *I hope.*

We sat that way for a while, only the sound of our breathing breaking the silence. I found him flipping the button in his hand, over and over, the same way I had. When I skimmed my thumb over its warm, smooth surface, he stopped. "Maybe you have connections here in Johnstown from the Revolution. That could explain what brought you here, why you feel so strongly about different places, things you've seen. Maybe somebody talked about your ancestors and you were too little to remember. It could still make a strong impression on you. I know my father branded me with local history. I couldn't shake it off if I tried. Have you tried looking into your genealogy to learn more about your background?"

"No, but you could be on to something. I'll ask my great aunt Jessica. She's the family memory keeper. If anyone would know, she would. It sounds like she and your father would really have plenty to talk about." Ben gave me a ghost of a smile. "Well, I guess I'd better get out of your hair. You've got work and so do I, though I'd much rather stay here with you."

He stood up, still a bit shaky and we walked hand in hand to the door. Every time he touched me, my feelings for him grew stronger. Being with this man felt right, fit perfectly like only one other man...and that had been a wild thrill ride too.

As I turned the knob, I stopped, squeezed his arm, fishing for any excuse to spend more time with him. "Would you like to go with me to the Fulton County Museum on Sunday? You can pretend you're Indiana Jones. Maybe we'll dig up a great find. "

His fingers threaded through my hair and he dipped down to brush my lips with a kiss. "I already have. Goodbye, Charlotte. Thanks for everything."

Slowly, Ben took up the cloak of his confidence and put it back on again, his back straight, his shoulders set. He didn't turn back all the way to his truck, taking sure strides. Once he reached the door, he broke and glanced at me, tossing me a smile. As he drove away, I pictured William's black horse, Raven, and Benjamin mounted on his back.

Ben's window opened and his hand waved, floating on the wind. I wanted nothing more than to run after him and grab it, let him carry me away. If only Benjamin and I had ridden off into the sunset and left Johnstown behind when he had the chance on our first go around.

# Chapter 19

*I THOUGHT OF THE BRICK BUILDING* that housed the Fulton County Museum as a home away from home. I'd been there countless times over the years, on occasion with both of my parents, mostly with Dad. His burning desire to instill a love of our past inside of me prompted him to bring me through every room, to marvel at each exhibit, to make new discoveries with each visit. I'd made many solo trips, losing myself for hours, always excited when any new additions were made. Today, the place reached out to me with open arms, extending an invitation. I only hoped that Ben felt as if he was welcome.

"Ready?" I asked as we sat in the truck, gazing at the museum. He slid me a grin, even as his hands ran over his jeans, over and over. I suspected his musket ball was in one pocket, my button in the other.

"Here goes nothing." I imagined it had to be nerve-wracking, never knowing when a flashback, feeling or impression would bowl him over, knock him flat, take him unawares. Like I had felt on that sunny, September afternoon when I found myself back in 1781 until that wretched day when the Battle of Johnstown shattered me.

He opened my door and took my hand, his fingers tightening on mine. I gave him an encouraging nod and we set off down the walk. Crows cawed loudly overhead and the dried leaves rattled in the branches of the trees. I could smell snow in the air and flipped up my collar, wishing I'd worn a scarf. Considerate as always, Ben drew me under his arm, sharing the warmth of his heavy pea coat and his body.

The door opened as we hit the first step and a familiar face greeted us with a big smile, blue eyes snapping, nearly as bright as the cloudless sky. The curator of the museum thrust out her hand to Ben first. "Welcome, welcome to the museum! Charlotte told me you were on your way. I'm always thrilled to have someone join us who has a true love of history."

She turned to me and gave me a hug. My breath came out in a rush at her touch, leaving me off balance. I stepped back and my vision blurred, the woman before me flickering in and out. At one moment, she was my fellow member of the Daughters of the American Revolution, a family friend who had sat at our table on many occasions, often with Maynard—I was sure they were an item. She was put together, as usual, her silver hair shorn close and stylishly layered, gold wire-framed glasses perched on her nose, her perfectly pressed pants suit a becoming lavender.

A heart beat later, I saw Grannie Brown with her white cap covering her curls, her ample figure wrapped in a long dress and apron. My mouth went dry and I had to find my voice. "Joan, this is my friend, Ben Wilson. Ben, this is Joan Brown, curator of the museum and close, family friend. She knows everything there is to know about this building, every nook and cranny."

*Brown?!* I wondered...if I were to trace the path of Joan's family tree, would I find a link to Grannie and Nathaniel Brown? As the elderly, yet surprisingly youthful, woman led us down the corridor, her hands emphasizing and punctuating every word, I couldn't help but think that she was another thread that tied in with my past.

"I do know a great deal about this place, although my mind does get a little fuzzy from time to time. Not quite as sharp as it used to be." She laughed and tapped her forehead. "My great grandfather established this museum and my family has played a major part in its growth and preservation ever since. I've inventoried every item, arranged most of the exhibits, and I'm always on the lookout for new pieces. Now tell me, what are you looking for?"

Ben shrugged, the darkness threatening to creep into his eyes until I gave his hand a squeeze. "I'm not really sure. I'm from Boston, but ended up here about two years ago, was drawn here as if a magnet was pulling at me. I've lost my parents and immediate family, so I don't know if there's any kind of connection to the area for me. I thought scouring through bygone years would be a good place to start."

He wrapped an arm around me, drawing strength and comfort. Whatever I had to give, I was glad to give it. Besides, I reaped countless rewards from being with him. Our effect on each other was reciprocal.

Joan rested a finger on her lips, eyes narrowed in concentration until they suddenly lit up with a cheerful sparkle. "Why, I've just the thing! Come back to the Colonial Room. It brings us to the beginnings around these parts so that's the best place to start, right?" She looped an arm through mine and the three of us walked together, like the Musketeers.

We stepped into a large room with brightly illuminated cases, each one holding carefully preserved artifacts. Clothing, documents, tools, drawings, and paintings were artfully arranged around the room, each accompanied by an identifying plaque. Great care and attention to detail had gone into every note. My father and Maynard Hughes considered it a labor of love and honor to be the authors.

Ben began to poke around, peering closely at each exhibit when Joan squeezed my hand

and squealed, "Oh, Charlotte! I almost forgot! We have a brand new piece. You won't believe it!"

She practically dragged me off to a display case that stood at the center of the room as the star attraction of the exhibit. Hanging on the torso of a mannequin was a navy coat from the militia, soiled and worn, bloodstained, with a hole in the left side of the chest. Bull's eye, over the heart. Each button proudly bore the letters *USA*. One was missing.

Next to the jacket, on a small pedestal, was a thick braid of hair, tied off with a blue ribbon. Breathless, I reached up and fingered one of my curls, glancing at it out of the corner of my eye. The color was the same as mine.

The room began to tilt, the blood rushing in my ears and I held on to Joan, even as my body went cold. My heart began to skip, my stomach rolling. Bile rose up, leaving a nasty taste in my mouth. I pressed a hand over my mouth as the tears slid down my face.

Ben was at my side in an instant. Whether he'd seen my reaction or responded to his intuition, his arm came around my waist and I buried my head in his chest, fighting not to weep. "Charlotte! You're white as a sheet! What is it?"

Joan rubbed a soothing hand round and round on my back. "I know it's upsetting, my dear. She always takes things very personally," the older woman murmured softly to my companion. "This coat dates back to the Battle of Johnstown, an actual relic from the field. An Elizabeth Cooper Bradley from Cooperstown donated it to the museum last week, said she found it packed away in a chest with a handwritten note. That document is there as well, next to the braid."

Shaking hard enough to make Ben quiver, I wiped at my cheeks and turned to read the faded piece of paper. A tidy, delicate script noted, "An undying symbol of my Patriot and his love...for our country, for me, and my love for him, full circle."

I was there again, on that terrible field, my heart ripped in two as I pressed the braid into Benjamin's hand, his button clutched in my palm. His heart thudded against mine and I didn't want to go.

Ben whispered something in my ear, bringing me back, if I had ever truly been back since all of this happened. I stepped forward and pressed my hands to the display case. I wanted to smash the glass, to hold the coat to my face, smell my Benjamin, feel his strength and bring back that brief flash in time. "Excuse me," I whispered and ran out of the room in tears, out to the truck where I buried my head in my hands.

Ben followed soon after, standing with the passenger door open, staring up at me, face twisted in concern. "What can I do?"

I felt terrible. This day that was supposed to help him had turned into a disaster. I rubbed at my face and fought to get a grip on myself. "Will you please apologize to Joan for me? Tell her I don't feel well."

It wasn't a lie. I felt horrible, as if I'd been turned inside out. Moments later, Ben returned, started the truck, and headed toward my house. When we pulled up to my front porch, he cut the engine and laid a hand on mine. "What did you see, Charlotte?"

I shook my head, mouth clamped shut or I'd start sobbing again. "I'm sorry. I can't tell you. I can't tell anyone right now or I'd be locked up in an insane asylum."

He pulled me into his arms. "All right. I think you're wrong, but I won't argue. Let me stay with *you* tonight, help you through this the way you helped me."

I didn't have the strength to argue with him. He picked me up and carried me into the house as if I was nothing more than a pile of feathers. Ben set me down on my bed, rummaged in my dresser, and brought me pajamas. He stepped out of the room, giving me a few minutes, finally tapping on the door. "Okay now?"

That was questionable. "I guess." I told him in a small voice. He turned the knob and stood at the doorway, staring at me, sympathy written all over him. Ben crossed the room, pulled back the covers, and covered me up. He kicked off his shoes and climbed on to the bed, next to me.

When I started to protest, he put a finger to my lips. "I won't take advantage of you. I'm just going to be here for you, give you something to hold on to."

I slid closer and took a deep breath, centering myself. One glance up and the warmth of his deep brown eyes was a balm for my soul, his slip of a smile steadying me. My Benjamin wasn't lost. I was convinced that he was with me now. If only Ben could be as sure. I closed my eyes and miraculously, the swirl of my thoughts stilled and sleep came for me, that much sweeter because it was someday and my prince had come.

"BETTER?" HE ASKED QUIETLY. Darkness had fallen and moonlight slipped in through my window. I awoke to find Ben lying next to me, fully dressed, on top of the covers, the picture of propriety. His hand reached out and stroked my hair, tucking a stray curl behind my ear. That simple action made my heart go haywire.

I nodded, found my voice. "Yes...I'm sorry, so sorry. I wasn't any help to you today. You had to pick up my pieces instead of the other way around." He had no one to catch him if he fell other than me. I had a network of family and friends. Above all else, I had him. I had to show Ben how much I appreciated him. I took his hand and pressed it against my chest. "I...I'm very thankful you're in my life, which reminds me. Do you have any plans for Thanksgiving? It's only two days away."

His chuckle rumbled all the way from the pit of his stomach. "I have a date with a frozen turkey dinner, the couch, and a football game."

I couldn't help it. I leaned forward and kissed him swiftly. "Well, if you don't mind real turkey, spending time with a family that can get a little over the top when it comes to history, and watching the Sons of Liberty marathon instead of the Buffalo Bills and the Cowboys, an invitation is open to come to my parents' place."

"Thank God. I hate football and frozen dinners. I'm not sure which is worse." Ben propped his forehead on mine. "And any place that you are is where I want to be...any time."

I became lost in his gaze and realized if a person could be a homecoming, mine was next to me now.

"What should I bring?" He continued to stare at me, hypnotizing me with his nearness. I couldn't think straight.

"Yourself." *And Benjamin's memories.*

*THE DAY OF GIVING THANKS.* Surrounded by the people I loved more than anyone in the world, under the umbrella of my parents' love, in the home that had sprouted roots in childhood strong enough to make me feel grounded right now, my gratitude knew no bounds. The day was crisp, clear with a hint of snow in the air. I wouldn't be surprised if I woke up to find a fresh blanket of white covering everything in the morning, wiping the slate clean...if only I could do the same.

My father and Ben hit it off instantly. My parents had always welcomed any of the boys I brought home over the years, but this was different, as if they were long-lost friends. The bond that had been forged between William and Benjamin had been ironclad, strong enough to

291

withstand the passage of time and several generations.

The moment we arrived, Dad kidnapped our guest, showing him this artifact and that. Right now, they were nearly forehead to forehead, bent over the book my father had written about the Revolution and used as a text for his class, American History: The Beginnings. They were having an animated discussion and based on what I could hear, Ben was surprising my father with some newfound nuggets of knowledge.

Standing in the doorway of the kitchen, listening to the words rolling off of their tongues, I thought back to all of the other dates that had come through my parents' door. They were far and few between. I was extremely selective and set the bar high. Realization stunned me, hard enough to make me grip the counter top at my side.

Every boy and man that I had spent time with had been tall, graced with dark hair and eyes. None of them had met my expectations because none of them were Benjamin. *The heart wants what the heart wants.* All through the years, I had been waiting for the right man to come along. This man. Ben.

"I like him." My mother slipped in behind me and looped an arm around my waist. We watched the two for a moment and then backed into the kitchen. She turned me to face her, her hands on my shoulders and I stared into her full, heart-shaped face, framed by a tumble of chestnut curls that stopped at her jaw, snared by her lively green eyes. I swallowed hard and the urge to cry was so strong I had to dip my head.

"Charlotte, what's wrong, sweetheart? You've been distant these last few days and that's not like you. You usually call me every day, usually several times a day." Her hand trailed through my curls and I looked up at her again. She pulled me into the shelter of her arms and gave me a big hug.

I sniffed and swiped at my eyes, laughing shakily. "Oh, I've just been working hard on a story and I haven't been sleeping well. I've had a lot on my mind."

She tilted her head and her smile bloomed. "I think I know what you've had on your mind. You light up when he's around...and so does he. I'd say Ben is a keeper." Mom patted my cheek and turned back to the stove. I joined in the efforts to put on a feast beyond compare, a Ross family tradition.

We sat down together, our heads bowed for grace. I held Ben's hand on one side, my father's on the other. Making the circle complete.

As the plates went round and round, I could sense the man beside me caught up in a net of powerful emotions. He took a sip of his wine, wetting a throat gone dry, his other hand clinging to mine under the table. "I...I just want to thank all of you. I haven't had a real Thanksgiving since my parents died, haven't truly felt a reason to have one...or give thanks. You've given that back to me and it means more than you know."

He turned to look at me and for a moment, everything else went away. It took supreme will power not to fall into him, let the tumble happen, head over heels, let him catch me in those sturdy arms, and kiss me into oblivion.

Ben gave me that crooked smile I'd come to love and squeezed my hand, the spell broken...for the moment. The low burn in the pit of my stomach would continue. A touch, a breath, a graze of his lips and I'd burst into flames.

A look of understanding passed between my parents, along with silly grins, when my father suddenly tapped himself on the forehead. "Now I know why your name sounds so familiar. It's the new headstone in the Colonial Cemetery! Maynard had me over there the day it was erected. Benjamin Willson. Any relation to you?"

I was about to blurt out an answer, but Ben beat me to the punch as he swallowed and wiped his mouth. "I don't know. The spelling is different. My last name is spelled with one 'L,' W-i-l-s-o-n." He turned to me and the line appeared between his eyes, the one that showed up any time he was torn, conflicted, confused. "By the way, I talked with my great aunt. No luck on my family tree past the Civil War. Confederate raiders destroyed all our records in 1865. I can't trace my way back to Colonial days."

My father's fingers formed a steeple as his face scrunched up in concentration. "Hmm. I know a few experts in genealogy and Maynard's good, damned good. He's our town historian. I'll see what we can find on the Patriot in the cemetery. You never know where it may lead."

I nearly choked on a mouthful of food and had to take a gulp of wine, hiding my face in my napkin until I could settle myself. How odd. We both were blocked from finding out exactly where our family trees would go, stopped by the road block of 1865. For some reason, we were not meant to have the hard facts in black and white. I would have to take a leap of faith.

*Believing is seeing.* I did not need a piece of paper to tell me what my heart already knew. Feeling the way I did the instant I met Ben, the moment I saw his face, when his hand took mine, obliterating everything else around me, I had no doubt. I belonged to him and he belonged to me. Our paths had been entwined together over 200 years before. We'd just taken a while to find one another again.

We spent the rest of the evening visiting in the living room, Mom snug against Dad in a giant, overstuffed chair, me sitting in the cradle of Ben's lap and no one questioned our familiarity. We watched Sons of Liberty, debated on a continuation, and stuffed ourselves with Mom's homemade chocolate pie. There was enough laughter and smiles to go around for everyone.

When it was time to go, my parents stood in the doorway, Dad's arm looped around my mother's neck. Ben stepped in and she grazed his cheek with a kiss before they both gathered him in a crushing hug. "Don't be a stranger, you hear?"

My father grinned and shook Ben's hand. "What she said. Seriously, come around any time. We can talk history."

Ben ducked his head, the flush rising up in his cheeks. "I'd like that. Thank you for a really special night. Good night."

I drove Ben home, right to his doorstep, when all I wanted to do was turn the car around, bring him back to my place, or follow him into his. These feelings I had for this man...they were so intense. Hard to handle. Nearly impossible to harness. Branded on my heart by Benjamin, they continued to seep deeper into the very fabric of my being, body, mind, and soul. The more time we spent together, the more I was overrun and about to come undone.

I was not the only one affected. My feelings might be so strong because of the memories that continued to be sharp in my mind. Ben was feeling the force of our attraction as well. I could see it when he didn't think I was watching him, in the longing in his eyes. Heard it in his voice. Felt it in his touch. When we were together, he began to vibrate as if his body was on a frequency that was in tune with mine.

His hand had found the way to mine many times throughout the evening. Under the table. On the couch. Walking me to the car. The entire drive to his place.

The car rolled to a stop and we sat motionless, still linked by each other's hands. Neither one of us wanted to say good night. Ben turned to me and his fingers drifted to my cheek, trailed through my hair, made me close my eyes and quiver as his lips connected with mine.

I saw sparks, like a shower of cinders dancing over a flame, heard musket and cannon fire, felt Benjamin by my side. I opened my eyes to find myself with Ben.

"Thank you for making me a part of your family tonight. I felt like...like I belonged." His forehead rested on mine and he stared into my eyes. I wanted to climb inside of him, never leave.

"You do belong...to me." My hands were resting on his chest and I could feel the unsteady thrumming of his heart. A gallop, a race, faster and faster until I thought it would explode.

I don't know how it happened. One instant I was in the driver's seat, the next I was in his arms, strong bands of muscle sheltering me, giving me something to hold on to before I lost myself, the sands of time shifting beneath my feet, past to present and back again. I turned in his lap and his mouth rested on mine. I couldn't breathe. I didn't care.

My hands couldn't stop touching him, had to run up and down his chest, to his neck where his pulse beat wildly under my thumb, to his hair, becoming entwined. Tangled. That summed what I was, with this man, had been for 233 years.

My mind took me back to the barn, surrounded by the scent of hay, warmed by a shaft of sunlight. That afternoon when I gave myself to Benjamin, set fire by his skin against mine, consumed by the flames of his touch. I would have given everything I had to him. My last breath. My last drop of blood. The last beat of my heart. I would do the same now.

If Ben asked me to come in with him. If he peeled me out of my clothes right now in the steamy confines of my car, shut off from the rest of the world, only our ragged breathing to break the silence... I would let him have me. Benjamin Willson had me from the start. What difference did the year make?

"Charlotte." His voice was raspy, like he had a sore throat or had inhaled smoke or run a long ways. Ben swallowed hard and his face was tortured for a moment before he forced it to smooth. "Charlotte, we have to stop. *I* have to stop before I make you think I'm a monster. I *won't* take advantage of you. You are a lady and deserve to be treated as such. Call me old-fashioned, but that's how my parents raised me. I won't let them down...or you either."

He pulled away and ran his hands over his jeans, over the slight rise of a button and a musket ball, finding his strength when put to the test. I no longer had the button to help me find my courage. I would have to rely on my own will power...and Ben.

Shakily, I laughed and skimmed a palm over his cheek. "I understand and I admire you for your restraint. Right now, I wish you were a less honorable man, but there will be a time that is right for us. Besides, my parents raised me that way too." I prayed our time would be soon, that I would not lose him again. My breath caught and my throat closed at the thought. I *could not* lose this man again.

In a rush, Ben gathered me roughly against him and kissed me hard, echoing my thoughts. "I pray I don't have to wait too long, Charlotte. I'm hanging by a thread. Good night." He practically sprinted to the door, glancing back when the knob turned. I thought he'd come back, give in to temptation, but the house swallowed him up.

I turned the car around and fought the urge to walk up his steps, pound on the door, throw myself at him and beg to come in. As I drove down his driveway, past the field, the smell of smoke was overpowering. I heard screams, shouts, grunts. The clamor of musket fire rang in my ears. A rag tag group of Patriot militia men scrambled across the tall grasses and Redcoats, equally frayed, came on.

I tried not to look, but my head turned as if pulled by a magnet to gaze at the far edge of the field. I saw a tall man with broad shoulders, painfully handsome in his blue jacket, clothed in loyalty. Dark hair whipped around his face and his eyes, usually sweet as chocolate, were black with sorrow. A shot exploded, so loud , as if by my ear, making me jump. In the space of a breath...a heartbeat...Benjamin fell to the ground.

The car almost ran off the road, straight into the stone marker with a plaque of Revolutionary shoulders, the victim of many reckless drivers. I slammed on the brakes and pulled over, my head coming down on the wheel and I broke, weeping for all I had lost. I cried until there was nothing left, until I felt like an empty shell. I started the car and kept my eyes trained straight ahead. I *would not* look back.

As soon as I made it home, I pulled on my pajamas, and crawled into bed. How I longed for Benjamin...or Ben. In my mind, they were one and the same. I lay there, staring at the ceiling, listening to the sighing of the wind in the trees, and my mind replayed the battle.

I wished I could rip that particular memory out of my head. I forced myself to breathe deeply, to reconstruct every beautiful moment I had with Benjamin and I slept. I dreamed. Of lying in Benjamin's arms, in the meadow, sitting on the stone, by the creek, in the hay, for all too short a time and the scene changed. I was with Ben, in his loft, entangled in sheets, bathed in moonlight, gazing at the starlight reflected in his eyes.

"How can you stand being here so close to where you lost everything?" My lip trembled and I almost began to cry. The losing him was a pain I would never forget.

He kissed me so tenderly, as if I was fragile and could break, then tucked me under his arm. "Because this is where I got everything back."

I came up out of sleep in an instant, as if someone had tossed a bucket of ice water over my head. My bed and my arms were achingly empty. I pulled my comforter around me and stumbled out to the kitchen to make my first cup of tea. As I sat with my mug cupped in my hands in my favorite chair, struggling to shake off the lingering traces of my dreams, I longed for someone to talk to. Someone who knew me better than myself because she was someone who knew me from my beginnings...in this life. Someone who would simply hold me even if I could not bear my soul. I craved some mother-daughter time.

The phone rang. A glance at the caller i.d. proved it was Mom, a mind reader once again as she had been countless times over the years. When I was hurting, she was the one who could numb the pain. "Hello?" I answered softly.

"I *need* more time with my daughter. I feel like we haven't sat down and talked in *ages*. How about lunch today at the Union Hall? See you at noon. Gotta run, sweetie. Your father is trapped inside a massive history book and I don't know if I'll ever pry him out. Love you, Charlotte."

"Love you too, Mom." She was my security blanket. I could always wrap myself up in her and be safe, warm. Never alone. I knew...if ever I lost my mother, we would find our way to each other again, some way, some place. A bond like that could not be broken. Benjamin taught me that lesson.

Pulling up my mental boot straps, I finished my tea, had a little something to eat, and showered. I put on my clothes and my brave face to go out and meet the day. No one waited on my steps, a disappointment, but I had a new motto: expect the unexpected.

# Chapter 20

*MY MOTHER WAS A CHEERFUL, PRACTICAL SORT,* the kind who made the best out of any situation and often told me, "If life tosses an ocean of obstacles in your way, build a boat." God bless her, but I needed her rock solid, unshakeable personality right now. She waved to me from a table in the corner of the Union Hall, rising from her seat to give me a hearty hug as soon as I reached the table.

"I'm so glad I could spring you. I knew the girls could handle the shop for an hour or two, even if it is Black Friday. Any runs on the shop this morning, people beating down the door, fighting each other off with their umbrellas?" Her green eyes twinkled, her dimpled smile reminding me just how much I loved my mother.

"No, although the latest installment in the Harry Potter series, JK Rowling's surprise release, just hit at midnight and we've already sold out of 500 of those. There wasn't a single drop of bloodshed and no arrests." I shook my head, laughing, until the breath was knocked out of me by another instance of déjà vu, a disorienting bout of double vision. My mother and Abigail Andrews flickered in and out, fuzzy around the edges, and I had to gulp down a glass of ice water.

Mom took my hand and squeezed it and she snapped back into focus. I wondered if I would ever get used to these strange experiences. "I'm glad to hear it. I know you live on the wild side in the Colonial Book Nook. You never know when some Revolutionary ghost might walk through your door."

That had me sputtering, choking on an ice cube. My mother helpfully patted me on the back and I covered my mouth with a napkin, all the while studying her features carefully, seeing the likeness with my friend from long ago. Faces the same shape. Dark curls. Merry eyes of green, brighter than the leaves in spring time. Clara Andrews Ross had always been more than a mother to me. She was my best friend. Could she be another connection to the past? Dad didn't do Mom's family tree. I'd have to look into it sometime, when my head stopped spinning.

The waiter came and we both ordered our favorite, a Cobb salad, tomato bisque soup, and an amazing crusty bread. The food, the company, and the atmosphere began to work on me, settling me. The Union Hall Inn was one of my favorite places to eat. Erected in 1798, it so happened to be one of Nicholas Stoner's favorite haunts as well. It might have come after the states won their independence, but it was close enough to Colonial times to bring me back to yesteryear.

Funny. While I was in the past, I longed for the future. Now, I ached for the simple, bygone times when I knew without a doubt what my heart wanted, when my world revolved around one small patch of earth and my Benjamin.

"How long have you known Ben?" My mother eyed me speculatively as she tore her bread into small, manageable pieces, a habit passed on to me. Cinnamon buns, muffins, bagels, donuts, cookies...it didn't make a difference. I always broke everything down.

I took my time with my piece, chewing carefully, putting off my answer in order to sound casual. "Since the end of October. We met at the ghost walk." I gestured in the direction of the cemetery.

Mom sat back and crossed her arms. "You two seem to have known each other forever. How comfortable you are together, the way you look at each other. Oh my." She picked up her napkin and waved at her face. "Let me tell you something. You generate a lot of heat and quite a bit of sizzle. What are you keeping from me? You can spill it. Did you elope? I won't be thrilled, but it's your choice in the end."

"Mom! Don't be ridiculous! I would tell you if I was married...and no, I am *not* pregnant. There's nothing to tell, really. We're still getting

305

to know each other." In the present day. I knew him inside and out in the past.

My mother tucked my hair behind my ear and cupped my cheek in her palm. "Don't push this one away, make excuses, or sabotage it, Charlotte. I think he's the one." She was right. I burned all my bridges with every boy or man in the past. Time to start building something of really sturdy construction, a bridge that could carry Ben to the past and back again.

I hugged her, my eyes stinging. "I hope so, Mom. I really do."

We finished and walked back to the bookstore, linked arm and arm. Main Street was decked out for Christmas, wreathes with lit candles in the middle hanging off the street lamps, storefronts decorated with Christmas trees and lights. Santa and his sleigh were parked on the grass and animated figures skated around the band shell. Snowflakes began to flutter down around us, dusting our hair, and I finally felt unruffled for the first time in over a month.

My mother entered the bookstore with me, greeting my girls and delivering a chocolate crème pie from the restaurant. "Enjoy, chickadees. I am off now. I think it's late enough to pick through the leftovers while I'm shopping without threat to life and limb. Toodles!" She called out to Erin and Trish who were already digging in with plastic forks, forgoing the formality of plates. She hugged me and kissed me on the cheek. "Love you, sweetums. Bring that young man back soon, you hear?"

A wave and she was out the door. "Love you too, Mom," I called after her. I turned around to face my girls. Erin offered me a fork. With a shrug, I joined in. *If you can't beat them, join them.*

At six o'clock, I closed our doors. The girls had scooted an hour before at my insistence. My feet were sore from standing most of the day since opening early at seven in the morning. I was ready to call it quits. I locked the door and stepped on to the sidewalk to find myself in the middle of a giant snow globe.

The first snow of the season continued to fall, fat flakes that looked like snippets of the sky coming down. I stood still, tipped my head back, and caught some on my tongue, like I had as a child. Hope sprang up inside of me. After my world had been turned upside down, maybe it was being set right again. A smile tugged at my mouth and I let it happen.

I turned in the direction of home and inhaled sharply. Ben stood on the corner, in front of the courthouse. He was unmoving and for an instant I saw Benjamin. I squeezed my eyes shut and opened them to see only Ben and he looked troubled, his gaze trained on the cemetery.

I crossed the street and approached him. He actually jerked at my touch. "Hey," I said softly. "I didn't think you could move after all of that turkey."

Ben looked at me and I saw a lost soul, making my hand tighten on his. "I'm sorry. I can't even remember why I'm here. I don't know what's wrong with me. I keep going to that

307

blasted cemetery." He tilted his head and focused on me. "Then I see you and I feel like I've known you all of my life, which is crazy because we just met." His fingers threaded through my hair and his lips brushed mine. His breath came out in a rush. "I *have* known you forever. My heart says so."

I leaned my head on his chest. The erratic flutter of every beat in my heart called out to his. "Then it must be right. Why don't you come to my place, have some tea, relax a bit and we'll get to know each other some more?"

He didn't argue. We walked, holding hands the entire way, coated with snow when I opened my front door. Ben sat on the couch while I fixed tea and brought out two, steaming mugs. Before I could hand him his cup, he took both of them away from me and snatched my hand. Something warm and hard was pressed into my palm. My fingers slowly unopened to reveal Benjamin's button on a gold chain.

I automatically pressed it to my chest. I wanted to kiss the tiny keepsake and was flooded with such a strong sense of relief, tears sprang to my eyes. "I couldn't keep it." He told me, his voice dropping down to a whisper. "Something kept telling me it belonged to you."

"Like you and your musket ball." I bent my head forward as Ben draped the necklace over my head and the button dangled under my shirt, against my heart.

His hand trailed to his jean pocket and a small bulge. "I've taken to carrying it with me all the time. I tuck it in my hand and roll it in my palm. Just knowing it's there holds back a sense of panic. You probably think I'm nuts."

I took his face in my palms and kissed him. "Never. I feel the same way about the button. Thank you for giving it back to me."

Ben's fingers became entangled with mine and his face became taut as he spoke. "You...you're the only thing that makes me sane. I feel like I have to see you every day, like you're..."

"The air that I breathe. Me too." I murmured.

He set his lips on mine and pulled me in close. "I'm easy in my soul when I'm with you. The images, flashbacks, nightmares—whatever they are, they fade away and there's only right now."

I saw another day, in a bed of straw and a splash of sunlight, our skin on fire from each other's touch. I grabbed hold of Ben's shirt, my fingers curling into the fabric. "I don't ever want to let you go."

"Then don't." I didn't know if Ben actually spoke the words or they were in my mind. It didn't matter. We came together and I kissed him as if I was smothering and each brush with his lips was a gulp of fresh air.

The tea was forgotten, replaced by wine and Ben was down for the count, asleep on my couch once again. I covered him with a blanket and turned out all the lights before going in to my room to change into pajamas. I stretched out on my bed, but I couldn't relax. My mind was too cluttered and the mere presence of the man in the next room made me want to go out there and try to shake some sense into him, make him remember.

Unable to sleep or act on my impulses, I sat down at the small desk in the corner of my bedroom and took out a notebook. I began to jot down all of the scraps I had learned, tangible evidence of my experience, and coincidences I had bumped into since my return. The button. Charlotte Ross Cooper and her branch of the family tree that continued with Benjamin Willson Cooper. The foundation of my cottage that had originally belonged to the Ross family. The musket ball discovered on the field where the Battle of Johnstown took place. Benjamin's coat and the braid. *Ben*!

I had all that I needed to confirm that we were in fact reincarnated, our spirits finding their way back to each other again. The question remained. Would Ben ever remember?

My memories were so raw and fresh, everything could have happened yesterday. For Ben, with the exception of his dreams and impressions, it was as if he suffered from amnesia. I rested my head on my arms as my eyes became too heavy to stay open. I didn't have any answers in all of this, didn't understand the why or where of it. I only knew that I loved Ben like I'd never loved any other man.

"Hey." His voice was soft in my ear and sunlight had tiptoed through my window. A bird was singing cheerfully nearby and Ben's hand was on my shoulder. He held coffee under my nose. "I think you need this. Extra cream, extra sugar, barely any coffee."

His crooked grin and chocolate eyes had me on my feet, accepting a kiss before he set the cup in my hands. "Just you would have been good enough for a wakeup call." Every one of my senses was wide awake, screaming for Ben.

Ben took my hand and led me out to the couch where we sat down together and he wrapped us up in a nest of blankets. "I was thinking the same thing. I woke up before dawn thinking about you. I finally had to take a peek and couldn't get over how cute you looked, sound asleep on your desk like that." He took a sip of coffee and shook his head. "You didn't look comfortable at all. Why didn't you go to bed?"

I waved him off. "Oh, I couldn't sleep and wrote for a while. That's when the Sandman snuck up and ran off with me."

Ben couldn't stop smiling. A few more sips of coffee and he took my cup. Once out of the way, he pulled me into his lap. "I'd like to run off with you. Since I can't, will you come with me to the Colonial Stroll tomorrow night? It looks like lots of fun, but I don't want to go alone. Of all the girls on my list, you're the only one I want."

"All the girls?" I asked, an edge giving my words a bite. "How many would that be?"

His talented fingers gentled me as they skimmed over my body and became embedded in my hair. "One. There's only you. There's never been anyone but you."

*THE COLONIAL STROLL.* A tradition in Johnstown for as long as I could remember, it signified the Christmas season was in full swing. Ben arrived at my door, wearing a jacket and breeches that would have been worn during an important gathering during the Revolution, very similar to what Benjamin wore to Richard Dodge's home. With its form-fitting cut that followed the clean lines of his body and his head held high, his hair brushed and smoothed away from his face, he stole my breath clean away.

He gave me that sweet smile that made me melt and took my hand, kissing my fingers before pressing my palm to his chest. "My heart. You have made it stop, completely. You are the most beautiful woman I have ever seen."

The heat rose up in my cheeks and I glanced down at my dress. I'd chosen a gown in a deep blue, something that would have been worn by ladies of importance during Colonial days. Ben skimmed his hand over the velvet fabric before following the map of my curls. "It suits you perfectly, complements the bloom in your cheeks, the honey in your eyes, the bright shine in these golden strands." His hand rested on the nape of my neck, toying with the few curls that had escaped the knot of hair on top of my head. "I'd love to let your hair down, run my fingers through it, see what would happen next." He grinned and brushed my lips with his.

I was quaking like a leaf caught in a windstorm. I gave Ben a trembling smile and took his hand. "We'd best be on our way then or we're both going to be a mess."

He walked me to his truck and picked me up at the waist, making my breath come out in a rush as I was settled in the front seat. A short drive of only a few blocks to town and we joined the other revelers meandering along the sidewalk. We were not the only ones dressed in period clothing. Ben took my hand and we took in everything. The tree lighting ceremony. The white wagon clopping by with Santa. The Christmas Music. Chestnuts and hot chocolate. Ben bought two cups of coffee from a vendor and told him, "Extra creamer, extra sugar, hardly any coffee." The inside joke had the both of us bent over in a fit of laughter, struggling not to let our cups spill.

A group of carolers went by and we trailed after them. Snow was coming down steadily and I couldn't resist poking out my tongue to catch a few. Ben gave in to temptation and did the same, sliding me a sideways glance from time to time. I made sure to snag some more.

I didn't even pay attention when we passed St. John's Episcopal Church and turned by the Colonial Cemetery. Ben squeezed my hand and pulled me toward the metal archway that stood over the entrance, filling me with absolute dread.

I planted my feet, my heart beating wildly, and yanked hard on his arm. "No! No, Ben, I will not go in there, not tonight." Terror sank its claws inside of me, made my stomach clench, and my lungs constrict. I did not want to go through that gate or near that grave marker again. I was too afraid I would go back. That Ben would be stolen away from me.

Ben was breathing hard, crimson stains burning his cheeks, his eyes glittering in the moonlight. "Here, Charlotte! It all began here for us!" *And ended here.* I nearly cried out.

He pressed me up against the stone wall, peeled the gloves from my hands, and I hooked them around his neck. "I have to get close to you."

"As close as two people can possibly be." His hand went under my cloak, skimmed up my sides, to my shoulders. His thumb grazed over the hammering of my pulse and then he cupped my face in his warm, strong palms, the calluses on his fingers grazing my skin. His mouth touched down on mine and fire ran through my veins. My body went loose and the heat of his touch consumed me. The chill of the air and the stone wall at my back couldn't even touch me.

His deft fingers went to work, pulling the pins from my hair, letting the curtain of my curls tumble down. "Dear God, Charlotte," he told me hoarsely. "I've never felt this strongly about a woman before. I feel like you are the other half of my soul, that you belong to me. I love you."

"And you belong to me. I love you too." We kissed until we had to breathe, Benjamin's button swinging beneath my dress, warming my skin. We were both shivering.

Ben snatched one more kiss and tucked my hand in the crook of his arm. "Let's go home." *I'm already there.*

Back at my place, sitting on the couch before a roaring fire, we couldn't resist getting a few more doses of one another. Finally breathless, Ben leaned back and tucked me against his chest. "I don't know why you have such power over me, but ever since the first time I laid eyes on you, since I had the first taste of honey in your gaze, since I saw your golden curls fluttering in your face, it is as if I've always known you...and I have to have you."

I rose up on my knees to take his face in my hands so I could stare deep into his eyes. "You already do." I buried my head in his chest and held on tight as his lips brushed my cheek. Every beat of his heart reminded me. *You are mine.*

# Chapter 21

*I WAITED BY THE WINDOW,* felt like I'd been waiting forever. Wine was chilling on the table, the candles lit. A fire flickered on the hearth, almost as bright as the flame burning inside of me. The tree was decorated, garland and white lights twinkling everywhere, and expectation was humming in the air. It was hard to take a deep breath and my heart was misbehaving, skipping at an unbelievable pace. Tonight. Maybe tonight Ben would cross the divide to Benjamin and truly recognize me. Tomorrow was Christmas with my family, but tonight belonged to us.

Snow was tumbling down, blanketing everything in white, and the world was quiet, waiting with me. A flood of memories played back in my mind, the movie projector taking me back to the night when a tall, dark stranger led me to a lonely grave marker. To a sun-kissed afternoon when I found myself in the past. To the first time I laid eyes on my ancestor. To the instant my Patriot touched my hand and I found my heart's content.

Footsteps sounded on the porch, pulling me back to the present and Ben stood at my door, gazing at me. I raised a hand to wave even as I gripped the windowsill to steady myself. He was so handsome, I bit down on my lip. His dark hair was disheveled from the wind, dusted with snow, his cheeks flushed from the cold, his navy pea coat failing in its attempt to contain such a man. He didn't bother to knock.

I crossed the room and opened the door, unable to make another move. I shouldn't have worried. If Benjamin could cross the barriers of time to reach me, Ben could handle such a tiny distance. One, great step and he took me in his arms, bringing the scent of winter with him, sealing my mouth with his.

He pulled me against his chest and set his chin on the nest of my curls. "I couldn't stand myself a minute longer. I had to see you, to be with you."

I laughed softly when I wanted to weep, the wanting was so strong. "Me too. Why don't we close the door before we freeze to death?"

Ben gave me his crooked grin and raised one finger, gesturing for me to wait. He stepped back outside, bent down to pick something up, and walked back in with a bouquet of red roses and baby's breath. The door closed with a click as he handed them to me.

They were a red as brilliant as the love that I felt with every beat of my heart, as bright as the crimson stain that bloomed on Benjamin's chest on the fateful day when he was taken away from me. I stomped on that last image, would not let that painful memory mar this night. I took the flowers and buried my face in them. "They're beautiful."

"They can't even touch you. My God, Charlotte, what you do to me." Ben took the bouquet from my hand and set it on the table by the door. His hand skimmed over my hair as he marveled at me and the blood was singing in my veins, my stomach tightening in anticipation. "You look so beautiful in that dress. I love the color of it. It's like the one you wore on Halloween."

I'd chosen a dress in a deep pink, a shade darker than the other gown. It hugged my body like a glove before flaring out at my feet as I perched on matching heels that brought me up to his chin. "I wanted tonight to be special. You're not looking too shabby yourself."

A navy sweater, calling to mind Nathaniel Brown's militia jacket, and loose jeans that fit him perfectly made me want to throw myself at him, lose all control, but we hadn't even eaten dinner yet.

I took his hand and slid him a smile with a promise in it. "Come sit down and get warm by the fire."

"I don't need the fire. I've got you." I could hear laughter in his voice, but beneath it was a need and wanting as strong as mine.

I led him to the couch and left him long enough to pour two glasses of wine. We sat together and sipped, the fireplace giving off sparks, while music played softly in the background. Ben managed a sip or two and he was on his feet, taking my hand, and pulling me into a dance. Through the living room. To the dining area. Into the kitchen where we were surrounded by the scent of dinner and the heat of the stove.

The song came to an end and I found myself pressed against his chest, listening to the unsteady drumming of his heart. "Charlotte...I'm only hungry for you. All the time. You're all I think about anymore."

"Me too." It seemed so inadequate, but I couldn't say more. We stood there in my kitchen and I waited for something to happen, for that lightbulb to go on, as I had been waiting ever since I realized who Ben was.

Nothing happened. I bit back my disappointment and pulled away. "I can't wait any longer. I've got to give you your present now. Dinner will just have to wait."

Back to the living room. Ben sat in my overstuffed chair, my favorite perch, while I picked up a long, narrow box from beneath the tree. I set it in his hands and sat on the arm of the chair, barely able to keep myself from ripping off the paper myself.

With painstaking care, he peeled off the wrapping. He didn't rip a bit of it. With each second of deliberation, my heart pounded even harder. I squeezed his shoulder. "Come on, Ben! Get on with it!"

He grinned at me and continued at a sedate pace. Finally down to the box, he lifted the lid...and froze. A Brown Bess lay in a bed of tissue paper and etched in the stock of the gun was an inscription. *William Ross 1776.* His fingers trembled as he ran them over the writing and he was choked with emotion when his words tumbled out. "Where...how did you find this?"

I couldn't resist touching the musket, my hand tracing the name that had become so dear to me in such a short space of time. An image of my forefather came to mind and I heard his voice, *"Charlotte, my blessing",* felt the warmth of his love as he kissed me on the forehead, each cheek, and on the mouth. My eyes were stinging and Ben snatched my hand, reminding me he was here.

"Maynard Hughes, the town historian? He found it. Someone actually called him out of the blue and asked him if he was interested." Another coincidence in a long string of coincidences. "A member of a family named Cooper in Cooperstown wanted to sell it. As soon as it arrived, he was beside himself with excitement and called me. He's a good family friend and we believe that this gun belonged to my ancestor."

I closed my eyes for an instant and pictured William and the Brown Bess over the fireplace. I had held that gun in my hands when I went to war with my men. It did not bear any writing, but there was another musket, the one that my forefather carried. It only made sense that he would commemorate the Declaration of Independence as he took up the fight.

"I can't accept this. It belongs to you and your family." Even as he said the words, Ben picked up the gun and marveled at it.

I laid a hand on his arm. "I want you to have it. So does my father. He already has a gun that has been passed down through the generations. Besides, he says you are like family."

Ben set the musket down and pulled me into a hug. "It's incredible. I don't think I can top it, but I'll try." In one fluid move, he was on his feet, shifting me to sit in the chair, and going down on one knee. One hand went in his pocket and a black, velvet box rested in his palm. Small enough for a ring. Big enough for his heart. "Go ahead. Open it."

My hands were shaking so hard I almost dropped it. Ben took over, flipping the lid, revealing a simple gold band with two hands clasped. He slid it on my finger and his hand closed around mine. "It's from the Colonial time period. 1776 is actually etched on the inside. I found it in an antique shop."

The words stopped and he was breathing hard, his face tipped up to mine. "I know it's not your typical engagement ring and if you want a diamond I'll get you any one you want, but this felt right when I saw it. It's called a heart in hand ring and you have held my heart since that first night I saw you in a halo of moonlight and I had to make you mine. Charlotte, will you be my wife and promise we don't have to be apart anymore?"

I nodded and the tears were making tracks down my cheek, splattering on my dress, on our hands. "Yes. I've been waiting for you all of my life." *And several lifetimes before.* I ran my finger over the shining band, turned it round and round. For an instant, I saw a simple, iron band crafted by my Benjamin in William's forge. The love welled up in my heart and spilled over.

Ben brushed the ring with his thumb and leaned forward. His hand threaded through my hair to cup the back of my head, his other hand at my waist, steadying me. "Then I guess I really will be family." His mouth came home to mine and we kissed until we were breathless. "I love you, Charlotte."

"I love you more," I whispered. I said the words, but knew his love was even stronger. My Benjamin had walked through the fire for me, died for me, and crossed over time to make his way to me. If only he'd remember. As Ben held me in his arms, my head against his chest, the beat of his heart reassured me that he was solid and real. I decided this was enough. I could be the memory keeper for the both of us...and my Benjamin was here.

*VALENTINE'S DAY. THE PERFECT DAY FOR TWO HEARTS TO UNITE.* We'd shocked everyone by announcing our wedding date with such short notice. Neither of us cared. There was a sense of urgency to do it and do it now before something got in the way. For me, it was an irrational fear that we would be torn apart, separated again. *Not going to happen, not now. This time, we're going to get it right.*

I stood with Ben on the field where the Battle of Johnstown took place, in the snow, with a stand of pines behind us and a scattering of houses around us. Sir William Johnson's would have been a more attractive spot with the Colonial flavor, but it went against the grain for both of us to marry in a place that housed loyalists, no matter what good they did.

My bridesmaids, two of my best friends from school days, wore red and blue. Ben's attendants wore the same colors in their vests and boutonnieres. My flowers bore the colors of our flag, in my hands, in my hair, and when I peeked under my groom's jacket, I had to laugh. His vest bore a pattern of the original American flag. My gown was from a vintage shop, a recreation of a Colonial wedding dress, what I would have worn if Benjamin had lived to see our wedding day. I was freezing, shaking with the cold, but I would not cover the dress. My groom *would* see me.

A small gathering of only our closest friends and family was here to share in an intimate affair, probably because they were the only ones crazy enough to come, including Maynard Hughes and Joan Brown. They huddled in their winter coats, hats, and gloves, their breath forming clouds around their heads. Many stomped their feet or held on to each other to fight off the bitter chill. Luckily for our guests, a table with hot coffees, lattes, and cocoa was waiting for them with a host of liqueurs and other forms of alcohol to light a fire in their bellies and thaw their toes as soon as the ceremony was over.

My mother and father were beaming. Thrilled from the moment we announced our engagement, they'd been all too willing to help us in planning for our day, treating us to the Union Hall Inn for our reception as our wedding gift. Mom flanked me on my right, a splash of red against a backdrop in white with her long coat that nearly went to her ankles and a matching beret. Dad held my arm on my left, wearing only his tuxedo. The stubborn man insisted that if Ben and I could manage to go without winter wear, so could he. I had chosen to depart from tradition; I needed both of my parents to give me away on this day. There was the slim chance that two time periods would merge once more and this would be the last I saw of them.

As a friend from high school played a hauntingly sweet tune on a flute, I finally reached my groom. Before I could take his hand, Mom kissed me, tears about to overflow, and gave me a desperate hug. She did the same with Ben and retreated, dabbing at her eyes.

My father sent me for a tailspin when he took both of my hands, kissed me on the forehead, each cheek, and on the mouth. "You have always been and will always be my greatest blessing. I love you, sweetheart."

He turned to Ben next and shook his hand before tugging him in for a bone crusher of a hug that had laughter spilling out around us. "You're quite a blessing yourself. Be sure to come around, *a lot!*" Dad joined my mother, leaving only Ben and I standing before the priest. My groom took my hand and I held on with all of my strength, my knuckles going white. I *would not* lose him this time.

The ceremony was short, both for the sake of our guests who were humoring two history buffs, forced to attend an outdoor wedding in the middle of winter, and for our sake. With each passing day, the intensity of our need for each other was becoming unbearable. We had been practically inseparable since Christmas Eve.

The vows came to a close, rings were exchanged, and somewhere in the distance, I heard those familiar words, "You may kiss the bride." Ben reached out, his hand skimming along my cheek and I tilted my face up to his expectantly. The sun burst out of the clouds, even as a gentle snow continued to flutter around us like pieces of heaven falling down, and the light touched the button on a chain around my neck, gleaming bright enough to blind us both.

His breath caught as he stared and grazed the warm, round disk with his fingers, tracing the letters...and in that instant, the rest of the world went away. Smoke blotted out the sun, booms of cannons sounded in the distance, musket fire crackled around us, and men were shouting. A flash of red coats raced by, heading off into the thick of the forest, Patriots on their tails.

Ben's hand gripped mine and I took hold of his lapel. "You stay with me. Do you hear me? You stay, Benjamin."

His eyes lit, his mouth pressed to mine in a fierce kiss that caused a tidal wave of emotion to rise up inside of me, and he smiled, even as tears threatened to break the dam. "*I told you.* I told you I'd find you, Charlotte, and I keep my promises."

His fingers brushed the button once more, the button Benjamin gave me on that fateful day of the Battle of Johnstown, when the grief of losing him stripped me to the bone. I felt my knees give and my mind became fuzzy. Ben took hold of me, kissed me again, and bowed me to the ground. The whispers of liberty faded away.

Only a plain field remained, covered by a blanket of snow, with a marker that stood by the road, a quiet reminder of the clash of enemies from centuries before. Our guests were laughing, clapping, shouting out, whistling for more kisses and the sun smiled on us.

Ben pulled me up and I set my hands on his cheeks. "You remember."

He nodded, his eyes filled with wonder. "Not all of it...but I remember what happened here...and I remember you, Charlotte." He held me close, his head bent to mine and finally, I felt whole again. Complete.

# Epilogue

*I'VE WRITTEN EVERYTHING DOWN.* From
the night Benjamin's ghost led me to his grave
until the day he found his way back to me at our
wedding. I want to get it down while my mind is
clear, before the images fade. Now that we are
together, some of the memories have grown soft
around the edges. Every night, I read my journal
aloud to Ben.

He has not been affected in the same way
that I have been. For him, it's more like feelings
at time, bouts of déjà vu, or impressions. Then
there will be those rare instances when a sharp
stab of memory pierces him and Ben will become
frozen. I'll take his hand, set my hand on his
cheek and gaze into his eyes, fearful that he is
slipping away. I'll see *my* reflection burning in
the middle of his pupils and he'll blurt out, "I
remember!"

We have vowed to make the most of right now. Having lost and found each other makes our love that much more sweet. I know with absolute certainty that death cannot part us. I have known my love in the past, in the present, and hold fast to the conviction—I *will* have my Benjamin by my side in the future, whatever that may be.

He is lying beside me, turned to silver in a shaft of moonlight, in our bed in the loft that overlooks the field where the Battle of Johnstown raged so many years ago. The whispers of liberty sing me to sleep as I hear their notes in the kiss of Ben's breath on my skin and the steady thudding of his heart when my palm rests on his chest.

As for our ghosts, they are laid to rest, deep inside of us, wrapped in each other's arms. Ben shifts and his fingers trail from my hip to the protruding mound of my belly, massaging round and round. A healthy kick is the response from my tiny occupant, making me snort with laughter. "I think we've got a firecracker in there. What should we call him?"

His fingers still and his voice is so soft I have to strain to hear it, but my heart already knows what he will say. "Jacob Cooper. Because of him, I found my way back to you."

I can't help but smile even as the tears begin to fall. Because of Jacob, I made it back to the cemetery. Back to 2015. "He brought me back to you too."

Our hands link on my belly and our baby responds, making them rise up as if riding on a wave on the ocean. Ben's mouth tilts up in a grin and he leans in to snatch a kiss. I am falling, the love rising up to sweep me away, snagged by my Patriot all over again.

# Afterward

*THE BATTLE OF JOHNSTOWN* really did take place six days after General Charles Cornwallis surrendered at Yorktown. If you ever venture into this sleepy town only an hour west of the capital of Albany in upstate New York, you will find many remnants of Johnstown's proud heritage. You can visit the James Burke Inn, the Union Hall Inn, and the original Tryon County Jail, which once acted as the garrison, Fort Johnstown. The Fulton County Courthouse, originally erected by Sir William Johnson in 1772, is still in service today. You can tour the Drumm House and Sir William Johnson's impressive estate that actually makes a cameo in the popular video game, Assassin's Creed III. Sir William's grave lies next to Saint John's Episcopal Church on North Market Street.

Stroll a few more steps to West Green Street and you will discover the Colonial Cemetery. Benjamin Willson is purely fictional and his gravestone is not there. However, many other notables from the novel, including Brigadier-General Richard Dodge, his wife, Ann Sarah Irving Washington, Talmadge Edwards, Colonel James Livingston, and John Little do sleep in this tiny patch of the past. Other Revolutionary soldiers rest here as well. They fought, sacrificed, and gave their lives so that we could live ours.

If you have a chance, walk amongst the stones, run your fingers over their cold faces, and read what time has not yet erased. If you are lucky, you may hear the whispers of liberty talking to you.

# About the Author

Heidi Sprouse is a teacher and writer in historic Johnstown, New York. When she is not busy teaching or spending time with her husband and son, she is whipping up the next story. Heidi dabbles in various genre, and loves to find the extraordinary in the ordinary as she focuses on small town men and women who overcome difficulties in life.

Previous titles:
*All the Little Things*
*Lightning Can Strike Twice*
*Aging Gracefully*
*Sunny Side Up*
*Adirondack Showdown*

## More Great Historical Fiction from Bygone Era Books:

*Immortal Betrayal*
*Immortal Duplicity*
*Immortal Revelation*
Daniel A. Willis

*Primitive Passions*
John N. Cahill

*Kilpara*
Patricia Hopper

*The Harlot Saint*
Susan McGregor

*And the Wind Whispered*
Dan Jorgensen

*The Prince of Prigs*
Anthony Anglorus

*Girl in the River*
Patricia Kullberg

*Bittersweet Tavern*
S. Copperstone

*Into the Hidden Valley*
Stuart Blackburn

*The Sands of Kedar*
Diana Khalil

*The Other Side of Courage*
Robert Nordmeyer